ALSO BY ELIZABETH BERG

Dream When You're Feeling Blue

The Handmaid and the Carpenter

We Are All Welcome Here

The Year of Pleasures

The Art of Mending

Say When

True to Form

Ordinary Life: Stories

Never Change

Open House

Escaping into the Open: The Art of Writing True

Until the Real Thing Comes Along

What We Keep

Joy School

The Pull of the Moon

Range of Motion

Talk Before Sleep

Durable Goods

Family Traditions

THE DAY I ATE
WHATEVER I WANTED

RANDOM HOUSE

New York

ELIZABETH BERG

The Day I Ate Whatever I Wanted

And Other Small Acts of Liberation

Por

Copyright © 2008 by Elizabeth Berg

Published in the United States by Random House,
an imprint of The Random House Publishing Group,
a division of Random House, Inc., New York.

RANDOM HOUSE and colophon are registered
trademarks of Random House, Inc.

The following stories were previously published: "The Only One of Millions
Just Like Him" appeared in *Bark* and "The Party" appeared in *Ploughshares*.

LIBRARY OF CONGRESS CATALOGING-IN-PUBLICATION DATA
Berg, Elizabeth.
The day I ate whatever I wanted: and other small acts
of liberation / Elizabeth Berg.
p.   cm.
ISBN 978-1-4000-6509-7
1. United States—Social life and customs—21st century—Fiction.
2. Women—United States—Fiction.   I. Title.
PS3552.E6996D39 2008
813'.54—dc22   2007034704

Printed in the United States of America on acid-free paper

www.atrandom.com

2 4 6 8 9 7 5 3 1

FIRST EDITION

Book design by Casey Hampton

To Matthew Sumner Krintzman

and

Katelyn Rose Krintzman

CONTENTS

THE DAY I ATE
WHATEVER I WANTED

THE DAY I ATE
WHATEVER I WANTED

—————

I began at Dunkin' Donuts. I hadn't gone there since I started Weight Watchers a year ago because I had to lose weight; my doctor *made* me go. I could have switched doctors, but who needs it with all the forms you have to fill out if you switch. You just wish there were a central headquarters with all your information that you write out once so that everyone who needs anything could tap into it.

Weight Watchers is a good organization, I mean it does actually work if you do the program and they try really hard to make you like you, which, as you may know, is a problem a lot of fat people have, they have low self-esteem. Skinny people look at fat people with disgust and have visions of them stretched out on fuchsia-colored silk sofas snarfing down Cool Ranch Doritos and Ben & Jerry's Chunky Monkey, but it isn't like that. What it is, is eating and eating with your shoulders hunched and your head down to scratch that itch that won't get scratched, and you have so much shame when you gobble things down you hardly even taste them. You start with *I want* and you end with *I want*, only now you have even more weight added to what is already too much and don't think we don't know it all, all, all the time.

But anyway, I went to my Weight Watchers meeting one day, and in addition to the usual annoying *emaciated* people who have no *business* there, there were two new members who absolutely blew my mind. Both of them on this same day. One was an old woman on oxygen with a walker taking about a thousand hours to get to the scales, and she was not to my eye fat at all. The other was a blind woman. Here is my question: When that blind woman looks into her mirror, what does she see? And anyway, she, too, had no visible blubber. I mean, I just walked out. I said to myself, No. Today, on account of those two women, on *behalf* of those two women, I am going to eat anything I want from now until midnight. And I drove right over to Dunkin' Donuts. You may be thinking, Why did she go to Dunkin' Donuts if she could have anything she wanted? Why didn't she go to Cinnabon? Well, because I actually like Dunkin' Donuts way more than Cinnabon. Cinnabon is just a whore, you know, no subtlety. I like almost all the donuts at Dunkin' Donuts and I really like the coffee though I usually just get regular coffee, milk, no sugar. But today I got coffee, heavy cream. "Anything else?" the counter person asked. She was Hispanic, about thirty years old, beautiful long black hair tied back in a ponytail under her Dunkin' Donuts hat and a really big caboose, what can you do, you'd have to be a weird person not to gain a lot of weight if you worked at D.D. Once when I was on a road trip I stopped at this great country kitchen place and every single person who worked there was really fat, I mean really fat. With good skin. And it was a happy place; everybody seemed to get along really well, they were just smiling, holding their little pads and pencils and I had one of those why don't I move here moments, like where I saw myself sitting in a chair by a window in my little yellow house, lilac trees outside and nothing hurting inside. Like, content at last, which I always think I'll be if I move, but which I know is a wrong assumption even though a lot of us have it, just ask any real estate agent. But anyway, the counter woman (her name tag said SIGRID, but I think maybe she just borrowed that name tag, it was put on with no care at all, for one thing, just hanging there perpendicularly). *Anyway*, Sigrid's fat looked good, truly, every now and then you see a person who wears fat well, it is that tight fat and just really looks kind of delicious and also their attitude is just great, like in your face: *I'm fat, so fucking what, get over your sanctimonious self.* It's usually the tight fat people who are like that, maybe it's a gene. Anyway, after Sigrid said, "Anything else?" I said, "Oh yes, I want some donuts." I cannot tell you how swell that felt.

"How many donuts?" Sigrid asked and I said I didn't know, I would know when the little voice stopped. "Pardon?" she said, and I said, "Just get a big box, please, but maybe we won't quite fill it." So she got out a big Dunkin' Donuts box and I just started *salivating*, like that experiment dog. Sigrid grabbed one of those tissue squares that I think we all take pleasure in using, and she raised her eyebrows and I said, "Okay. A bow tie, a chocolate-frosted cake, a Key lime, a powdered cake, a Boston Kreme, a lemon bark, a maple-frosted, a coffee roll, a maple-frosted coffee roll, a cranberry muffin, a bagel and cream cheese

and butter, too, on the bagel, and a plain Dunkin' donut."
And then before she tallied it up I handed her a fifty and
said just keep the change and walked out. My back was
feeling kind of hypervisible, like I was walking away really cool from a crime scene where I'd been the criminal.
My heart was racing and my mood level had shot way,
way up.

I got in my car and I opened the coffee and had a deep
whiff and a taste. Actually, I guess I have begun to prefer
milk in my coffee because the cream tasted *whoa*. Next I
opened the lid on the box and had a good whiff of the
donuts. And then I looked around and there was no one so
I ran my tongue along every single surface of every single
donut. Man. It was sexual in a way, but more yeasty and
better. Then I sucked the filling out of the Boston Kreme
mixed with a little chocolate frosting. I dipped the powdered cake in the coffee and had one bite; ditto the chocolate-frosted. I went on in this manner until I would say
about a third of the donuts were gone. And then I am sorry
to say I threw the rest away. I would like to say I ate tidily
and cut off where bite marks were and gave the rest to a
homeless person along with a couple of finskis, but I did
not. I threw them in the garbage, where maybe later they
were found by a homeless person anyway or at least by pi-
geons, who, depending on where they live, can actually
have it pretty good. Though sudden violent death is always
a problem for them. But probably they have no attach-
ments, which helps.

I was pretty full, so I went for a walk in a park to make
room for lunch. It was a nice day and there were joggers,
with their determined, miserable faces, and lovers lying in
the grass thinking it would last forever. There were lots of
dogs and one was a bulldog puppy, which, please, has cor-

nered the market on cuteness. The owner was this very thin woman who looked sort of bitchy, which, think about it, most very thin women do—even when they smile, it's like grimacing. Fat people are often miserable, too, but at least they *look* jolly even though it's really mostly them apologizing, like, "Sorry, sorry, sorry I'm taking up so much room," "Sorry I'm offending your idea of bodily aesthetics," "Sorry I'm clogging my arteries and giving the thumbs-up to diabetes." And spilling over airline seats, which, come on, even for skinny people those seats are ridiculous. Metal girdles.

Lunch was a problem, like do I sit down or continue to fast-food it. Because I really do appreciate good food, but fast food is what I always *want.* Drive past a White Castle? See myself opening one of the little burgers with the onions all square. Go past KFC? See the big bucket, lift off the lid, see the one corner of one breast just loaded with coating that you pull off and pop into your mouth. Wendy's? Regular with cheese, just a plain regular with cheese and it is *good.* The buns are still good at Wendy's, they're not those weary things other places give you that are like bread out of an old person's bread box who never throws anything away and it was cheap bread and not good in the first place. Generic.

Hot dogs? Well. I live in Chicago, where we know what hot dogs *are* and how they should be *served.* I know someone who used to fly from Boston to San Francisco once a month on business and she always stopped in Chicago so she could get a red hot. She said she told people she needed a walk but really she needed a red hot. She ate them in the first-class cabin and all the people used to get pissed off at her. She said they got pissed off because the onions stunk the place up, but I think they got pissed off because they

didn't have the foresight to bring a red hot on board themselves. A flight attendant can put all the French words in
the world after "beef" and it still tastes like airline food,
which tastes like jet fuel smells.

They don't have red hots in the airport all over the
place like they used to. If you come to O'Hare and you
have a bit of a layover, get in a cab and tell them Superdawg at Milwaukee and Nagle, it's only about ten minutes
away. Get the regular hot dog, but you might also want to
try the Whoopercheesie or Whoopskidawg. There is only
one Superdawg and it was started by a guy and his wife,
they fell in love in high school and now they're probably in
their eighties. You can see her working the booth, she sits
there in her black nylon windbreaker and you shout your
order into the little metal box by where you park. Everybody gets their own speaker and their own menu, which
has humorous descriptions of the food.

Portillo's hot dogs are also good, and their tamales, oh
my. You eat them with a plastic spoon, which adds to the
flavor, as does the light orange grease stain on the wrapper.
But the Portillo's are not as close to the airport, you might
not have time. Although if you said to anyone who knew
Chicago, "I missed my flight because I had to go to Portillo's," they would say, "Oh, I know, did you get a tamale?"
If you're debating, which should I go to?, pick Superdawg,
because they are not a chain. Always pick the thing that is
not a chain, is one way to try to save the world.

I decided I'd go for lunch to this café I know where the
butter is real and the syrup is real and the waitresses do not
in any way judge what you order. I got there at 12:30 and
got a table in a good booth because it was across from
where Ivy was sitting. Ivy is a regular in her nineties, and
she wears a little old lady dress and a sweater and sneakers

and a white baseball hat turned frontways. Long gray hair tied back in a skinny ponytail. She orders a little something and then falls asleep before it comes and then after about half an hour her home health aide comes to wake her up and take her back home.

I ordered a bacon cheeseburger, fries, and a chocolate malted, and I loaded up the fries with salt and made a neat pile of catsup. I had whipped cream on the malt and I ate some by itself and then mixed the rest in. When the waitress asked, "Will there be anything else?" I *almost* ordered two over easy with hash browns because I just wanted one bite of the potatoes mixed with yolk, but no, that would have been too much wastefulness in one day.

But. Because this was a day purposefully given over to gluttony and greed, I walked over to a bookstore, where I looked at cookbooks. You may think, Right, she looked at dessert books, but that's where you would be wrong. Because guess what? Vegetarian. And some Mediterranean and Indian. And okay, then I found this one? The cake doctor? Which so made me in the mood for a piece of cake, not a fancy one, just a yellow cake with chocolate frosting. And vanilla ice cream, vanilla enough to be a bit yellow in color. So I went and got that at another café, but I could only fit in half.

By now I was feeling the shame but also defiance. Like here, I'm carrying the banner for all of you who cut off a little piece wanting a big one, who spend a good third of your waking hours feeling bad about your desires, who infect those with whom you work and live with your judgments and pronouncements, you on the program who tally points all day long, every day, let's see, 7 for breakfast, I'm going to need only 3 or 4 for lunch, what the hell can I have for so little, oh, I know, broth and a salad with very little dressing. And broth is good! Yes! So chickeny! That's what we tell ourselves, we who cannot eat air without gaining, we who eat the asparagus longing for the potatoes au gratin, for the fettuccine Alfredo, for the pecan pie. And if you're one of those who doesn't, stop right here, you are not invited to the rest of this story.

In the afternoon, I rented two movies. *Big Night* and *Tortilla Soup.* Which made me starving again even though I wasn't. How many people went *running* out for Italian food after *Big Night?* Hands? I think movies like those are very beautiful, because in addition to food as art, you get love of the family variety and more. I returned the movies, stopped at the very famous Petersen's ice cream parlor for a turtle sundae, extra caramel sauce, and made out my grocery list on a napkin. When I paid at the cashier, I got a bag of Cheetos because there was one of those chip racks and every time I see a chip rack I want some chips. I love Cheetos so much it kind of makes my butt hurt. Every time I fly, I buy a bag of Cheetos (not the puffy kind, eww) because you never know, and if I go down, I'm going to at least have had a bag of Cheetos.

Okay. Dinner. I was going to make dinner. I was going to have steak and mushrooms and a loaded baked potato and Caesar salad because I make better Caesar salad than any restaurant I've ever been to. And apple crisp and crumb-topped cherry pie. And a baguette with that European butter that starts with a "P." After I got it almost ready, I was going to sit on my front porch with a martini with blue-cheese-stuffed olives, and potato chips with Lipton onion soup mix dip, which I love, it has that same thing going for it as Kraft macaroni and cheese. The cheese in the envelope in the box, I should say, the old kind

in the box where you yourself must mix the milk and butter and powdered cheese in. Here is my favorite recipe:
Buy two boxes of Kraft macaroni and cheese. Make one
box of macaroni but use both cheeses. Telling you this, I
just remembered this woman I really liked a lot who died
and she loved egg salad more than anything and didn't eat
it for years because it was *bad for her* and then when she
was on her deathbed and could have anything she wanted,
she was given an egg salad sandwich and she couldn't eat it
anymore.

So dinner. You can imagine it, can't you? The mushrooms sautéed in butter lying seductively over the steak.
The potato, buried under butter, bacon, green onion, and
sour cream. The two desserts sitting side by side, can you
see them? I knew after the day was over, I'd have to go back
to the plan, go back and confess at my meeting. Which is
okay, it's fine, you can say anything at a meeting. Once
someone said she had cheesecake left in her refrigerator
from a family dinner and everyone was saying, "Oh, my
God, get rid of it, give it away." Someone else said, "Just
throw it away." And this other woman said, "Well, I'm sort
of embarrassed to admit this but I have actually taken food
out of my garbage and now I've learned that I have to pour
water on it before I throw it away."

I myself put coffee grounds over food I throw away,
that'll do it. Sometimes at a meeting, a person will take up
practically the whole time telling how she fell off the
wagon. And all of us at the edges of our seats, eating it all
with her in our imaginations. And also feeling a little bit
smug that we didn't fall off the wagon. This time.

I ate the dinner, the whole thing, just like I said. And
then I took a wooden mallet and I beat the shit out of my

scale. I wanted springs to pop out like they might in a cartoon, but all that happened was it didn't work anymore
and it had a few dents. Still.

The next day I went to a Weight Watchers meeting,
and the blind lady was there again. "How are you doing?"
I said to her and she said, "Okay. How about you?" "Okay,"
I said. I never confessed. I got weighed and I was four
pounds up and they were just like, "Well, that happens,"
and I bought another scale and that night I had turkey
burgers for dinner. Seven points and actually very good
and I had spinach and a two-point ice cream thing though
I don't think it's really ice cream, it's probably chemicals
that kill you faster than fat. And I drank lots of water.

I have to tell you this funny story about water and
Weight Watchers that our leader told us. She said she was
telling a new member the rules and she guessed she talked
too fast. Because she told the woman be sure to drink six to
eight glasses of water a day. And the woman came back the
next week saying, "I did everything you said, but I just
can't drink sixty-eight glasses of water a day." Imagine her
at the sink, upending yet another glass of water, wide-eyed
and discouraged: *This program is* hard!

I would like to end this by saying that it felt really good
to cheat all day, to eat whatever I wanted. But it didn't. All
that happened was that I felt hollow-eyed. I felt like one
time when I was a little girl and I sat on the porch steps
one summer evening with my dad. We were watching the
neighborhood kids riding bikes with no hands or roller-
skating or turning one-handed cartwheels three in a row
or chasing each other up and down the block at breakneck
speed. "Some of them are real athletes, huh?" he said. And
I stared at my knees and said, "All of them are."

"Well," he said. And he took my hand.

I was already really chubby and he was a very fat man with pretty blue eyes. A couple of times I was with him when people made jokes about how fat he was. He would laugh like he thought it was funny and his belly would shake, it went up and down when it shook, but their remarks hurt him, I could see it—he registered pain in those instances by one quick jerk of his right eyelid. But that night he took my hand and I moved closer to him. Inside the house, hidden between my mattresses, was a stockpile of Butterfingers, and I couldn't wait for bedtime. I thought there was a delicacy to the way I licked the chocolate off my fingers. I thought it was beautiful. I wished someone could see.

RETURNS AND
EXCHANGES

It wasn't until she got outside into the sunlight that she realized her socks didn't match. At least one of them was navy and the other black. Only last week, she'd crossed her legs and realized she was wearing one kneesock and one ankle sock. It was not Alzheimer's, causing this. It was not a senior moment. It was not menopause or peri-menopause and it certainly was not PMS. PMS was years ago, and she remembered it now as rather charming, uniquely and daintily feminine, all ribbons and lace, though of course it was not. Rather, it was her coming home from the grocery store, slamming innocent cans down onto cupboard shelves, tearing into a party-size bag of Ripple chips and finishing half of it before she realized what she was doing, then bursting into tears because she was a fat pig. Ho. That was a laugh, thinking of herself as a fat pig when she weighed 126. Now she was a fat pig at 176. Recently, in a hotel room with an unfortunately positioned bathroom mirror, she'd seen herself sitting naked on the toilet and thought she looked just like Buddha.

So, no, there was nothing to blame this forgetfulness on. Absentmindedness was . . . well, it was just *her.* In kindergarten, she'd once forgotten to wear underpants. When the children had spread their blankets out for nap time, Agnes had lain down, stuck her thumb in her mouth, and, when the breeze coming through the open window had blown her little blue dress up, revealing her nakedness and making Sister Theresa gasp and the girls giggle and the boys shout, when that had happened, she had meekly followed her teacher to the principal's office, imagining her white soul stained by sin. The principal, frowning, had phoned her mother, who'd soon arrived at the school with a pair of underpants stuffed into a plastic bag, which was stuffed into a brown bag, which was stuffed into her purse, which was stuffed into a gently deteriorating large floral tote. "I'm so sorry," she'd told the principal. And then, "Agnes, did you apologize to your principal?" "No," Agnes had said, and her mother had said, "Well, *apologize* to your principal."

"I'm sorry I forgot my underpants," Agnes had said, and something about it had struck her as funny, and she'd smiled.

"Do you find this *amusing?*" Sister Mary Catherine had asked, but she had not been looking at Agnes when she said it. She had been looking at Agnes's mother, who'd been looking at Agnes. "Apologize *right,*" Agnes's mother had said, and so Agnes had said, "I'm sorry I forgot my underpants" with a deeply sorrowful face, achieved by imagining her kitten smashed under the front wheel of her father's car. It was something she occasionally worried about.

"All right, then," Sister Mary Catherine had said, and Agnes's mother had said stiffly, "I'll see you at home, Agnes." Agnes knew what that tone of voice meant. Sometimes it meant that her raven-haired doll, Veronica, would be put on the high shelf in Agnes's mother's bedroom closet. Sometimes it meant no *Mickey Mouse Club*. And sometimes it meant a spanking with her grandmother's ivory hairbrush. Occasionally Agnes was allowed to pick her own punishment, and always she picked not watching *The Mickey Mouse Club*, even though she had a big crush on Jimmie. She'd had a crush on Jimmie for a long time, with his manly torso under his tight T-shirt. These days, she would go for Buffalo Bob, with his funky leather outfit and cozy paunch. "Buy me a drink, Buffalo Bob?" she might say. In heaven, perhaps, this could happen, she could sit on a barstool between Buffalo Bob and Elvis.

Agnes believed in heaven, though she was too shy to tell anyone, especially her husband, Harold, who believed in nothing but believing in nothing. His favorite thing to say was "You believe that? What, are you nuts? You *believe* that?" She had stopped going to church on account of Harold, a difficult thing for her to do at first, but in the end she had not minded so much. She actually preferred celebrating the glory of God in other ways. Sometimes, aware of some transcendent moment disguised as ordinary life, she would whisper to herself, "Hallelujah."

But Agnes still liked believing in heaven, liked imagining a starry firmament as background at night, and clouds infused with pastel colors during the day. She liked imagining a sense of perfect contentment, as well as an ability to reach those still on earth, should one desire to do so. No harp music—who could bear to listen to harp music unless you were having high tea at the Palm Court? No, the music would be jazz, Diana Krall style. And endless trays of fried foods floating by, garnished with pink magnolias, with white peonies, with deep purple orchids slashed by lines of gold and freckled with black. A million house-trained puppies who stayed puppies, and children who never got older than five. That was heaven.

Agnes had a daughter, Nancy, who was twenty-seven and hated her. Agnes knew this because, in the interest of personal integrity and owning one's feelings, her daughter had called one night to tell her so. "I hate you now," she'd said, "but my therapist says I might grow out of it. For the time being, though, it's better if you just leave me alone." Agnes also had a son, a thirty-year-old highly successful advertising executive who adored Agnes and who said, about his sister, "Aw, fuck Nancy, she's a wreck." "Andrew," Agnes would say, offended by the language and the senti-ment, "please." "Ma, she's a *bitch*," he would say, "and you spend way too much time worrying about her. Forget about her. Let me send you to Paris, you want to take a little trip to Paris?" "No thank you, sweetheart," Agnes always said. She didn't like to travel. The pillows always smelled funny, and no matter what wondrous sight she was beholding, something at the base of her brain kept whispering, *Home*.

Agnes was on her way to work. She'd recently started a dating service for people over fifty. So far it wasn't doing too well, but she figured it would take off when people found out about it. "You believe that?" her husband had said. "What, are you nuts? You actually believe that?"

"Yes, I believe that," Agnes had said. "I *know* it. And when it does become successful, I'm not sharing any of the money with you. I'm going to spend it all on me. I'm going to spend it all on *hats*." She knew this would get Harold's goat. He hated her loving hats, particularly since she never wore one. She once spent an hour and a half looking in a hat store in New Orleans while Harold paced and fumed outside. Periodically, she would stick her head out and say, "Why don't you go look somewhere else?" but he wouldn't. He wanted to stay and get madder at her.

Oh, he wasn't all bad. He wasn't! They'd had wonderful times in the past. They were fifty-eight now, the razzle-dazzle was gone; but there was something to be said for comfort, wasn't there? Something to be said for saying to your partner, about something on your body, "What *is* that?" and having him take off his bifocals to have a good look for you, then offer blind reassurance. There was something to be said for someone waiting for you while you had your colonoscopy. For someone to be dismayed with you when your basement flooded, when your car acted up, when your old dog died, when your lipid level rose. It was good to have someone with whom to share, when you wanted only half of the remaining piece of strudel. Agnes was not unhappy. But she was a hopeless romantic, and she opened her dating service because she wanted people her age to fall in love and act foolish.

After she walked the six blocks to her office, her only form of exercise, she sat at the desk to check her e-mail. Nothing. There was, however, a message on voice mail. A man named Jon Vacquer, calling to see if there were any women who were blond and blue-eyed and exceptionally fit and dying to meet him—he who was blond and blue-eyed and exceptionally fit. If he was the same Jon Vacquer, he was someone whom Agnes used to know.

It couldn't be. But it *could* be.

Agnes sat back in her chair, closed her eyes, and let herself remember the first boy she'd ever loved. She'd just finished high school, and her family was moving away from Oklahoma, where they'd lived for a mere eighteen months—Agnes's father was an IBMer, in the days when IBM stood for I Been Moved. Two days before she left, she'd met Jon Vacquer at a party. He was Beach Boy cool— shaggy blond hair, eyes that were a gorgeous green-blue, and don't think he didn't know it. *Staggeringly* handsome. All the girls were crazy about him, and so Agnes made no move toward him. She was cute enough, in those days, but she was not an A. She was a good, solid B, and she knew what she should strive for and what she should not.

But this Jon. He stood in the corner of the room and a crowd gathered around him. He was smoking Lark cigarettes and telling jokes and everyone was laughing. Then he said something cruel, Agnes can never remember what, but she spoke up; she reprimanded him. That was the start of their romance. She'd reprimanded him, and so he noticed her, and they began to talk and . . . what? Why did they fall so hard in love? Probably it was because Agnes was moving. It was so tragically romantic, how little time they had. She snuck out of the house for the first time in her life to meet him in the middle of the night; he visited her three times in Minnesota, where she was in college, and on the third visit she lost her virginity to him. It was a small motel room where it happened. It had hurt—she couldn't stop trembling. He'd kept saying, "Are you all right?" and she'd kept saying, "Keep going." Afterward, she had sat in an orange plastic armchair with her robe tied tightly around her tiny waist (though at the time she had called it enormous) and she had crossed her legs and tossed back her hair and said, "Well. I'm glad *that's* over." And he had come to kneel beside her and he had kissed one of her kneecaps and then the other, and he had said, "I love you, you are a very odd girl, and I love you so much," and he'd had tears in his beautiful, beautiful eyes. And then, two months later, he'd gotten a girl pregnant and he had called to tell Agnes that he had to marry that girl, and then he had never called her again.

Agnes had spent every night for a month sitting on a rock at the edge of the Mississippi River, trying to remember that the world was vast and had very little to do with Jon Vacquer. But mostly what she thought about was how pure a love they'd had, and how his stupid mistake would cause both of them to suffer forevermore. And she thought about how he had been the first. In the usual fashion, his mark on her heart was permanent. In the usual fashion, he became the standard by which she measured every other man.

And now, forty years later, here was this name and this voice, which just might be his own. She listened to the message again. Yes. Yes? Yes, maybe so.

She called the number back, and he picked up on the first ring. She identified herself using her married name, Agnes Miller, the owner of 50 + 50. "Ah!" he said. "Yes, I called you!"

"So you did."

"*Do* you have anyone of that description?"

Agnes did not. "Yes, I do," she said. "There are several women in whom you may be interested. But first I'd like a little information about *you.*"

"Retired, rich, divorced, handsome, and healthy. And bored."

"Bored" was the man's word for lonely, that much Agnes had learned.

"Would you be willing to come in today and fill out an application?" she asked.

"Well . . . maybe online, can I do it online?"

"We'd need to meet you in person." Agnes had no partners; she worked alone, but she thought the pronoun "we" offered a certain sense of legitimacy. "It's a guarantee to our clients that we meet with every person we keep on file. Frankly, Mr. Vacquer, we don't take just anyone—we strive for a certain quality. You'd have to come in for an interview. Have you time today?" Her toes curled inside her shoes at this last. My God. What if it were the same Jon Vacquer? She would see him! And he would see her. Uh-oh. The socks. And the rest of her outfit . . . Well, she didn't care about nice clothes—she preferred to spend money on antiques. And on cheese.

"I might be able to come in," he said. "Can you hold on for a moment?"

"Certainly."

She looked out the window, thought about the gift he'd given her that she still had. Part of a dollar bill—he'd torn it in half the last time he'd seen her, asked her to keep it forever. "You'll have half and I'll have half. It's light. You can always carry it with you."

"All right," she'd said. He was like that. An English major who liked lousy poets, what could you do. A boy creating his own Rosebud, she supposed. But then he'd said something else. He'd said, fiercely, "No matter what happens, I'll keep on loving you. Always, for the rest of my life."

He must have known, she realized later. He might have been awaiting pregnancy test results—or even known them. He had kissed her that last time so soulfully and sweetly; her heart had fluttered and sighed, then locked permanently on the position of him. And then she had never seen him again.

She heard him pick up the phone. "How's four?"

She was supposed to get a temporary crown at four o'clock. "That will be fine," she said. "Do you know where we are?"

"I think so. I'll be there."

Agnes hung up the phone and looked at the clock. Six more hours.

"Not too poofy," she told her hairdresser. "Don't make me look like Loretta Lynn. Make me look like Emmylou Harris."

It was three-fifteen, and Agnes was getting the last touches to her coiffure. She had long hair, inappropriate for a woman her age, she knew that, but it was beautiful hair, still thick, and the gray was silver—it shone in the sunlight.

"It's *not* too poofy," Lorraine said. "You look fine. You look *good.* Oh, God, I'm so excited for you!"

Agnes had told Lorraine the whole story, such intimacy necessary for maintaining the proper hairdresser-client relationship. And Lorraine had told Agnes about the boy she'd lost her virginity to—a preacher's son with breath so bad it could peel off wallpaper. "But a good kisser nonetheless," Lorraine had said. "And I wanted to do it with him because I thought then it wouldn't be a sin. The one I really wanted to sleep with was a kid who came to school on a motorcycle every day. Big greaser. But oh, those eyes."

"Oh yeah?" Agnes said. "Well, you should come and see

this guy's eyes. If it's the same guy. In fact, you should come in and pretend to be a client—he's looking for a woman like you."

Lorraine did fit the bill—blond, fit, over fifty but not so that you could prove it: she used every piece of equipment in the gym with extreme intention.

"I'm married!" Lorraine said.

And Agnes said, "So am I," and so Lorraine said, all right, she would come, she'd wander in about four-thirty.

"Make it five," Agnes said. And then, standing up and handing her plastic cape to Lorraine, she said, "Don't look *too* good."

Lorraine stepped back, cocked her head, and looked Agnes over. "*You* look great," she said. "I'm not kidding."

Agnes looked at herself in the mirror. She did look kind of great. Considering. She'd been to Max Mara for a new black suit. She'd been to Tiffany for a gold necklace and a matching bracelet. At Ralph Lauren she'd found a pair of stunning black heels and a V-neck silk blouse, a wonderful eggshell color, so elegant, only a sliver of it would show. Tomorrow it would all go back. She felt a little bad about that, but that's what they got for being so expensive. She'd been to a makeup counter for the application of a good twelve products, none of which she had purchased, and she'd gotten an elegant little bottle of Chanel No. 5, which was what she'd been wearing when she met him, and which he'd said he loved. A girl could always use a little Chanel—she'd hold on to that. Or maybe she'd send it to her daughter, with a note on some sweet piece of stationery: *Nancy, sweetheart, enjoy this—pretend it's not from me.*

At three-thirty, Agnes returned the two calls that had

come in while she was gone. Two women, all fired up about her service, how wonderful that she was exclusively for more *mature* people, when could they come in and fill out an application. Business was picking up.

At quarter of four, she brushed her teeth again in the little lavatory at the back of her office, careful not to disturb the lipstick the makeup artist had put on her, which had cost thirty-five dollars a tube, no *thank* you. She straightened a few strands of hair that didn't need straightening. She took down the hanger with the clothes she'd worn in that morning, brought them to the filing cabinet, and shoved them in. What if he asked to use the lav and saw those clothes? Then she went back to the mirror and smiled and said, "Hello, I'm Agnes Miller." How did she look saying this, she wondered. Well, how did the she she was *now* look, compared with the she she was *then*. Answer? She couldn't imagine.

At five of four, the door opened and a man walked in. Her husband. *He* walked in.

"Harold!" Agnes said.

He turned from closing the door. "Agnes. Hey! *You* look nice."

She fingered the necklace. "Yes, well . . . just trying this out. I think I'll probably return it."

"It's great. Keep it."

"Well, it's . . . you know, it's very expensive."

"Keep it. I'll buy it for you."

"Well . . . *thank* you, Harold. We'll see. But . . . sweetheart? What are you doing here?"

He smiled, sheepish. "I don't know. I left work early. I thought maybe I'd take you out to dinner."

"You did? Well, I'd love to, but it's . . ." She looked at her watch. "It's only four." *Four!* Her stomach tensed; she could feel the prickle of perspiration starting under her arms.

"I thought you could knock off early, too. I thought we'd take a walk down Michigan Avenue while it was still light, and maybe then we could head over to Gene and Georgetti's—get there early, get a good table."

"Well . . . I would *love* to do that, but I have some work to do first. Maybe you could go do some things and I could meet you on Michigan, right by the Wrigley Building, right in front."

He sat down in one of the chairs along the wall. "Just go ahead and finish up. I'll read the paper—I never got around to it this morning."

She should never have gotten that subscription for the office. It was two minutes after. "Harold? Would you mind running a couple of errands for me?"

He shrugged. "Sure. What do you need?"

What did she need. ". . . Paper!"

"Paper for what? What kind of paper?"

"Oh . . . every kind. Copier. Fax."

"You just *got* fax paper. Last week when we were at OfficeMax, you—"

"Listen, Harold," she said, "this is my office. I am the boss. And if I say I need fax paper, I need fax paper. Now will you get it for me or not?"

She snuck a look at her watch.

"I'll get it," he said, sighing. "I'll come back for you at five."

She watched Harold leave, then checked her e-mail to see if Jon had left a message saying he wasn't coming. When she looked up again, another man was coming in the door. And it was Jon. It was. He was fifty-nine, and not nineteen, but it was he.

Her heart moved up into her throat and blossomed. She spoke around it. "Mr. Vacquer?"

He took off his elegant black coat, shook it. "Hey there. Sorry I'm late." He wasn't in such good shape. A paunch, the three-months-pregnant look.

He came over to her desk, shook her hand. "How do you do?"

Did he not *recognize* her? Well, of course not. He needed some context.

"So!" Agnes said. "How about we talk a bit and then—"

"Before we do that, I wonder if I could see some pictures."

"Of . . ."

"The women. The blondes."

"Oh!" He would not be interested in the two blond women Agnes had on file. "Well, we don't show anything to anyone until we've had an interview." Her heart spoke quietly within her: *Jon. Jon. Don't you know me?* Bette Midler sang mournfully in her brain, *Don't you remember you told me you loved me, baby?* Agnes smiled. "If the interview goes well, you fill out an application."

"Oh. I see. Well, all right then, fire away."

She pushed her hair back from her face, that old gesture, did he remember? "Why don't you start by telling me where you're from."

"Oklahoma."

"Uh-huh." She leaned forward. "I used to live in Oklahoma."

"Did you. Well, I lived there until ten years ago, then I moved here to Chicago."

Ten years he'd been here! She took in a deep breath. "Jon?"

"Yes?"

She stared into his still-beautiful eyes for a long moment.

He shifted in his chair and said, "You know, I . . ." He stood up. "May I be honest with you? This doesn't exactly look like the kind of place I had in mind. I'm sorry. I don't mean to offend you, it's just—"

"It's quite all right," she said. *What?* What was it? The wallpaper? The carpet? The furniture? Oh. *Her.*

"I just always know right away if something will work or not," he said, "and this . . . I think I need a larger agency. But I'm glad we were able to . . . I'm glad we didn't waste each other's time."

"Yes." She stood, looked at the clock. There was time to call Lorraine and tell her never mind, tell her everything. There was time to take her things back to the stores before they closed.

"Thanks anyway," Jon said.

"You bet." He was almost out the door when she called his name again. He turned, politely impatient.

"Could you hold on for just a minute?"

He waited while she got her wallet. She took out her half of the dollar bill and crossed the room to hand it to him. He looked at it, then at her. "What's this?" he asked.

And she said, "Nothing."

He half smiled, and left.

Agnes sat down at her desk and rearranged the pictures of her wildly imperfect family, her son, her daughter. And Harold. "Hallelujah," she whispered. She got the clothes she'd worn to work out of the filing cabinet and went into the bathroom to change back into them. She left the jewelry on.

She'd get a martini—Bombay Sapphire gin, extra dry, three blue-cheese-stuffed olives. She'd get a huge steak,

French fries, sautéed mushrooms, and creamed spinach. A nice Cabernet. She'd get a rich chocolate dessert, complete with whipped cream and chocolate shavings. She weighed 176 pounds and her socks didn't match, and she was going out with the man who really loved her. "Harold," she might say. "I believe in heaven. Did I ever tell you?"

THE PARTY

here were a bunch of us who had drawn together into a corner of the dining room. It was a big party, and none of us had met before. But a tiny core of women of a certain age had attracted more women until there were enough of us that we needed to be democratic about talking—each of us needed to be careful not to take up too much airtime.

We were talking about kissing, and we spoke rapidly and excitedly and laughed loudly. This was T-shirt and jeans laughter, not cocktail dress laughter—it came from the belly, not the chest. It was size fourteen and not size two. When one of us made moves toward some wilting hors d'oeuvre, the rest would stall, so that nothing good said was missed by anyone.

We seemed to like best telling about our first times.

There was a glamorous blonde wearing huge diamond stud earrings who said she first kissed at age eleven, while playing spin the bottle on a hot Texas night. The rule was that, after the spin, the chosen couple would go into the kitchen, stand by the washing machine in the corner, and kiss. No tongues. The blonde modified the rule to include no lips, only cheeks. But a certain Paul Drummond was too fast for her that night, and he smacked a kiss right on her mouth. She said she'd intended to get angry but instead backed up in pleasant shock into the washer hard enough to make a noise that roused the supposedly supervising parent from sleep. The kissing stopped; the party broke up; and the blonde went home, where she stayed awake much of the night reenacting the scene in her mind, and telling herself that the sin was venial, venial, venial.

A woman named Vicky said she spent years practice-kissing with her best friend, Mary Jo. "We would put a pillow between our faces, kneel down on my bed, rub each other's backs, and kiss that pillow to *death.*" We all laughed some more, because we'd all kissed pillows, it seemed.

One woman wearing a seductively cut black dress that now seemed beside the point ventured bravely that she and her best friend, Sherry, had dispensed with the pillow and gone at it lip to lip. You could tell from the ripple effect of lowered eyes that she wasn't the only one. I thought of fourth grade and my friend Mary, whom I asked to be the wife so I could be the husband. I liked to be the husband—you got to say when about everything. While Mary dusted, I went to work. When I came home, we kissed hello for what became long enough that we decided we'd better start playing outside.

There was a serious, shy-looking woman named Jane, who hadn't said much of anything, and who, when she laughed, had actually put her hand up over her mouth. "Oh, honey," I wanted to say to her, when I saw her do that. "Sweetheart, come here and let's give you some tools." She wore a dress with buttons that went high up on her neck, and each one was closed. I was pretty surprised to hear her say, "Oh well, kissing was one thing, but do you remember the first time you touched a dick?"

Now we were all into high gear. We were beside ourselves in our eagerness to share our experiences. We drew closer.

A roving rent-a-waiter dressed in tight black pants, a blindingly white shirt, and a black bow tie offered us little bundles of something from his tray. All of us, to a woman, took one. The waiter seemed very pleased. I waited for him to move on, then greedily spoke first: "I was forced. This guy called Telephone Pole Taylor, for the very reason you might suspect, pulled my hand down and held it there until I had touched it for five seconds. We counted together. I almost threw up. I was a serious virgin, and I damn near passed out at the thought that that kind of thing would someday . . . But after I got over the size, I became kind of intrigued by the texture."

Vicky's eyes widened. "Yes! Like damp velvet, right?"

Jane, standing next to me, sighed quietly. "I don't know," she said. "Men's bodies are just not *pretty*. That makes it difficult. I think women's bodies are, though, and I'm not, you know . . ." We knew. She took a sip from her drink, leaned her head against the wall, frowned in a contemplative sort of way. "It turned out that penises weren't so bad, really, although it did take me a long time to get used to that rising and falling routine. I mean, it was grotesque the first time I saw an erection. It was like a monster movie."

The gorgeous blonde spoke up. "I *liked* it! I thought it was so *magical.*" But then, as though protecting Jane, she added hastily, "But not beautiful of course." We drank to that.

"It's the balls that get me," Vicky said. "They're like kiwi fruit gone bad." We burst out laughing again. I think we felt that we were becoming dangerous, careening in our conversation, and we liked it. We were ready to reveal anything about ourselves. Almost imperceptibly, the circle tightened again.

"I think it's all a matter of cultural conditioning," I said and was met with a friendly collective groan. "No, I mean it. If we'd been taught to go after a penis by a mother who winked at us when she talked about it, and if all the boys at those drive-in movies had covered their privates with both hands and moaned little protests into our ears, we'd have been *wild* to touch them. Instead, we pulled their hands down from our tits and up from their crotches."

Jane put her empty glass on the floor. "I think men and women are just hopelessly different. It's a wonder we get along at all. Sometimes the smallest things can bring out the biggest things. I had a horrible fight with my husband last night, and you know what started it?" We were all listening hard, and we didn't notice the approach of Jane's husband from across the room. But Jane did. She stopped talking and stared at him: in her eyes, it was as though a shade had been pulled.

He stood at the edge of our circle, a little wary. "What's going on over *here?*"

There was a beat; no one answered. And then Jane said,

"Oh, you know. Just girl talk." I think we were all miffed by her response, but no one challenged it.

Her husband looked at his watch. "It's time to go."

Jane didn't budge. "I'd like to stay for a while."

"Oh?" He put his hands in his pockets. "All right. That's fine." He didn't move. Another beat. Silence all around. Then two of us simultaneously moved toward the food table. Someone else walked off toward the bathroom. Vicky waved to a man across the room and started over to him. Our group fell apart in a sad, slow-motion sort of way, as when petals leave a blossom past its prime. And then I heard Jane say, "I guess it is late."

I listened to her say good-bye to the people around her. I was dragging a piece of pita bread through the leftover hummus tracks at the bottom of a pottery bowl. I was hoping the potter had used no lead. I was wondering what my children were doing.

I thought about what I had to do the next day as I finished my drink. Then I looked around for my husband. He was in the living room discussing the Middle East conflict with a short, mildly overweight, balding man. I imagined the man in the front seat of a car at a drive-in, thirty years ago. I gave him hair, but otherwise I didn't change him much.

I sat in a chair close by and heard my husband say emphatically that Israel fought only defensive wars. I fiddled with the hem of my skirt and wondered what it was Jane and her husband had fought about. Several possibilities occurred to me. I heard the short man ask my husband what he did for a living. Sports would be next. I turned my head away from them and permitted myself a yawn.

I thought, *Here is how I feel about men: I am angry at them for the way they sling their advantage about—inter-*

rupting, taking over, forcing endings, pretending to not un-
derstand what equality between the sexes necessitates, thus
ensuring that they are always and forever the ones who say
when. But I feel sorry for them, too.

I remembered a red-eye flight I was on recently. At
about four A.M., I fell into one of those poor-quality sleeps.
I woke up about twenty minutes later and took a stroll
down the aisle. The plane was packed with businessmen,
and they all lay sleeping, their briefcases at their feet like
obedient dogs. They had blankets with the airline's imprint over them, but the too-small covers had slid to one
side or the other, revealing gaps between buttons on the
dress shirts, revealing fists slightly clenched. They looked
so sweet then, so honest and vulnerable. I felt a great love
toward all of them, and smiled warmly into each sleeping
face.

OVER THE HILL AND
INTO THE WOODS

———

Seventy-five-year-old Helen Donnelly is kneeling beside a box in the upstairs storage closet, hiding from her children. Not that she would admit that. No, she tells herself she is searching for the Thanksgiving platter that used to belong to her grandmother. It was dropped last year by Helen's daughter Melissa, and it broke into so many pieces there was no hope of gluing the thing back together, even to hold the lightweight, sentimental baubles Helen provides her family as gifts every holiday. "Now, this is just for fun," she always says, her hands kneading each other, as they open them. "Nothing serious, just a joke." As though they needed to be told that wind-up chattering teeth that walked on little plastic feet were anything but that.

One year, when she was cleaning up after Christmas

dinner, Helen found two of the gifts thrown into the trash. Whoever was responsible hadn't even bothered to wait until they got home. The Santa magnets had cost only eighty-nine cents each, and all right, Santa's red lips *were* painted rather wildly off the mark, as though he had been given a quick kiss in passing, but still. It wasn't the cost. Hadn't she thought about them? Hadn't she spent the time and the effort? Don't bother, her husband, Earl, had told her. Nobody wants those gifts, sweetheart, don't waste your time. They want them, she'd said. You don't know. *Some* of them want them. And when he'd asked, more curious than confrontational, *who* wanted them, she'd said, Never mind. Tightened her lips and picked a toast crumb off her lap. Just forget it, she'd said.

The dish shattered spectacularly, dropped as it was on the new Italian tile kitchen floor. She knew she shouldn't have gotten that floor. *Italian* tile! When it came from Beloit! There was not a thing in the world wrong with her old linoleum floor. But there was Marjorie Beauman over for lunch one day, talking about how there was a sale, talking about how tile could make over a whole room, that you could even get heated tiles! "Think of it," Marjorie said, her voice low and very nearly sexual, "you come out in the middle of the coldest winter night and you think you're in Daytona Beach!" And Helen fell for it, even though she would rather be in her little Wisconsin town than Daytona Beach any day, summer or winter.

So yes, Helen knows very well that Grandma Ute's platter is gone, thrown out in the trash last year with the unwanted food left on the plates (so much *cranberry* sauce, after she'd gone to the trouble to make the garlic-cranberry chutney that that Susan Stamberg had raved about on NPR). For the first time, the giblets and the neck of the turkey had been in the trash, too, because the cat, Gertrude, had walked away from them, no longer able to enjoy such pleasures.

When Melissa had dropped that platter, Helen had gotten so angry she'd begun to shake. Appalled by her outsize reaction, she'd run to the bathroom to sit on the edge of the tub, where she'd folded and refolded a hand towel embroidered with a lovely Thanksgiving cornucopia—not that anyone had noticed—and tried to calm her breathing. And Melissa, outside the bathroom door, "Mom? You're not crying, are you? Mom? It's just a platter, I'll get you another one!" That had just made Helen madder. Get her another one! Another one that Grandmother Ute had washed with care in her old farmer's sink and then dried with one of her flour sack dish towels? A platter she'd bought from Goldmann's the first year she was in this country, had paid for on layaway with money she saved every week from her housecleaning job? Yes, Melissa would just run over to *Fifth Avenue* and buy Helen a platter exactly like that, sure she would. Put it on her *platinum* card, and Fed*Ex* it to her.

Melissa has no appreciation for her great-grandmother. No appreciation for family history. Unless it is a person of color, perhaps. Or a person of persecution, then the history matters. And Melissa had shown no sign of remorse when she broke the platter, either. Even if she did think she could replace it, shouldn't she have felt bad for having broken it? Was it really so bad to feel bad? Helen thinks more people should feel bad for more things. There should be a kind of revolution to bring guilt back into the mainstream. More guilt, more feelings of worthlessness. All this self-esteem crap was making for a society of selfish people who were careless with everything but themselves. It was making for a bunch of people who felt entitled to speak their minds when no one wanted to hear their opinions, people who paraded their sexuality and politics before the whole wide world when no one cared, couldn't they see that no one cared? Helen is *not prejudiced,* no she isn't, but there's a time and a place, really, there is a time and a place and why do those gay people have to tie up traffic that way with their endless marches? Oh, not just the gays, of course. All of them. The formerly disenfranchised who now can't get enough of the spotlight. Just go home, she wants to say to every single one of them. The environmentalists. The vegans and animal rights activists. The transsexuals and the transvestites and evangelicals. The AIDS activists and the antiwar people. The prochoicers and the anti-choicers. The Hare Krishnas snaking along the sidewalks, stinking up the place with their incense. Just go home and shut up. As for the homeless, to whom she used to hand dollar bills and smile at all softeyed? Now she wants to grab them by the shoulders and shake them, shouting, "Oh, God bless your*self.* Get a *job!*"

She hears Earl calling her from downstairs, and pretends not to hear him. Sometimes if she ignores him he gives up, not having been that much interested in her responding anyway. If he's calling her to see some golfer on TV. If he needs some help on his crossword, not that Helen is any good at crosswords, anymore. These days, words fly right out of her brain.

"Helen!" Earl calls again, from the foot of the stairs. "The kids are here!"

"I know," she says, in a voice he can't possibly hear. She had seen when the car pulled up, the rental car Melissa and her husband got because they thought their parents were too feeble to drive to Milwaukee and get them at the airport. Just because of that time she and Earl had gotten lost and ended up in Fond du Lac. One lousy time. Plus, all right, another time they had an accident, but it was not their fault, people had no manners on the freeway.

"Hon?" Earl calls.

"I *know!*"

She hears him walk up a few of the creaky stairs—are they ever going to get those stairs fixed? Not that anyone would fix them properly. Someone would come and charge a fortune and say that they were fixed but they wouldn't be. "Aren't you coming down?" Earl asks.

"Yes! I'm looking for something and then I'll come down." *And don't ask what I'm looking for,* she thinks.

"What are you looking for?" he asks.

She sits back on her heels and sighs.

"Helen?"

"Are Michael and Elaine here, too?" she asks. Her older daughter, the one who deigned to stay in Wisconsin, though in Milwaukee, of course. House on the lake big enough for thirty people. Elaine is fifty-four years old. How could her daughter be so old? Coloring the gray in her hair and getting those shots in her face!

"Yes, Elaine's here." Earl calls up. "Say . . . Helen?"

She comes out of the closet and goes to the top of the stairs to look down at him. There he is, dressed in the shirt she told him not to wear, it is too small and it makes him look ridiculous. A black knit, for God's sake. Who does he think he is, James Bond? A black knit, and he has also put on the tan pants she has told him a million times to throw away. There is a stain at the crotch plain as day, one little round circle and then two smaller ones, no mystery as to what *that* is. Throw those pants away, she keeps telling him and he keeps telling her, No, I like them.

"What *is* it, Earl?"

His smile fades—he'd been smiling at her, his holiday smile. "What are you doing up there?" he asks. He starts up the steps, and she holds up an arm, traffic cop style. "*Don't!*"

He looks up at her. Oh, fine. The hurt face.

"It's a surprise," she says.

"*What's* a surprise?"

"What I'm *looking* for, Earl. It's a surprise. I'll be right down. Just start the relish tray. Give them that. All you have to do is take off the plastic wrap. Can you manage that?"

He turns around and heads back downstairs, shaking his head.

"Oh, pooty pooty *poo!*" Helen says and returns to the storage closet.

She sits down and leans against a large cardboard box, crosses her ankles and closes her eyes. She hears Melissa ask, "Where's Mom?" and the low tones of Earl answering. And then Melissa says, "What's she looking for?"

What is it with these people? Don't they have anything else to talk about? Has the art of conversation disappeared entirely? Well, yes. Yes, it has—Helen knows the answer to that question. It is the fault of television. Television and computers, where all anyone wants to do is keep everything passive and abstract and moronic unless it is about sex where there is nothing abstract at all and everyone is naked. She could teach those people a thing or two about what was really sexy and guess what? It has nothing to do with nakedness.

Something rises up in her. A scary feeling. A thought that she cannot go downstairs. She cannot.

"Mom?"

Melissa.

"Don't come up here," Helen calls.

A pause, and then the stairs creak. "Don't come up!" she says again. But there is her younger daughter before her. "Hi, honey," Helen says. "Happy Thanksgiving."

Melissa crosses her arms. "What are you *doing*, Mom?"

Helen stands, feeling one knee buckle briefly, and brushes off her behind. She's wearing pants, an old gray wool pair, and a white blouse and a red cardigan sweater, an outfit she could just as easily wear to Sears to get a replacement gasket for the washing machine. She has given up on getting dressed up for family dinners: her silk dresses and double-strand pearl necklaces, her theme sweaters. *They* never get dressed up. "I'm looking for something," Helen says. "I told your father to serve the relishes, is he serving the relishes?"

"Yes, they're out. We're eating them."

"Well, then, that's fine. That's all. That's all for now. Go and eat some more."

"Ma, do you . . . need some help?" And there it is, Melissa is looking at her strangely.

"How's Clayton?" Helen asks. "Is he feeling better?" Melissa's husband.

"Oh, my God, he's fine now; his temperature has been normal for two days."

"What a relief, huh?" Helen does not now nor has she ever liked Clayton. Chews with his mouth open and doesn't he just know the answer to everything, just ask him. Insisted that his son be named Rolf, his daughter Enya, never giving a second's thought to Helen's suggestion that his son would be regarded as a neo-Nazi and his daughter a New Age lightweight. Not that she put it quite so bluntly when informed of the name choices. She offered her opinion in Wisconsinese. She said, ". . . Oh?"

"I brought some flowers," Melissa says. "Where's your pumpkin vase? That smiling pumpkin?"

Helen sees that smirk. Don't think she doesn't. She tells Melissa, "Well, it's the flowers, isn't it? It's not what holds them. Just put them in anything."

Melissa says in a voice not quite her own, "All right, Ma." Then she heads back downstairs.

Helen sighs and sits back down again. She hears the muted clatter of pots and pans. Someone's in the kitchen. Earl, probably, though it could be Clayton, who could have been a famous chef, just ask him. Though Clayton did comment on the Susan Stamberg cranberry chutney last year. Commented favorably. He was the only one.

And now here is the smell of turkey, always her favorite smell. So Earl has taken the bird out of the oven; it is time to make the gravy and put the side dishes into the oven, the green bean and mushroom soup casserole, the candied yams, the cloverleaf rolls that don't taste anything like they used to even though the company insists it hasn't changed a thing, Helen wrote to them asking what they were doing differently and they said nothing.

Now the creak of the stairs again, and Elaine is standing before her, saying softly, "What's wrong?"

Helen tries to laugh. "What did Melissa tell you? Did Melissa tell you something?"

"Is there something to tell?"

Helen puts her hands over her face and begins to cry, and Elaine gasps. "*Mom?*"

"Oh, for heaven's sake," Helen says. "No." She wipes at her eyes and smiles. "It's nothing. I just need a minute. Go help Dad."

Elaine stoops down next to her mother. "What's going

on?" She looks around the closet. "Are you really looking for something? Or is it something else? Are you okay?"

"So many questions!" Helen says.

"But are you?"

"Give me five minutes. That's all. Please."

After Elaine has gone downstairs, Helen looks at the garment bags, at the out-of-season clothes in their dry cleaner shrouds, at the things she can't decide what to do with and so leaves here year after year. More and more accumulating, all the time. Helen's friend Winnie told her about a woman who went into every closet in her house and threw out everything she found except for four pair of pants, four blouses, her vacuum cleaner, and her scrapbooks. And she didn't throw out the scrapbooks only because she thought she'd get in trouble with her children for not keeping them. She herself didn't want to look at them anymore. They made her sad. She only wanted to think about the here and now. Not yesterday. And certainly not tomorrow.

What's in these boxes anyway? Helen can't even imagine the contents of most of them. She slides one toward her and sees behind it a huge dust bunny. *Is* it a dust bunny? Helen moves closer to it, blows on it experimentally. Did it move? Her eyesight isn't what it used to be. It could be a nest of some sort. Mice? Rats? Bats, do bats have nests?

She comes quickly out of the closet, slams the door, and pauses for a moment—reflexively, really—to regard herself in the mirror over the dresser. Old woman. She is an old woman. She is aware suddenly of a crushing feeling, centered in her chest, centered right beneath her breastbone. A heart attack? Now she'll have to go to the

ER, where no one will speak English on a holiday, for sure.

She sits nervously on the edge of the guest bed and puts her fingers to her pulse. It's fine, so far as she can tell. If your heartbeat is okay, can you be having a heart attack? Well, now the pain has gone away, anyway. Just like that.

From under the bed comes a bedraggled Gertrude, her coat full of knots. It makes you feel a little ill to pet her now, all those bumps and lumps reminding you of tumors; even if they are only clumps of hair, they remind you of tumors. You can't brush her anymore; she won't have it. She bites you if you try to groom her, gentle Gertrude, the cat who used to act like a dog, following people around from room to room. Now she hides, comes out only to try to eat or use her litter box, and it's getting harder for her to do either. And those baby-faced vets, last time Helen brought Gertrude to them for her stupid shots, which she probably didn't even need anymore, "You might want to consider putting her down." All they wanted was money. If they weren't telling you to murder your pets, they were telling you to torture them. Give cats anesthesia so they could have their teeth brushed. They were animals! What next, nose jobs? Put Gertrude down! Maybe she isn't the same, but she still has her place in their family, yes she does! Helen gently picks up the cat and lays her in her lap. "You're just fine," she says. "Aren't you?" She strokes a small triangle at the top of the cat's head where there are no lumps. "My beauty," she says.

A burst of laughter from downstairs. Helen stands and pulls down on her sweater, checks to see that her blouse is tucked in, rubs her lips together to even out her lipstick, assuming that she's remembered to put it on. A few nights ago, she had a dream that she was outside in her ratty bathrobe and pajamas, lost. Asking directions of the strangers she met on the street, explaining that she couldn't be far, she had walked, so she couldn't be too far, she kind of recognized things, she was just a little disoriented. And the people looking at her so strangely. In the dream, she held a spatula, egg yolk dried at the edge in a thin yellow line.

She really must go downstairs. But what can she bring to justify her having been up here for so long? She can't go down empty-handed—if she does, she'll have to say she couldn't find "it" and they'll all want to know what "it" is. No, she has to bring something along with her.

She goes back into the closet and opens the box closest to the door. On top, a pink elephant, an old stuffed animal that her daughter Elaine used to keep on her bed when she was a little girl and had named Mona Massengill. Mona wore pop-bead pearls around her neck and various outfits—clothes that Elaine had outgrown. Elaine wrapped scarves around Mona's head; earrings dangled from her elephant ears. Sometimes, when Helen was tucking Elaine in at night, she asked what Mona had done that day. The answers varied but were really the same, because what Mona had always done was be a perfect mother. More specifically, Mona had let her children do what Helen disallowed. So Elaine might have said, in answer to Helen's question, "Today Mona drove her children to school in a solid gold limousine." This because Helen made her children walk the four blocks to school. Or "Today Mona and her kids went swimming at the country club." Or "Today Mona gave her daughters fashion outfits because she doesn't think they're expensive at all and also she let them play with *Barbies* because she *knows* it will not *hurt* them."

Helen hates this elephant, actually. She is not pleased to

find her lying at the top of the box in all her weird stuffed-animal self-righteousness. It is in Helen's power to throw her away—no one would know. If they found out, Helen could claim mildew. Instead, she brings the elephant downstairs. No one is in the dining room yet, and she seats Mona at the head of the table and ties a napkin around her neck. Let her finally be seen as the idiotic thing she always was.

And now here they all come, filing into the dining room, calling out "Hello!" to her as though she is some invited guest and they are welcoming her to her own table. And then Elaine sees Mona Massengill. "What's this?" she asks, and Helen says, "That's what I was looking for. That's the surprise. You remember her?"

A tick-tock of silence, and then Elaine moves over to gently touch the elephant, and she says, "Oh, *yes*," with a kind of longing that makes Helen's back teeth ache.

"It was just a joke!" Helen says. Elaine picks Mona up and sits her in the extra chair in the corner of the dining room. Helen has a mind to pick the elephant up by its trunk and swing it around her head, lasso style.

But here is ten-year-old Rolf, pulling at Melissa's skirt and saying, "Can we eat now?" Six-year-old Enya, wide-eyed in her little brown dress, her thumb in her mouth. Helen rushes over to kiss their soft cheeks and say, "*There's my grandchildren!*" and then everyone begins talking and they all take their places. Well, everyone but Earl and Helen, of course. The waitstaff. Earl goes into the kitchen. Helen stands at the table for a moment, looking around at all the faces. Who *are* these people?

"Hey, Mom," says Clayton, though Helen is not his mom and never will be. "Where are the gifts?"

"What gifts?"

"*You* know." He winks at her.

"There are no gifts this year," she says. "You don't any of you like them, and I'm not getting them anymore."

A general *AWWWWWW!*

Well, they are making fun of her, of course. She smiles and goes into the kitchen to help Earl serve the whole ungrateful lot of them.

Earl is at the stove, a dish towel tucked into his trousers, stirring the gravy. Helen sits down at the kitchen table and sighs.

"What's the matter, love?" He comes over with a tablespoon of gravy. "Here. Taste."

She waves him away. "I'm sure it's fine."

"Come on; everything's getting cold. I need you to taste it."

"No, you don't. You don't need me at all. No one does except Gertrude."

He looks at her, astonished. "Is that it?"

Helen rests her chin on her hand and looks out the window.

"Helen?"

"What."

"Is that what's been bothering you? You think no one needs you?"

She drops her hand and stares accusingly at him. "No." It sounds like a question, the way she says it.

"So . . ." He is floundering. He loves her.

"It's . . ." Her mouth goes dry. "You know, Earl, it's like you live your life opening doors. One after the other. You open a door onto a hallway, which leads to another door, which leads to another hallway. But then one day you open a door and it's to a closet. It doesn't go anywhere. And it's dark in there."

"Boo," Earl says.

". . . What?"

"I say, 'Boo!' I'm right in that closet with you."

"No you're not, Earl. In that closet, everyone is alone." Her eyes fill with tears.

"Oh, sweetheart." Earl bends to kiss her forehead, careful not to spill the gravy. "You're just a human being. Now, taste. Tell me if it needs more salt."

She tastes the gravy and nods. "Good. It's really good, Earl. Just right."

He turns off the flame with a flourish. "Okay, then. Let's eat!"

She starts to stand but then sinks back into the chair. Earl comes over and takes her face in his hands. They smell good, his hands. Like turkey and gravy and bread. And Lifebuoy. "Helen," he says. "What do you want? Do you want me to send them all home?"

She sniffs. "Yes."

A moment and then, "Really?" Earl asks.

"Yes. Well, not you. I'll do it. I'll tell them I don't feel well. I don't feel well, Earl."

He straightens his too-tight top, removes the dish towel from around his waist. "All right. If that's what you want. I'll go with you."

"Let me say it, though." She reaches for his hand, and together they go into the dining room.

Helen clears her throat and taps a fork against the side of a water glass. "May I have your attention?"

They all turn to face her. She hesitates, then says, "You know, Earl worked very hard on this lovely dinner. He won't talk about how hard he worked. But he did. All his life. I wonder if any of you know how—"

"*Hel*en," Earl says.

"No!" she says. "I think they should know!" She looks around the table. All of them silent and staring.

"Okay, then," she says. "So, thank you, Earl, and let's eat."

"Mom?" Clayton says. "Before we do? In our family, we used to do the alphabet of thanks as a way of saying grace. You go really fast, just say anything when it comes to your turn."

"I don't want to," Helen says, and Clayton says, "Well, see? That's *okay*. That's the thing. You can say 'pass,' if you can't think of something."

"I don't want to say 'pass.' I don't want to say anything."

"And *that's* okay, too," Clayton says. "So! *I* am grateful for *apples* in the fall." He looks at his son. "Rolfie? Can you say something you're grateful for that starts with a 'B'? Buh-buh-buh . . . What starts with a 'B' that you're grateful for, sweetheart?"

Rolf stares at him.

" 'I am grateful for . . . *buh* . . . *buh* . . .' " Clayton says, and Helen wonders if she can possibly keep herself from leaping over the table to pummel him.

"Butterflies?" whispers Rolf.

"Good!" says Clayton. "Good job!" He looks expectantly at Melissa, seated next to him.

"I'm grateful for *climbing* stock prices," Melissa says, and everyone but Helen laughs. Melissa looks over at Enya and says, "What are you happy about that starts with a 'D'? *Duh . . . Duh . . .*"

I am going to scream, Helen thinks, but then Enya says, "*Dogs!*" with such innocent triumph and joy that Helen can only stare into her lap, ashamed, and wait for it to be over. On and on it goes. And each time it is her turn she is silent. Until they get to "S." Then she starts thinking, *Well,*

*for heaven's sake. How bad can it be. It's just a game, look
how the grandchildren are enjoying it.* And so when her
turn comes around again and they are at "W," she says,
"Okay, I'll do one. 'W.' . . . All right, I am grateful for walking catfish."

"*Huh?*" Rolf says.

"Because they are able to breathe out of water," Helen
tells him. "Isn't that something? You'd never expect that,
would you?"

". . . No," Rolf says, and they go on playing the game.
Helen watches her children, thinking, *I am their mother,
forevermore.* Not Mona Massengill but a real flesh-and-
blood screwup, like every other mother. A human being
who rocked and raised her babies and worried and hoped
and failed and often felt the fullness of her love pushing
out against her ribs. What does she expect? That her children will one day come to her with a long list of things for
which they finally want to thank her? No. They will not do
that. Nor will they come to her with a long list of slights.
She will hide her list and they will hide theirs. They will
go on having holidays with Helen until she can no longer
have them. Another few years, maybe, and then she will
not be able to do holidays anymore and it will be someone
else's turn and then she will be the wrinkled old lady who
comes shuffling in with her terrible toenails and baffled
expression.

When they have finished eating dinner and are ready to
take a break before dessert, Helen asks Earl if he wouldn't
mind running an errand with her. She doesn't want to
drive; she has developed night blindness. "Of course," Earl
says and tells the kids, "We'll be right back, Mom needs
something."

She asks Earl to take her to the twenty-four-hour truck stop, and when she gets there she walks the aisles until she finds something: light-up pins for Christmas, little trees you pin on your coats and the lights flash on and off, on and off. She buys one for everyone, including Mona Massengill. "You're just a stuffed animal," she'll whisper when she pins the tree on the elephant's chest, and she'll say it with superiority, and irony, and—it can't be helped—a little bit of envy.

On Christmas Eve, just before they are to leave for Elaine's house for dinner and gift opening, Earl takes Helen by the hand and leads her upstairs. "What?" she says. "Where are we going?" A thought runs through her brain: *He's going to punish me. He's going to bring me to the bedroom and say, "Stay here; I'm going without you."*

Truth be told, Helen wouldn't blame him. Her attitude, if one might call it that, has not improved. She remains caught in a sinking kind of despair. At Earl's urging, she has made a doctor's appointment, and he has said he will accompany her and afterward they will take in a movie and after that they will have dinner and after that they will go to another movie. "Why would you do all that?" Helen asked and he said, "I like movies."

But now he leads her into the guest room, then to the storage closet. He turns on the light, pulls her in behind him, then shuts the door tightly.

"What are you doing?" she asks. "Earl?"

"Shhhhh!"

She starts to move past him, and he grabs her hand. "Helen, don't. Just wait."

"For what?"

He smiles at her. "Do you trust me?"

"Oh, for heaven's sake. Yes, I *trust* you, Earl. Do you need to bring me to a closet to ask me that?"

He pulls her close to him and then turns off the closet light. "Sit down," he whispers.

"Where? I can't see a blessed thing." She is whispering now, too.

"Just lower yourself down, it's all right."

"Earl."

"Let me help you." He guides her into a sitting position, and then they are both on the floor.

"It's so dark in here!" she says.

He doesn't answer.

"Earl?"

"*Shhhhhh!*" He takes her hand between his own.

Resigned, she draws in a breath and leans against him. They sit quietly, and after a while all the fretful questions banging like moths against her brain seem to fall away. Inside, there is only the cottony feeling of peace. "Thank you, Earl," she says. And then, "Earl? I only got you a new pair of tan pants. That's all I got you for Christmas. I'm sorry."

"I love tan pants. As you know. They're exactly what I need. And that's not all you got me. You also gave me this lovely light-up Christmas tree."

He pulls it from his pocket and turns it on, and now their faces are rhythmically presented to each other in carnival flashes of red and green. She laughs and he kisses her cheek and stands, then helps to pull her up.

"Crepitus," she says, of her complaining knees, and Earl says, "*Et cum spiritu tuo,*" and she laughs again.

Downstairs, they put on their coats and go out into the

night. It is icy, and Earl puts his hand under Helen's elbow to steady her, though in truth it steadies them both.

Once they are off the slick side roads and onto the freeway, Earl turns on the radio, where Christmas songs are playing. He sings along so softly Helen wonders if he knows he's singing. The light-up pin he has put on his coat lapel turns off and on. Helen watches it, aware that, cheap as it is, it may stop working at any moment. But it goes off and on. Off, then on. Off. On.

Eventually, she grows tired of watching it and turns her attention to what she can see from her window. It is a dark night, the new moon only a parenthesis in the sky. But the snow offers soft illumination, and every now and then there is the lovely asymmetry of a split-rail fence, or a family of rock-eyed snowmen, or the swift flight of some animal moving deeper into the woods, toward safety.

FULL COUNT

It is a hot morning in August 1960, and Janey's family is driving from Texas to North Dakota. The trip has hardly begun—they're just past the outskirts of the Army base where they live in a row house not far from the PX. Still, Janey leans over into the front seat to ask her mother if she can have a piece of pie. She knows exactly where it is. In the way back of the station wagon, next to her father's suitcase, in a red food chest with a silver clasp, and she can very easily reach it. The pie is nestled on top, as it should be, being far more vulnerable than the roast beef and fried egg sandwiches, the apples and oranges, the bottles of RC Cola packed below.

It's a mince pie, Janey's favorite. Usually they have mince pie only at Thanksgiving time, but Janey made a special request for this road trip and her mother said yes.

There are starlike designs on the pie that her mother made using fork tines, and sugar is sprinkled liberally over the top and it has collected most heavily and caramelized near the edges of the perfectly crimped crust. Janey thinks the pie is a work of art. And she should know. Only twelve, she has already won prizes for her watercolors of her mother's garden, for her pottery bowls imprinted with geranium leaves, for her charcoal drawing of her embattled Keds. "Shoes?" one of her classmates, Ben Green, asked. "You won an award for a picture of *shoes?* I don't get it. So strange." He says the word "strange" with that southern accent that hikes up a word in the middle and gives it an extra kick. "Striange."

Janey has been living in Texas for over two years now, and she supposes she has a southern accent, too. She can't help it. It just happens that wherever her Army officer father is stationed, she picks up the accent. When they lived in Wisconsin (ages seven to ten), Janey said, "Okay, then" in that Wisconsin way, and also she said, "You betcha," and when she hung up the phone she said, "Bye, now." When they lived in Germany (ages three to six), she spoke more German than English. She still says *Ja* for yes.

Last night, Janey came into the kitchen, the screen door banging behind her, and asked, "Are we fixin' to eat?"

Her mother turned to look at her and laughed.

"What?" Janey said. "Idn't it five-thirty yet?"

"Oh my goodness," her mother said, laughing louder, and turned back to the stove. She was dishing up potatoes. It *was* time to eat. So what was so funny? When Janey asked, her mother affected a southern accent to say, "Well, y'all have just gohn raht out 'n' turned inda one of 'em. Mah lands."

Janey wasn't sure what to do. First of all, "y'all" was

the plural form of "you," not the singular. She stood still, half smiling, and her mother sighed and came over and kissed the top of her head and told her to go wash up. "Don't be so sensitive," she told Janey. "It's kind of sweet. Are we *fixin'* to eat."

In the bathroom, Janey looked deep into her own eyes. She likes doing this, but she has to be careful not to look too long or she can go crazy. Mary Beth Croucher told her that, and it is true: if you look too long, all of a sudden it's like you are floating and your brain goes cobwebby. But Janey likes to look because, when she does, she can see herself as a woman. She falls down the rabbit hole of her own eyes into a brighter future, where she is grown up and no longer oversensitive. There she is in a short-sleeved sweater and tight skirt, her hair in a French twist, pearl earrings firmly screwed on. Red lipstick and rouge. The woman Jane.

She is getting there. Recently, boobs came. They are not pointy enough, they are more like fat pads, but they are still boobs and she has a bra with a sweet pink rose sewn onto it. Soon she will start her period and there will be no arguing then: she will be a woman because she will be able to have a baby. She doesn't like to think too much about actually *having* a baby, it makes her a little ill, but the fact of being *able* to, that's the thing.

Last night, after Janey looked into her eyes just up to the point of going crazy, she washed her hands and dried them hastily on the towel. She did this to obey her mother; Janey herself thinks using towels is wasteful. Why not just wipe your hands on your clothes? It's only water. Even after baths, Janey sits in the tub to air-dry. There's only the tiniest residue of dampness on your bottom when you do that, and pajamas easily absorb it. And then the towels: pristine, unbothered.

Next Janey went to sit at the table with her parents and eat dinner. It was then that she asked about the pie for their trip tomorrow. She saw a look pass between her parents; then her mother said, All right, yes, she would make a pie. Janey wasn't sure what the look meant, and it was times like this that she longed for a sister with whom she could compare notes. If she were the older sister, she could be flip and ask, "What the hell was that look?" If she were the younger sister, she'd have to be more deferential, of course. She'd have to ask permission to come into the sister's room, permission to sit on her bed, and then say, "Why did Mother and Father look at each other that way?" But Janey is an only child, and so she lay in bed that night and asked the question only of herself. Maybe because baking the pie would heat up the kitchen? Or it would be too messy to eat it in the car? Had she said "pie," "pah"?

But now, "Go ahead," her mother says. "If you want pie, have some. If you're that hungry."

Janey is not hungry. It has nothing to do with that. She reaches into the back and carefully opens the food chest, carefully cuts a piece of pie, carefully puts it on a small paper plate, carefully gets out a fork and a napkin. "Do y'all want any?" she asks.

"No thanks," they say together, and her mother is smiling that smile again.

Janey looks out the window while she eats her pie. It tastes wonderful; her mother knows how to keep mince pie from being too sweet. She puts in apples and lemon juice. She puts in butter and salt. Janey rubs her tongue against the roof of her mouth to squeeze out all the flavor she can. She sits up straighter and puts her knees together. Good food makes her do that. Dogs do it, too, begging for a bite. They sit up very straight and still. Janey takes small bites, so that the pie lasts longer, so that it seems like there is more. She has heard you should chew at least seventeen times, but if you do that, all you're doing is chewing spit. Janey has observed that she chews mostly four times and usually begins swallowing at three and a half.

When Janey has finished her pie, she checks the rearview to see if her father is watching. As he is not, she licks the plate. She considers asking if she can have more. No. She'll ask later. When they stop for gas. She throws her dirty dishes in the trash bag her mother has put on the floor of the backseat. Janey's thirsty now, but to make up for asking for more pie later, she won't ask for a drink now.

She stretches out along the backseat and closes her eyes and thinks of her grandfather, called Bampo, from the first grandchild's mispronunciation. She'd never tell her parents, but she loves him more than she loves them. He wears cardigan sweaters and suspenders. He makes gravy beyond compare, and he gives Janey mashed potato and gravy sandwiches and eats one right along with her so that she doesn't look stupid. He slides his lower denture plate out with his tongue, then bites it back in like a snapping turtle. (When he first showed Janey this, she didn't know his teeth were false, and she thought he was an awfully talented man.)

When Bampo greets you, he shakes your hand really fast in a way that undulates your whole arm and says, "Howdohowdohowdo!" until you are helpless with laughter. You always laugh around Bampo, he makes everybody laugh. He talks to strangers and they talk back to him. He is the star of the whole extended family. Janey thinks sometimes it must be hard for her grandmother, but her grandmother is a good sport about it. She has her role. She stands in front of Bampo to be the first to welcome those who come to visit. She answers the phone and she makes the coffee and toast in the morning. She cleans the birdcage and vacuums the rugs, she decorates the bathroom with fluffy pink toilet tank covers and toilet seat covers and rugs. There are also pink ruffled curtains, and a doll wearing a pink crocheted hat and a wide skirt that hides the extra toilet paper. The doll has a pink parasol, which Janey longs for, though she has no idea why—what would she do with such a thing? Her grandmother is the only one allowed to touch the porcelain poodles on the end table, a white poodle dog and two puppies, all linked together with fine gold chain. She sits at the kitchen table with her daughters and talks to them about how to manage husbands and children, and sometimes she reads their fortunes in tea leaves, oh, she can be vibrant in her usefulness.

But Bampo is the star, and he loves Janey the best of all his grandchildren. He lets her sit on his lap no matter what, even if he's listening to baseball on his transistor radio; he loves his baseball and will not suffer interruptions during a game. Janey does not love baseball except when she's with him. Then, she listens to the game, too. She likes when the announcer says, "Annnnd it's three and two, full count." Janey likes a full count, because then something is forced to happen—the guy's safe or he's not.

There are other reasons Janey knows she's her grandfather's favorite. If she gets a cut or a scrape, he's the one to put on a Band-Aid. If she's dizzy after a ride at the state fair, he'll sit things out with her on a bench with his arm around her for as long as it takes. Once, he burned a tick off her head with a lighted cigarette. He put the cigarette to the tick's butt, and the thing backed right out. When she drives somewhere with him, he lets her turn the steering wheel. He sent her a bottle of Friendship Garden perfume for her tenth birthday, when no one else thought to give her perfume, which she loves. He knows her secret, and keeps it.

Janey often has night terrors, where she wakes up from a sound sleep with her heart racing and her breathing all but impossible. The idea of her own death seems to assume wretched form, and it sits on her chest, pries open her eyes, and mashes foreheads with her. The walls close in and the ceiling lowers. Darkness deepens. She does not hear but feels the words:

YOU   WILL   BE   NO   MORE.

Sometimes it lasts only a minute or so, and she falls back asleep. Other times, it lasts longer. When it used to happen, she would cry and whisper, "Please." But last time her family came to North Dakota, Janey and her grandfather were for some reason alone in his house, and she told him about it. She said, "Sometimes I wake up at night, and I'm so scared of dying." She laughed a little, embarrassed.

Bampo said, "Oh, that's an awful thing. What do you do about it?"

"Nothing." She swallowed hugely.

"You don't tell your parents?"

"I can't." She looked down. "I don't want to."

She expected that he would argue against this, tell her she should awaken them so that they might comfort her. But he didn't say that. Instead, he said, "Well, next time it happens, here's what I want you to do. I want you to go very quietly into the kitchen and turn on the light and sit at the table and eat an orange. Will you do that for me?"

She nodded solemnly. She thought it could work. She could see herself at the kitchen table in her pajamas, swinging her legs, peeling an orange, the scent rising up for the cure. She could hear the low hum of the overhead light burning steady and bright, chasing away the shadows and illuminating the cheerful Mixmaster, the long line of her mother's cookbooks on the counter.

And indeed Bampo's suggestion did work. When Janey awakens now with that particular kind of panic, she goes each time to the kitchen and turns on a light. Once they were out of oranges, but an apple did the trick. It wasn't the fruit anyway, Janey had decided. It was the getting up.

So, yes, her grandfather treasures her: she holds it in the teacup of her heart. But there are other good things in North Dakota. Janey has cousins there whom she really likes; they are like brothers and sisters. Her parents always stay with her grandparents, and Janey stays with Aunt Peggy and Uncle Jim. They have five children, three boys and two girls—her parents' siblings all have large families, her family is an anomaly; she doesn't know why.

Janey spends time with the girl cousins who are her age, but she also spends time with the boys, and she prefers this, it seems a privilege; boys do not otherwise seem to like her. They seem, in fact, to like her less and less. Boys and girls from her school go roller-skating together and then to Boogie's for hamburgers, or they meet at the movies, and sit together. But then they just go their separate ways right afterward, and their eyes seem empty of the near memory of one another, so Janey doesn't think she's missing all that much. She believes she'll catch up soon. She hopes so.

Janey especially likes her cousin Michael, Aunt Peggy and Uncle Jim's oldest, and her cousin Richie, who is the oldest of Aunt Ruth and Uncle Henry, who live nearby. Michael is a year older than she, and Richie only three months older, and they both greatly admire the way she can draw. Last time they wanted tanks and airplanes, infantrymen dead on the ground, bullets flying. This time she suspects they'll want spaceships or beautiful women, amply endowed—this is what the boys in her art class ask her to draw. She can do either.

Her parents will probably deliver Janey to her aunt and uncle late at night, they usually do, and Janey thinks how Aunt Peggy will show her to a bed made up in sweet-smelling linens from the sheets having hung on the line to dry in the wind and the sunshine. She thinks too of how Aunt Peggy—everyone, really—will comment on how much she's grown. They haven't seen her for two years— last August, Janey got her tonsils out and they couldn't take their annual trip to North Dakota. Janey got all the ice cream she wanted in the hospital, but it didn't make up for the burning pain. Everybody said it would, but it didn't.

Janey sits up and spreads her map across her lap. Every time her family drives to North Dakota, she follows along on a map, x-ing out the states as they pass through them. This time it will be Texas. Oklahoma. Kansas, Nebraska, South Dakota. She already knows that South Dakota will seem the longest because it's the one before you finally get there.

She yawns, considers car bingo, with its insulting juvenile pictures of cows and railroad crossings, rejects it in favor of watching the telephone poles whip past, birds on the wire occasionally rising up in a great flurry of flapping wings, a choreography of surprise and fear.

At the restaurant where they stop for lunch on the second day, the silverware is in an envelope of waxed paper, and the waitress calls her father "honey." She doesn't know not to be so familiar; he's not in uniform, and he is using his vacation manners: no orders, no yelling, no gruff inquiries as to where he left his burning cigarette. He winks at Janey's mother, and her mother smiles back. They are always in their own club.

Janey asks if she can have a hamburger, and her mother says of course. "Cheeseburger, I mean," Janey says, "and can I have French fries, too?"

Her mother ignores her, so she asks again for French fries. "If you *want* them, *get* them," her mother says. Janey holds one hand with the other and squeezes it.

"Get them," her mother says, more softly now.

Janey shrugs.

"We'll share," her mother says. "How about that?"

"Okay." Janey doesn't like to share food. It makes her nervous, deciding how much she can take. She'll let her mother have all the French fries.

While they wait for their food, Janey looks around the room. Big fat guys dressed in bib overalls and plaid shirts, hats on the table beside them with sweat stains on them. Not many women; there's one woman two tables over sitting with a little girl wearing a blue sundress and red shoes. The girl is cute: curly blond hair, pink cheeks, a hectic kind of energy that has her playing with the salt and pepper shakers, arranging and rearranging her silverware, changing her position from sitting to kneeling to sitting.

Janey waves at her, and the little girl stares. "Hi," Janey says, but the girl says nothing back.

"So," Janey's mother says, "are you excited?"

About lunch? Janey wonders. *The trip?* She nods.

"Me, too," her mother says, and then turns to her father.

"Hi," Janey says to the little girl. "Hi, there." No response. Janey looks out the big plate-glass window in the front. Across the street, a grocery. A dry cleaners. Dust rising up in the street from the occasional truck passing by; there are far more trucks than cars in this town.

And then the cheeseburger comes, and the French fries are good ones, so Janey does have a few. Four. And then when they go back to the car her mother and father both want a slice of the pie, so it's not so bad for Janey to have one, too.

It is indeed late at night when they finally get to Aunt Peggy and Uncle Jim's house, and after changing into her pajamas in the bathroom, Janey is shepherded quietly to her cousins Vicky and Doreen's bedroom, to a cot beneath the window that has been made up in the very way she remembered: the linens are a summer day. Janey holds the fabric against her nose and falls asleep quickly. She dreams of riding in a car. Wheels turning and turning and turning, asphalt humming, radio stations coming in and fading out, the clouds a motion picture playing out for miles across the sky.

In the morning, Janey awakens before Vicky and Doreen. She sees how they have changed: ten-year-old Vicky's face has lost its baby fat, and her blond hair is very long; eight-year-old Doreen is much taller, and she, too, now has long hair. Janey tiptoes out of the room and heads downstairs; she can hear the voices of the boys in the kitchen, Michael's in particular (so much lower now!), and she is eager to see him. She wants to ask what they'll do that day but decides against her own presumptuousness; she'll let him offer, and whatever he offers, she'll say she wants to do.

"Good morning!" Aunt Peggy says. She is in her robe, her hair in rollers, standing at the stove, where she is making pancakes. "Look who's here!" she says to Michael and the six-year-old twins, Ben and Harry. Ben and Harry do not look alike at all, something that confounded Janey until her father explained the difference between fraternal and identical. But they are all nice-looking children, and Janey sees that Michael has grown handsome, even manlike, and it makes her pull down on her pajama top and wish she had brushed her teeth.

Aunt Peggy offers her a plate with three large pancakes stacked up tall. "Hope you're hungry!" she says, and Janey is. She sits at the table and pours syrup over her pancakes, though the truth is that she prefers jelly on them. But this is travel: you accommodate yourself to others' preferences.

Michael stares at her, then looks away when she looks over at him. Janey smiles, then asks, "How is your summer going?"

Oh, how the question hangs in the air. Finally, he shrugs and says, "Okay." And then he smiles, and she feels better. She remembers now this period of awkwardness that she always goes through, her cousins looking at her like she is a rare zoo animal. But it passes quickly. Soon they will be comfortable with one another, and all the cousins will push en masse to be first for one of Uncle Ray's perfectly burned hot dogs at the family picnic. Janey will spend time with this cousin and that during her visit, but mostly she will be here, and she thinks now that maybe she will say something about the day, claim her place at Michael's side.

"What are you doing today?" she asks him.

"Swimming!" Ben and Harry say, and Michael says, "Bampo's taking us to the lake."

"All of us?" Janey asks, wondering how they'll fit in Bampo's car. They are used to sitting on one another's laps, but still.

"No, just us and Richie," Michael says. "Richie always comes. He should just live in this family."

"Well, I think he'd miss his own, don't you?" Aunt Peggy asks. She sits at the table with her own pancakes, cuts them into neat squares, and douses them with syrup. "I wish we weren't out of bacon," she says, and then, to Janey, "I'm sorry we're out of bacon."

"Oh, I don't mind," Janey says and can feel herself blushing.

"I seem to remember you really like bacon," Aunt Peggy says, her mouth full. She swallows, then says, "Don't you?"

"I do, but . . . I don't mind." She puts her arm up to try to hide her already empty plate.

Michael stands. "I'm going to get ready."

"Me, too." Janey rises so hastily she scrapes her leg painfully against the underhang of the table. Important not to show it. "Race you upstairs?" she asks Michael. He snorts, but it's not derisive; it's friendly.

They go upstairs, Michael ahead of her, and he turns back to say, "I hear you won some awards for your artwork or something?"

"Yes."

"That's good."

At the top of the stairs, he says, "See you."

Janey tiptoes into the girls' room, but they are awake now. "Hi, Janey," Vicky says. She sit up in bed, tosses her hair back over her shoulders. "You're here again."

"Want to see my new doll?" Doreen asks. "She's a fashion doll with blue eye shadow and she has lots and lots of clothes."

Janey will hurry with Doreen and Vicky; then she will go and find Michael, and she hopes they will wait outside together for Bampo, away from the others. She is glad she'll not be seeing her parents all day, indeed not for three days, when they will have the family picnic; it was a long drive.

The lake water is a deep green, and Janey can see the seaweed undulating beneath the surface. She doesn't like seaweed, and she doesn't like the rocks on the bottom of the lake, even when they are tiny. She has gotten used to swimming in the pool at the Army base, where the bottom is smooth and the water looks turquoise and the diving board sparkles with a rough white surface that looks like diamonds. Janey has learned to do a half gainer, but there are no diving boards here.

She is wearing her swimsuit under her clothes, and the straps are cutting into her shoulders; she will need a new one before the season is out. But for now she is sitting with Bampo at a picnic table while all the others are in the water. He watches them, but he talks to her. She has told him about her favorite and least favorite teachers. She has told him about visiting the Alamo. He has asked if she's famous yet for her art, if she has a boyfriend who drives a convertible and can crack his knuckles ("*No?*" he said, when she laughed in response), if she has seen many movies lately, he envies her the cheap cost of movies on the base. He has shown her a card trick using the miniature deck he always carries, and she has agreed with him that it will thrill the little ones.

Janey feels mature, sitting at a picnic table with her hands clasped and talking this way with Bampo, and indeed he has been the first to comment on how she's grown, calling her a real young lady now. She smiled when he told her this and did not blush, everything that comes from Bampo is easy to hear.

She is about to ask him how his baseball team is doing when he sits back suddenly and says, "Here now, don't you want to swim? Don't you want to go into the water?"

She shrugs. "I don't like the seaweed."

"Well, I'm going in. It's hotter than the devil's pitchfork. Come with me, why don't you?"

She might as well, what is the alternative but to sit alone and watch, something she is overly familiar with. She takes off her pedal pushers, her short-sleeved blouse and sandals; he takes off only his socks and shoes—for Bampo, swimming means rolling up his pants legs, wading into the water up to his knees, and then staring out at the horizon with his fists on his hips. She walks hand in hand with him to the shoreline, and then they separate. *"Bampo!"* Ben and Harry call out, and he waves at them. Doreen and Vicky are practicing mermaid dives, and they yell for Bampo to watch; Michael and Richie have swum out to the dock, and they too call out to their grandfather.

Of all the people Janey has seen thus far, she thinks Richie has changed the least since she last saw him. Still on the short side, still innocent-looking, with his big blue eyes and rosy cheeks, still sporting a crew cut, and his voice is still that of a boy. Still giggles when he laughs. Not like

Michael, to whom so much has happened. In Bampo's car on the way over, Janey noticed fuzz on Michael's upper lip. He was wearing his swim trunks and a T-shirt, and Janey saw the dark hair on his legs, and it revolted and thrilled her. She herself has begun shaving her legs, though her mother got angry about it the first time she did it. Two months ago, Janey came downstairs with little pieces of toilet paper stuck to her ankles, to her knees, and along her shinbones. Her mother was sitting on the sofa reading a magazine, and she looked up and gasped and said, "Don't you dare do that again, you are too young!" But then, right afterward, she said, "You know, once you start that, you have to keep it up!" so Janey kept it up. She likes the look of shaved legs, though she realized after looking at Michael's legs that stubble had grown on hers—it has been three days since she's shaved. She decided that later she would ask Aunt Peggy if she might borrow a razor. Really, she should have her own.

She stands still, a little cold, her arms crossed over her chest. Out on the dock, she can see Michael standing, staring at her. He says something to Richie, and then Richie stares, too.

"I'm going in!" Janey yells and splashes out farther in the water. She swims over to Doreen and Vicky; she knows how to mermaid-dive, and she can teach them about keeping their legs together, their toes pointed. They will be all right to play around with, the girls, but the main thing is this: Michael has noticed her. He is her cousin, but he has noticed her in a new way. Janey feels like she did one time when she was much younger and was outside with a group of kids playing horse. She was the leader, a young stallion, and she was wild and free and beautiful, satiny black with a white star beneath her forelock. She neighed and pawed the earth and flung back her head and ran faster than she ever had before, and her hair streamed in the wind behind her. This moment is like that. She feels it in the same low part of her body, the way she has come suddenly to a place of beauty. Bampo may have seen it as well, for he, too, stares. First at Michael, then at her. Again at Michael, then at her. It's all right, she wants to tell Bampo. We're cousins. Nothing will happen. We've just grown.

After everyone has come out of the water, they play hide and go seek, all of them together, the bigger kids and the younger ones, and even Bampo, who volunteers to be "it" first. He leans against a tree and covers his eyes and counts aloud, and the cousins spread out to hide. They are still a bit wet, all of them still dressed in only their bathing suits. Bampo has said that, after they're dry, he'll take them to Dairy Queen. He had his arm around Janey's shoulders when he said this, and she dared not move lest he take his arm away. She hoped the others didn't mind his preference for her, they really shouldn't, she was there so infrequently.

Now she stands still behind a tree that is very close to Bampo; she learned long ago that the best place to hide is close to home. The person who is it always assumes that people will hide far away and, after counting, moves quickly forward to begin the search. If you hide right behind base, you can quick run over and tag yourself in. Not this time, though, for as soon as Bampo stops counting, he heads directly for Janey's tree. She can't run back to base; he'd beat her. So she surrenders even before he finds her; she steps out from behind the tree, giggling, and says, "I give up. I'm it."

He stares at her, and Janey can't quite read the look on

his face. Disappointment? *Anger?* "Ah, now, Janey. I hadn't even seen you. I might have walked right past you!"

She shakes her head. "No, you were headed right for me." She holds up her hands. "I surrender." Her bathing suit is really bothering her. It feels too high at the bottom, and again the shoulder straps are cutting into her. She will be glad to get home and change out of it.

"I got caught; I'm it!" Janey yells. "Everybody come out!" She is glad to be it, really; Bampo shouldn't be running all over. He takes heart medication.

The cousins come out from their hiding places, and Janey leans against the tree to count. After she hits one hundred, she yells, "Ready or not, here I come!" She can't really remember if she is supposed to do this; she hasn't played hide and go seek for a long time. Oh, but what difference does it make, it's such a gay day, her happiness is tight in her throat, she loves being here.

Janey stands still and looks around for a telltale sign: a flash of clothing, movement of some kind, a muffled giggle. And there, in the bushes across the way, she sees a rustling. It's so obvious she thinks it must be intentional, a ploy to be found so everyone will be that much closer to Dairy Queen. She knows what she's getting: a Peanut Buster parfait. Last time she babysat, she used the money to buy herself two.

She walks over to the bushes, laughing. There they all are, every one of them, including Bampo, crouched in the greenery and peering up at her. "I see you," she said. "Y'all come out of those bushes."

A kind of guffaw, and then there is the sound of Michael imitating her, saying in a high voice, "Y'all come out of those bushes!" All the cousins laugh. For a moment, she holds the smile on her face, the bright happiness she was enjoying still inside her. But then Michael comes crashing out of the bushes and walks past her with a look of disgust on his face. "Lard ass," he mutters.

She jerks back a breath. *Lard ass.* What does it mean? She imagines a person with a big round behind, shiny and metallic like the Crisco can, galumping along and looking sideways at all the people she passes. And then she thinks of the Three Stooges, running into one another and all falling down. Dominoes standing upright in a line, and then one gets pushed. She imagines a net breaking, a bag tearing, the contents falling and falling.

She is not a stallion, wild and free. She is a girl whose bangs were cut crookedly last time and whose mother told her to stop complaining. Her teeth are too big and her eyes are too small. She sleeps with a silk slip stuffed between her mattresses, and in times of need she scratches it and sucks her thumb. She does not have any friends, really. And here, the last, she understands now that she has gotten fat. She understands the reason for the looks that pass between her mother and her father when she asks for pie, for French fries, for more.

Janey walks beside her grandfather to the car. He has not heard Michael, and she will not tell him, for along with her other realizations, she has seen that Bampo cares equally for all his grandchildren, she is not the favorite, she is simply loved. It is good, but she had thought it was more.

At Dairy Queen, they sit at one of the outdoor tables, and her cousins place elaborate orders with Bampo; swimming does make you hungry, and it is long past lunchtime. Janey's stomach feels hollow; she is so hungry she is light-headed, but she says she doesn't want anything. Bampo is surprised. He asks if she's sure, and she says yes. Up her spine, a zip of approval, of solace, of strength. She crosses her arms over her belly and looks away from the softly melting ice cream being delivered to her cousins. She thinks of the last time she was in North Dakota and all the cousins were in Bampo's basement, playing war. Michael and Richie and the other boys were the fighters, Janey and the other girls were nurses. She remembers how she knelt beside the injured, sympathizing with them over grotesque wounds, which they described to her in detail. She thinks of how she advised each patient not to go back into battle, but to surrender, and how they all ignored her and went back to fight. Janey understood the futility of war, the terrible cost. She knew her strength was that she did not believe in fighting. But now she wonders if it is her weakness, too.

She hears the sounds of the cousins eating their sundaes, their plastic spoons scraping. She knows the feel of butterscotch in her mouth, the perfect mix of sweet chocolate and salty peanuts. If she were eating, she would put the spoon in her mouth right side up and pull it out right side down.

She stares into the glare of the sunstruck cars in the parking lot and imagines herself back at home, ensconced in her room with a clean white sheet of paper. She is painting a watercolor. She is trying a new technique, using lovely pastels so thinned with water you can barely see them on the page. Look how beautiful they are.

RAIN

———

I used to have a friend who lived in a house he built with his own hands. I'd first met Michael at a party in the late sixties, when we were single and in our early twenties, both of us living in Minneapolis. I was singing in a rock band, making enough money to get by, and he was writing ad copy for junk food and making more money than he knew what to do with. Michael drove a Morgan, wore clothes right out of *GQ*, dated a succession of beautiful women, and lived in a tastefully furnished apartment in a hip part of town where he was utterly miserable. The last time I visited him there, he was standing in front of an open cupboard in his kitchen, wearing one of his Edwardian suits and pointing to boxes and boxes of Snackin' Cake. "This is my *life*," he'd said.

"Well, what can you do?" I'd asked, rhetorically, of

course. And he'd looked over at me, and it seemed as though I'd given him the missing piece to an equation that had been keeping him up nights at the blackboard for a long, long time. "Quit," he'd said. And grinned.

He was gone in a week, apartment sublet, car and furniture sold, clothes, too, for all I know. He moved far up north in Massachusetts, to some acreage that had been in his family for over one hundred years. There was a graveyard there, he said, but nothing else. Michael intended to build a house and live off the land. It took a long time for it to happen: for the first five years after he left, he rented a cheap apartment in a little town nearby and lived off his considerable savings while he built every part of his house, learning as he went along. We wrote irregularly to each other during those years—I talked about my marriage to Dennis, the birth of my son, the guilty ennui of any young mother. He wrote about swimming in the ice-cold pond on his property, wetting down his hair to comb it for the pretty women at contra dances, picking enough blueberries to fill a large silver bucket and then sharing his bounty with friends who returned the favor by dropping off a pie. The time he wrote me about coming home to that pie (*I did the sensible thing and brewed up a pot of coffee and ate it for dinner*), I held his letter and stared out the window, thinking of what it must be like to live somewhere where you could come home to a pie left on your kitchen table. It was so different from our way of life. We had friends, Dennis and I, but we also shopped in grocery stores for our small and overly expensive boxes of blueberries. Most prohibitively, we kept our doors locked when we weren't at home, and oftentimes even when we were. That Christmas, I sent Michael an engraved card with an enclosed photo of our little family; he sent a handmade card on butcher paper he'd decorated with a potato stamp: *Note the folksy unevenness of the points of the star,* he wrote. *No small effort went into making this appear effortless.*

Seven years after Michael moved, he sent me a letter saying he had completed building his house, and I really ought to come and see it. A trip like that seemed impossible, but I really wanted to go, and finally I talked to Dennis about it. There was some discomfort at first, as I'm sure there would have been if Dennis had wanted to go and visit an old female friend. But in the end, he told me to go the next weekend and even to use his frequent-flier miles; he and two-year-old Will would manage fine without me. I had suggested initially that we all go, but both of us knew I didn't really mean it. In truth, Dennis didn't want to go; he didn't even know Michael.

I left Minneapolis early on a Saturday morning in late spring and flew to Boston, and much of the time I was on the plane, I thought about Michael. I remembered once when we were driving together in his car and I had pulled out a tube of lipstick and put some on. When I finished, I held out the tube, saying, "How about you? Need to freshen up?" He put the lipstick on—not a playful dot, he moved carefully from one side of his mouth all the way around, then handed me back the tube. And we drove on. I loved it. I loved that he put lipstick all over and then didn't take it off right away. I loved how far he was willing to go, but something about it bothered me, too.

I thought about the cold winter night when he picked me up and we drove onto a frozen lake. We spun around in circles and slid sideways, completely out of control. I laughed until I was out of breath, but my scalp prickled with fear. "Don't you ever worry about falling through?" I asked, and he said, "Of course. That's the fun."

I thought about how handsome he used to be, and I thought about how I used to look in those days, too, my black hair nearly to my waist, my clothes as Janis Joplin–ish as I could get them: feathers and pearls, bell-bottoms so wide they looked like ball gowns, patchouli-scented velvet-and-lace tops, beneath which my breasts moved freely. Michael and I had flirted with each other, and I think at various times had contemplated having a relationship— a look across a room, a certain tone to our voices when we spoke on the phone—but we hadn't. I told myself it was because we were never between relationships at the same time, but I also sensed that, if I moved too close to Michael, I'd lose him.

He picked me up at the airport. In those days you could wait at the gate for passengers. When I emerged from the mouth of the Jetway, I saw Michael standing off to the side—he was easy to spot; only a few other people were waiting there. But he was jumping up and down and waving his arms, saying, "Over here! Over *here*!"

I walked up to him, a little embarrassed. "Clown," I said, and he touched my bobbed hair and said, "Ah well. You're still beautiful."

I touched his ragged beard. "You, too."

We drove a few hours on the highway, then on some back roads, and finally turned down a heavily rutted dirt road where the dust rose cinematically. Then we were there. I stepped out of the car and was, for the first and only time in my life, literally rendered speechless. "Go in," he said.

There was a small front porch with a rocking chair on it. There were stained-glass inserts that ran on either side of the front door in the colors of light green, orange, red, and yellow. In the kitchen was a wood-burning stove, two chairs, and a beautiful bird's-eye maple table. The table was stationed before a bank of tiny-paned windows. I stared at the windows, just stood there for a while taking in the view of the woods and the wildflowers outside, but mostly I was admiring the craftsmanship of those many panes. "Got those windows at the dump," Michael said. "Lots of stuff here came from the dump." I put my hand to the smooth surface of the kitchen table and looked over at him. "Yup," he said.

Along the kitchen walls were open shelves holding pottery dishes—he had traded firewood for those, the potter who made them lived not so far down the road. There were plastic bags with granola, dried fruit, whole wheat flour, walnuts. There was honey complete with comb, olive oil and blackstrap molasses, and Mason jars of coffee that had been hand-ground by some ancient kitchen tool bolted to the wall. Michael had depleted his savings and now made money for groceries doing odd jobs, mostly carpentry—building a porch here, putting in a cupboard there. He had told me about this in his letters, but seeing the evidence—food he'd gotten for labor—seemed a kind of miracle to me. There was a small refrigerator with Deco styling, it too rescued from the dump, where it had been tossed for the crime of being too old, but it was fine in every way. Inside was a block of butter, cinnamon bread that appeared homemade, fancy cheeses, speckled brown eggs in a pottery bowl. There were vegetables in colors so vibrant they looked fake: deep purple eggplants and carrots the orange of construction workers' safety vests, rosy red tomatoes. Beer and wine, milk and cream. Half a jar of anchovies, the fancy white kind.

Michael let me look, he let me snoop. He followed me

around, available for questions, you might say, but mostly he just enjoyed my seeing everything for the first time. It let him appreciate things anew, he said.

A ladder led to a loft-type bedroom, where there was a mattress on the floor, covered with an Indian-print bedspread. His bed was neatly made, and I admired this about him, that such a manly man (his descriptions in letters of cutting down trees with a chain saw! Lying under his truck to grease it!) would also take such care in straightening bed linens, in placing pillows just so. The bed was stationed directly beneath an uncurtained window, and a hummingbird feeder hung outside it. Finally, I spoke. "Do they *come?*" I asked.

"All day long," he said.

There was a little hot plate in the loft so he could brew tea without getting out of bed. There was an oil lamp that let him read by the kind of gentle golden light he preferred, and there was a stack of tapes—classical music—to listen to. Nails on the wall held all the clothes a person needed, really. Orange crates served as bureau drawers for socks and underwear. There was an old-fashioned girlie calendar on the wall directly opposite the bed, featuring well-endowed Vargas-type women: curly-headed, apple-cheeked blondes wearing see-through negligees and cha-cha shoes, their mouths naughty O's. "Lonely up here?" I asked, and he smiled.

"This is where you'll stay," he said. "I'll sleep in the hammock outside." When I started to protest (though I wondered if I didn't sleep there where I *would* go), he said, "I like to sleep outside in the summer. Mosquito netting is the trick, there."

The living room was outfitted with an overstuffed sofa

and chair, a 1940s floor-model radio, and bookshelves spilling over with offerings of classical fiction, history, poetry, and all manner of how-to manuals. No television.

I even liked the outhouse—it was clean and full of light from the crescent moon–shaped skylight. The walls were papered with pages from an old Sears catalog: wringer-type washing machines, boxy men's suits, women in cone-shaped brassieres. There was a wooden toilet seat, complete with lid, and there was very good toilet paper. A framed sampler on the wall said DO CHECK FOR SPIDERS. DON'T BE AFRAID.

Outside, there were acres of woods and open fields. Now that he had finished the house, Michael told me he intended to make penned-in areas for lots of animals: chickens, sheep, rabbits, even a pig.

Seeing Michael's place filled me with conflicting emotions. I was happy for him, glad he'd stood in the middle of his kitchen one random day and pulled the veil from his heart's desire. But it distressed me to understand suddenly that this kind of life was what I wanted, too. Everything about it—the natural beauty, the deliberateness of every choice, the apparent congruency of heart and soul and mind—spoke to some fundamental longing in me that had never been brought into focus before. But it was too late for me to live like this. Dennis wouldn't want to. Will was all set to go to good schools—we'd chosen our suburb with that in mind. We liked our neighbors and friends, liked living near the city. Dennis and I watched the late-night talk shows together and often held hands while doing so. Sometimes I would be wearing some weird-colored facial mask, and I would think, *Forget the romantic notions of marriage. This kind of comfort, this kind of safety, that's the thing.* But on the day I first saw Michael's house,

I regretted the way I'd gone, and wished I'd come with
him all those years ago. Of course he hadn't asked me to,
and if he had I wouldn't have said yes. I wouldn't have
known to—everything that let me appreciate what I saw
around me now was unripened in me then.

And so I stood having my petulant little memorial service for the self that never got to be. And then I let it go,
moved back into the head and heart of a monogamous
married woman with a child who loved her husband and
son and her granite kitchen counters and knew how much
she had to be grateful for.

We kept the weekend friendly, and we kept it safe: we
cooked together; we talked about old times; we walked for
many miles. On Saturday night after dinner, we sat in the
living room listening to a symphony performance on the
radio—Michael put on a tie for this, and I did, too. On
Sunday, we had breakfast and then drove back into Boston
so that we could go to the Gardner museum before he took
me to the airport. He kissed me on the mouth when we
said good-bye, but only briefly.

I saw him standing at the plate-glass window inside the
airport as the plane backed out of the gate and then began
taxiing down the runway. He held his hand up, and I
pressed my own hand to the airplane window, though I
doubted he could see me. *Over here!* I thought.

A couple of years later, Dennis got a job offer he
couldn't refuse, and we moved to Boston. Michael and he
finally met and truly liked and admired each other. We
drove up to see Michael a few times a year, and he came on
occasion to see us. Once, when he was desperate again for
money, we hired Michael to stain our deck. My next-door
neighbor, Suzanne, spent a fair amount of time standing in
the backyard and talking to Michael while he worked. His

style might have changed: he cut his own hair—badly—
and wore thrift shop clothes, but he was still a very attractive man. He had streaked blond hair, eyes so blue they
were navy, and he was in the kind of enviable shape you
enjoy when you use your body for real work. Michael had
taken his shirt off that day, and Suzanne stood with her
arms crossed and watched the muscles move in his back. I
thought I knew a little about what she was thinking. And I
had the misplaced proprietary feeling of a married woman
who has a handsome single man for a friend.

One day in August, when I was seven months pregnant
with my second child, Dennis, Will, and I all went up for a
visit. Michael had lots of animals by then, including a big,
fat pig named Sally. I had always been beguiled by pigs, or
at least by the E. B. White–ish idea of them, but standing
right beside Sally, no fence between us, made me a bit nervous. She ate huge mounds of scraps every day, and it is
something I would have happily paid to see, the pig's ears
coyly over her eyes from the way she bent down to attack
her dinner, her grunting sounds that made anyone watching smile, you really had to. The curly tail going round and
round and then stilling for a certain kind of pleasure: a
hard scratch to the hindquarters, or coming upon something delicious to her in her slop pan—bits of blueberry
pancakes, perhaps, Sally was inordinately fond of blueberry pancakes. Bizarrely enough, she also liked bacon.

There were lots of cats and dogs by then. The cats were
nearly feral, and came close to the house only at dinner-
time. They formed a semicircle not far from the door and
waited, and Michael put out food for them and then sat in
a lawn chair, smoking a cigarette and watching them.

The dogs were another matter: they loved all hu-
mankind, all the time, and they lived all over the house.

Michael favored cocker spaniels, and it seemed that one of them was always having puppies. The one he named Señorita Rosalita Carmelita had delivered seven fawn-colored puppies—all boys—on the day before we visited, and Michael let my then five-year-old son hold one of them. Will was overwhelmed with the pleasure and the responsibility: he sat still as a statue, afraid to move, afraid even to breathe. When my husband asked him to smile for a photo, the most he could offer was a twitch of one side of his mouth. Rosa watched my son anxiously but did not move from nursing the rest of her brood. When the puppy was returned to her, she eagerly sniffed him everywhere she could reach, and then Michael turned the puppy on his back so that Rosa could leave no spot unexamined. "Everything appear to be in order?" he asked. Rosa looked up at him and wagged her tail, and Michael put his hands on either side of her head and kissed her full on her mouth.

"Eww," Will said, but he had the courtesy to whisper, and I think, too, that there was some respect and understanding mixed in with his squeamish commentary. It occurred to me to make some flip remark about Michael being lonely up here, just as I had years ago, but it seemed as though it wouldn't be funny anymore.

I remember we went into the house afterward, and I made spaghetti sauce from the riches of Michael's garden: onion and garlic that were sautéed in olive oil, basil and oregano and tomatoes still warm from the sun. I added a little honey and a little red wine and we let the sauce cook down, and then we ate outside, watching the sky redden, then purple, then go black and starry. Maybe it was the wood-burning stove, but I have never tasted better marinara. We had salad, too, butter lettuce also from the garden dressed simply with lemon juice and olive oil and salt.

Michael had Hershey bars from his last trip to town, and we ate those for dessert.

After that we moved back inside the house, and I lay Will down on Michael's bed, where he always liked to fall asleep. I did the dishes while the men sat in the living room and talked. At one point, Michael came into the kitchen, moved close behind me, and put his arms around me. "You and Rosa," he said quietly, and there was less irony than admiration in his voice. He put the flat of one hand to my belly, and I laid my hand over his, pressing down, so that he could feel the baby move. "Ah," he said and kissed the back of my neck, then moved to the refrigerator for beer. "Heineken?" he yelled, and Dennis yelled back, "Great."

When I finished the dishes, I came into the living room and waited for the evening's entertainment: Michael had finally broken down and gotten a phone and had left a message on a more forward-thinking friend's message machine to call him when she got home so that he could hear it ring. We waited, idly chatting, until it did ring, and then we all stared in wonder at the thing—we had slipped into Michael mode, as people often did when they visited there. You walked onto his land, and within a few minutes, the rest of the world fell away. So when Michael's new phone rang, it was as though a Martian had landed, and I suppose in some respects it had—Michael had by then gone a very long time without a phone—for years he'd had to walk half a mile down the road to his neighbor's if he needed to make or receive a call. But he hardly ever did need to. He wrote letters, is what he did. He wrote, *You'll forgive my silence. Winter is knocking at the door and I'm far away from completing fall's chores. Firewood in these parts is not a lux-*

ury. In deepest summer, he wrote: *A picnic lunch on the newly erected breezeway of Anne and Peter Sullivan. Rhubarb crisp took first place here, followed closely by the sweet corn, then by the honey wheat-berry bread, served still warm from the oven. No offense to the tomatoes, which also deserved a high place in the running, but which are too often and easily praised.* Often, he wrote about his inability to stay with women: *Disheartening to see how soon the straw begins to suck air. I suppose I admire your willingness to hang tough in your marriage, despite your complaints. I never could argue for trying to force a relationship. Once my mind has decided there's no future, I'd rather read a book. Still, it's awfully humiliating to find oneself masturbating his way through his forties and into his fifties. Especially on those nights I beg off to my own self, pleading the proverbial headache. I'm afraid that the state of my love life might best be summed up by the state of my refrigerator: I have plenty of margarine, but I'm low on the high-priced spread.*

Once, sadly, he wrote, *I came home to find little Sophie dead at the side of the road. She had gotten out of the house somehow and engaged in her bad habit of car chasing. She was a pretty dog, with a pleasantly blocky face and silken ears, and she was full of life and good humor, as Rosa's puppies always are. Her dance card turned out far shorter than I'd anticipated, and I buried her this morning with a regret that seemed barely able to be contained. I put her next to Mona, who lived a far longer time but less happily, I think. (You might remember Mona as the Lab mix I got at the shelter who never would lay off licking her forepaw. On a hot afternoon, it could get on your nerves.) Sophie lies not far from the brook she loved to swim in. I expect it will take a while before I can visit her there. But you know one of her virtues was patience. That and licking the grease off the hamburger wrapper without ripping it up, allowing for a much appreciated ease of disposal.*

His stationery moved from blue fountain pen on brown Eaton pages to pulpy lined paper he found at the dump (*Reams!* he said. *If you like, you can have some, too. It makes you feel young to write on this*) to the back of flyers and of solicitations that came in the mail. Then he began reusing envelopes from those solicitors, ironically highlighting their gaudy call outs in one way or another before he taped the envelopes shut. When he visited, he gently chided me for the paper cup dispenser I had in the children's bathroom. Dennis suggested at one point that Michael was going round the bend; I hotly defended him.

The fall after we'd moved to yet another, bigger, house (the last one! Dennis and I promised each other), we invited Michael and several others of our friends for Thanksgiving dinner, and Michael didn't show. Finally, we all sat down to eat without him, and the phone rang. "It's Michael," I said. "Go ahead and start." I had been fearful that we had fatally offended Michael with this last acquisition—it was a really big house—and that he was calling to say he'd decided he'd rather not be faced with yet another evening of values clashing. I figured he'd say, as he often had before, that it worked best when I came up to see him, and why didn't I do that, soon. But it was not Michael on the phone. Rather it was his brother, Sam, whom I'd never met. He told me that Michael had asked him to call and explain that he'd not be able to come to dinner. He was in the hospital. He'd been diagnosed with a brain tumor. And what did I do? I laughed. I said, "*What?*" Then I burst into tears, and then I immediately stopped crying and apologized. I said, "What can we do to help?" Dennis came into the room and put his hand to the

small of my back, a question, and I grabbed on to it and
squeezed. Michael's brother said it might be nice if we visited him at the hospital, but not that night, as he'd had a lot
of visitors already. I said we'd go tomorrow, and his brother
said maybe in a few days would be best: his surgery was tomorrow.

I hung up the phone and said to Dennis, "Let's just eat.
I'll tell you later."

After we got into bed, I told Dennis what Michael's
brother had told me. We said the usual things: How could
this be, what did this mean, what if he dies. We talked
about the last time we saw him, how he had seemed *fine*.
And then Dennis said, "I always wondered. Did you ever
sleep with him?" I said no. He said, "Maybe you should."

I stared at him. "Are you serious?"

He shrugged. "I don't know. Yeah."

"Well, which is it? 'I don't know' or 'Yeah'?"

"I guess it's 'Do you want to?' "

"*No*, Dennis."

"I'm sorry," he said. "I don't know why I said that." He
turned out the light and rubbed my arm. "I don't know
why I said that. I guess I always thought you two were attracted to each other. And now that he's . . . Never mind. I
don't know why I said that."

We lay awake, silent, for a long time. Another episode
of off-the-mark communication, a problem in our marriage, as I supposed it was in countless others. So many of
us dream of complete honesty in our love relationships,
believing it to be the way to achieve true intimacy. Then
we discover that the truth can be dangerous, even cruel,
and we struggle with what to offer and what to withhold.

It wasn't true that I didn't want to sleep with Michael.
I'd always wanted to sleep with him, and all these years

later, I still did, and I thought I understood the confused generosity of my husband. He was making an offering of his wife against sorrow and fear, and in deepest friendship. He had assumed, for a moment, at least, the wide perspective that the prospect of death can bring.

And so the cards. The phone calls. The visits to the hospital bearing homemade soup, books, funny slippers. The hope that the tests would come back one way, and they came back another. The hope again, that maybe he would defy the odds. Then, finally, the end of the road. Everything tried; nothing successful. What was left was for him to go home and try to keep comfortable for as long as possible.

We visited often at first, Dennis and I. All Michael's friends did. But our visits fell off: the distance, the necessity of living our own lives, the way one becomes used to anything, even a good friend dying.

In mid-July, I got a call from Michael's brother asking if I could drive Michael to the hospital the next day; he couldn't stay at home any longer, even with all of his friends and neighbors checking in on him, it wasn't safe. His doctor had called Sam that morning and told him it was time. Sam asked if I could deliver Michael to Mass General tomorrow by four; Sam couldn't, because he himself was hospitalized for a hernia repair. He could ask one of Michael's other friends, but they'd already done so much, and they were all so busy at this time of year. Could I do it? Yes, I said, yes, of course.

"When was the last time you saw him?" Sam asked.

I confessed, guiltily, that it had been a few weeks.

"Be prepared. He's pretty bad off now. He might need help with . . . He might need help. He's not walking too well."

"I'll take care of everything," I said and hung up the phone as though it were made of thinnest glass.

I arrived the next day much later than I'd intended; there'd been a bad accident on the turnpike that had stopped traffic, then slowed it for miles. I pulled up to the house and saw Michael on the front porch, in the rocker. I stepped out of the car, and he watched me walk over to him. His hair was cut wildly unevenly; shocks of it stuck up here and there amid areas that had been shaved close to his head. "Hey," I said.

"Come for the gipper, huh?" He lit a cigarette.

I sat on the steps beside him and stared out into the woods. This view. This land. This house.

"I'm not going," he said.

I turned to face him, and he leaned in closer to me. "Do you blame me?"

"Michael," I said.

He held out his pack of Camels. "Cigarette?"

I had never smoked. "No, thanks," I told him. "I'll wait for you to finish. But then I have to take you to the hospital. I'm sorry I got here late; we'll have to leave right away, I'm afraid."

He squinted up at the sky, a cloudless blue.

"I have to pee," I said. "I'll be right back." I cut through the house to get to the privy, and saw Michael's calendar on his desk. He'd written things on there, but it was not his usual penmanship, and things were grossly misspelled: *Simfhoany with M.!* he'd written on one of the days. I put my hand over my mouth and looked at other entries, all misspelled and some completely unintelligible. Then I moved to the window and looked out at the back of Michael's head, those tufts of hair. He moved the rocker gently back and forth. He was wearing untied sneakers, a pair of gray corduroy pants, and a pink dress shirt, the sleeves unbuttoned. There was a plastic bottle beside him with what looked like sediment from apple juice coating the bottom. I wondered if he'd eaten. I wondered if he could answer accurately if I asked him. I wouldn't ask him. I'd just make him something and offer it to him, and then we'd have to go.

When I went back into the house, I opened the refrigerator. A terrible stench came from there—it seemed as though every single thing in it was rancid. I closed it quickly and moved over to the shelves, looking for crackers. There were some wheat crackers, and I brought the box outside. I held it out to Michael, and he said, "What's this?" in a way that made me wonder if he was asking literally. "I thought maybe you might want to eat something," I said. "Got some crackers here. Are you hungry?"

He pooched his lips out, as though he were considering, then said, "When was the last time *you* were flossed?"

I half laughed. "What—?"

He reached out and grabbed my crotch.

"*Michael.*" I pushed his hand away.

He turned from me and stared straight ahead. He lit another cigarette, though one already burned in the ashtray. "You know, you've got one going," I told him.

A car came down the road, pulled into the driveway, and a man stepped out, slammed the door, and looked up with a big smile on his face. It quickly disappeared. "Michael?"

Michael stood, and I saw that his pants were barely hanging on. He'd lost so much weight. He hiked them up, then stood there with his hands on his hips. "I know you."

The man nodded. "I was your summer helper a few years ago."

"Don."

"Well, it's Bradley, actually."

"Bradley," Michael said. "I remember."

I introduced myself. I was trying to think of a way to tell the man what was happening here. But then Michael said, "I've been sick. Had a little brain surgery."

Bradley nodded vigorously.

Michael put his arm around me. "This is a friend who's come up to visit." He stumbled and sat back down heavily in the rocker. "Christ."

"Well," Bradley said, "I won't keep you, then."

Michael rocked in his chair. "No."

"I just was out here in the area and remembered you, and thought I'd stop by."

Michael rocked and rocked.

"It was a nice summer," Bradley said. "I don't think I've ever met a man who knew so much about so many things. I still miter corners the exact way you showed me. I still play the Mozart tape you gave me, play it most every morning while I shave."

Michael stopped rocking and stared sadly ahead.

"So anyway. Just wanted to stop by. . . . I'll come back another day, I know this isn't a good time."

"Another day," Michael said. "Yes."

"Okay, then, take care, Michael." Bradley got back in his car and drove off. I had seen a wedding ring on his finger, and I imagined the conversation he'd have with his spouse later on. "Jesus, can you imagine? I didn't know *what* to do."

A great tenderness arose in me, and I embraced Michael from behind, put my arm loosely around his neck and kissed the top of his head. "Yup," he said.

"We have to go, sweetheart."

"Where?" he whispered.

"I have to take you to the hospital. Sam was going to do it, but he can't."

"Hernia repair," Michael said.

"Yes." I closed my eyes. "Yes, that's right."

Michael stood and started for the house. "Be right back," he said. I waited on the porch for a while, wondering where Sally the pig had gone. Michael's friends who lived in the area had done a lot to help, and one of the things they'd done was to find homes for the animals. Not a single one was left, not even a dog. The grass grew high in the pens; the gates were all open. The potter down the road had told me they'd left the oldest cocker with him for a while, Lilly was her name, but he hadn't been able to care for her—forgot to feed her, to let her in and out. "I bring her by to visit," the woman had said. "Lately, though, he doesn't really seem to care."

From inside, I heard a crash, and I ran into the house. Michael was by the refrigerator, loading things into a box. A bottle had broken, and the contents were spreading out over the floor. I grabbed some of the newspaper he used for paper towels and began mopping up what looked like it might have been salad dressing. Michael continued packing the reeking contents of the refrigerator. I sat back on my heels. "Michael."

"Yeah." A cigarette dangled from his mouth, the ash long.

"What are you doing?"

"No point in everything going to waste."

"It's rotten."

He ignored me, continued packing. I stood and put my hand on his arm. "Michael, it's *rotten*."

He kept on putting things into the box: limp vegetables,

greenish bacon. His hands were shaking. "Let me," I said, gently. "I'll do it for you. Wait for me outside in the rocker, okay?" He shuffled away, and I continued mopping up the floor. I was hoping that he'd forget about this—that when I was done cleaning up, we could just get in the car and go. I felt terrible that I was doing such a bad job at the relatively simple task I'd been assigned. I gave the floor one last swipe, put the food back into the refrigerator, and went outside. No sign of Michael. I came back in, climbed the ladder to the loft, and saw him lying on his bed, smoking.

"Okay," I said. "I'm ready." He didn't move except to tap ashes off his cigarette and onto the covers of the unmade bed.

I stepped closer. "Might not want to do that."

He took in another drag, exhaled upward.

"Michael?"

He looked over at me.

"Do you want me to pack anything?"

"For what?"

"To bring to the hospital?"

He lay his cigarette down on the bed and pulled the half-full pack from his pocket to shake out another one.

I leaned over and grabbed the cigarette he'd put down. It had burned a small black hole into the spread.

Michael flicked his lighter and tried to light the other cigarette. I took it and the lighter from him. He stared at me as though he were contemplating what he might do next. But then he just shut his eyes and turned onto his side.

He was a big man. I couldn't haul him out of there. And I couldn't leave him. I sat on the bed beside him. "Michael, will you please come with me? Please."

He sat up but raised a finger, *wait.* He turned toward the open window. Outside, you could hear the whistle of a cardinal. The leaves shifting in the wind made for kaleidoscopic patterns of light and shade against the side of Michael's face. Then I heard the thrilling buzz of a hummingbird. It appeared at the feeder in its tiny, jewel-like splendor, drank, then flew quickly away. Just when I was going to say again that we had to go, Michael stood up.

He went down the ladder first, and I followed. He stopped at a mirror he had stationed on a wall above the kitchen sink and regarded himself. He licked one hand and smoothed down his hair, then went over to the refrigerator, opened it, and stood there, blankly staring.

"Please leave that," I said.

He reached in and pulled out a softened and lopsided orange, then faced me. He rubbed his hands gently over the fruit, kissed it, and began peeling it.

"You can bring it in the car, okay?" I pulled the keys from my purse.

He leaned against the open door of the refrigerator and continued peeling. Then he split the orange almost in half and began licking at the center in a way so specific it made me blush. He moved his face in closer to the orange, closed his eyes, and worked his mouth slowly, rhythmically. And then he fell down.

I rushed forward and asked him if he was all right; it was a hard fall. He looked up at me, one eye closed. "Ow." He blinked, rose slowly, refusing my assistance, then stood tall to say, "Well, anyway. Et *cet*era." He leaned forward, pressing his forehead against mine. "Was it as good for you as it was for me?"

I smiled.

"I *could* offer you a banana," he said.

Now I laughed. "I'm fine."

He closed the refrigerator door and looked at it as though it were a relative he was awfully fond of. "Let's go," he said.

He took nothing with him but his beat-up wallet. He did not lock his door. He did not look back, not before he got in the car, not after. I pulled slowly away, then, after the house was no longer in view, picked up speed.

We didn't talk much on the way to the hospital. I was thinking of what I'd tell Dennis about this day, what about it belonged to him and what about it belonged to me and what about it belonged to Michael, and I decided it all belonged to Michael.

At the last tollbooth before we got off the turnpike, I reached in my cup holder for two quarters to pay the fifty-cent charge. Michael said, "You know, I've always found that one quarter works just as well." I tried it; I put in one quarter, and the gate lifted.

He leaned his head back and closed his eyes. "I've always meant to tell you that. I have no idea why it took me so long."

I said nothing. To acknowledge all that was in that remark would be to put a fist through the dam. I drove the short distance to the hospital and pulled into a parking place near the entrance. I cut the engine and touched Michael's arm, gently called his name. He started—apparently he'd fallen asleep—and looked out the window. "Big place," he said. Then he said, "Okay. I'll be wanting to go in alone." He sighed, and pointed at me. "You," he said.

I pointed back at him. "You."

On the way home, a light rain fell. It wasn't enough to require using the wipers. But some drops gathered along the side of windshield, and when I came to a stop sign I noticed how they captured light and refracted it, how a whole spectrum of possibility was contained within a single drop of water.

I visited Michael a few more times, but he was often sleeping, and then he became difficult or impossible to understand. He died the night after some friends had taken him outside briefly on a gurney to see the few flowers that grew on the grounds, and to watch for birds, which never came.

THE DAY I ATE NOTHING
I EVEN REMOTELY WANTED

Those Weight Watchers meetings are murder. There's always a bunch of brownnosers who get little presents and applause for the pounds they lost. Sometimes a little whoop, too, there's this one woman at my meetings who whoops for people. And the leader always makes this announcement at the end of the meeting about how many pounds were lost this week by our whole group. I sit in the back staring at my lap because week after week I mostly lose nothing. Well, one time I lost three pounds. I'd had the flu, and the whole time I was embracing the toilet, a part of me was saying, *"Yes!"* Next meeting, two and a half pounds had come right back on, saying, "Hey there, Bubbles, did you miss me?"

Still, the meetings do work for getting me motivated over and over again. They make me feel like when I was a little girl and went to confession every week. All the way home, I used to walk so slow and tight to keep my soul spotless, but as soon as I came in the door, there was my brother. Same thing with the meetings: each time, I vow it's going to be different this week, and then on the way home I see a Krispy Kreme, no line. Or, you know, my kitchen.

"It's okay," my leader always tells me. "We all slip up once in a while. You come to the meetings every week; that's a *great start*!! Just try to eat less, now." Her eyes are kind; her belt is cinched a bit too tight, but, hey, let her take credit where credit is due. One thing about those leaders: I always wonder about their personal lives. I mean, are they always like this? If so, do their co-workers at their real jobs want to slug them? Sometimes I wonder so hard about their personal lives it keeps me from paying attention to the meeting, which always has a little allegory of some kind, some story you're listening to, wondering what does that have to do with anything, and then *whump!* A diet lesson has been delivered. I feel kind of sorry for my leader. She tries so hard. So yesterday, just for her, I tried to eat right.

I began breakfast with coffee and skim milk. Do you know what drinking coffee with skim milk is like? It's like asking for a dress and being handed a slip. Also I had toast, which was equally disgusting because it was toast made the new way, using diet bread, a.k.a. cardboard. Here is my recipe for toast made the old way: (1) Go to the bakery and buy a loaf of freshly baked white bread. (2) Take two slices from the middle of the loaf and toast them to just light brown. (3) Lay the toast out on a beautifully patterned antique china plate that has a rim of gold and must be washed by hand, but it's worth it. (4) Saturate the toast with a rounded tablespoon of Plugrá butter (European-style, higher fat content), which has been melted in an old cast-iron skillet that your grandma gave you that never was and is not now all that clean. Just to be clear, that would be a rounded tablespoon of butter on each piece of toast. All the way to the corners and then some. (5) Cut the toast on the diagonal into four lovely pieces. (6) Dunk in hot chocolate you've made with Dutch-processed cocoa and cream, and over which you've sprinkled fifty or sixty little mini-marshmallows, very fresh and boingy ones. (7) Eat, while dialing the number for the Buddha. When he answers, say, "You want contentment? I'll show you contentment!" So that is toast, made the old way.

When you make toast the new way, you spray it with some chemical stuff that comes in a cheerful can and is colored yellow and that is supposed to make you think it tastes like butter, but it does not, it tastes like chemicals and it reminds you of jaundice.

Along with the toast, I had some fruit that I bought in a plastic container at a fancy health food store whose nickname is Whole Paycheck, because I wanted a mix of fruit and didn't want to spend a month's rent on an assortment of whole melons and whole baskets of berries. So I bought this mix that looked very appealing, the cute little blueberries and raspberries mixed with other things like cantaloupe and honeydew (which, wait, what does "honeydew" *mean?*), but guess what? The fruit had *no taste.* Zero. It was all texture, no taste. And the texture was slimy. And forget bringing the fruit back to the store. Because they are trained to make you feel bad. They say, Sure, we'll give you a store credit, but look at their nostrils: flared.

Here is a quiz: What does the dieting woman have for lunch? Right! Salad! And what kind of dressing? Right again! Almost none!

It is said you can get used to salad with no dressing. Well then, why call it a salad? Why not call it grazing? I will admit that sometimes a strip of red pepper can taste good. But that's usually because you've added salt, which helps just about everything, even chocolate, as they have finally discovered. But when you're dieting, what must you cut down on, in addition to everything else? Which reminds me: Have you tried air-popped popcorn? No butter, no oil, no salt? I believe it began as a practical joke, but then the diet people heard about it.

Okay, so I had salad with vinegar and an atom of oil. So boring. I had to make up a fantasy to get through it. Which was that I had to eat really fast because I was on my way to an all-expense-paid trip to Japan, where I have been wanting to go lately, so who cared what I was eating, it was just fuel (something else dieters are encouraged to think, that eating is just fuel rather than, oh, a reason to get up in the morning). I had to hurry and eat to catch the plane, where I had a first-class seat. But then my fantasy led to dangerous waters, like, hmmmm, first class, don't they serve freshly baked chocolate chip cookies on those flights? I wanted to make some low-cal, low-fat coconut custard after that, which really is actually not too bad tasting except you feel like you're in an old folks' home when you eat it. But I didn't make the custard because what usually happens is I eat all of it, not just one serving, and I was *not* going to cheat. One day at a time, as the AA people so wisely tell themselves every day. I modify this to: one meal at a time. So instead of coconut custard, I had an apple, which, like most apples these days because they're stored for two hundred years, tasted like mush. *"Ummmmm!"* said I, to fake myself out. So appley, so not at *all* in need of baking with butter and sugar and cinnamon in a cunning little crust.

Oh, the hours before dinner. Made worse by the exercise obligation hovering over me. *"Get moving,"* said this one pamphlet I got at Weight Watchers. That really gets my dander up. *Get moving!* Like all I do is lie around. No. I do exercise.

My exercise plan, by Melody Peterson: Every day, take a walk unless you are too tired or it's cold out. Do not pass grocery stores. Or bakeries. Or restaurants. Basically, walk in the woods and worry that someone will kill you for recreational sport before you've even come close to your target weight. You might try "Oh, Mr. Murderer, please don't kill me, I have only fifteen pounds to go." It *might* work. Because he has his own troubles, obviously, and he might relate.

The afternoon passed, the clock finally said four-thirty, and I could think about cooking dinner. I had to make something I didn't like so as not to eat too much. What? Liver? No, I *extremely* don't like liver, plus it can't be good for you if its role is to filter out toxins, can it? I never got that. Why would you ever eat liver once you've seen and touched it? My mom used to make liver and onions, which I have to tell you made me feel like committing suicide. I would walk in the door after coming home from high school, with all its troubles of where to sit in the cafeteria and pimples and physical education teachers, and say, "What's for dinner?" and my mom would say, "Liver and onions!" all cheerful like Avon calling, and I would just deflate like a cheap balloon.

For dinner, I decided on plain chicken, not even oven-roasted, which just carries that buttery connotation plus when you roast a whole chicken you get crispy skin, which no one can resist except New York women. I think the French women do eat it. But their secret is they eat a little tiny bit of it and then a little tiny bit of chocolate and a lot of wine and they go off and have affairs, which of course burns off all the fat.

Crispy chicken skin being the worst for you, it tastes the best. It is just diabolical, how this is all set up, that the best-tasting things are the worst for you. Isn't it hard enough here? I hear all the time that once I make the change and get used to eating right, an orange will taste like dessert. "It really will!" they say. To which I silently respond, "Are you talking to me?"

This is a true story. One time I met a chef from a really fancy restaurant, a really expensive one, too. And I asked her what her favorite food was. You know what she said? "Pork rinds. But homemade ones, which are greasier." Which just goes to prove all kinds of points.

So. A plain baked chicken breast, I thought, maybe a little barbecue sauce, even though barbecue sauce makes me think of baked potatoes, loaded, which is the natural accompaniment, the Mrs. to the Mr. of baked chicken. No. No loaded potato! A plain baked potato, one half, with that damn spray again. Yellow spray. Maybe it doubles as insect repellent, it certainly could, a mosquito would hold up its hand(s), coughing, and say, in its high little whine, "Okay, okay, I surrender, jeez, what *is* that?"

For my vegetable, I would have broccoli, all the broccoli I could eat. Here is my recipe for broccoli: Cook it any way you want, it doesn't matter, it will never taste really good without hollandaise sauce. Chew it fast with your nose plugged. Done. I did squeeze some lemon on the broccoli, which kind of helped. So I squeezed on some more. Quite a bit more. Basically, my vegetable was green lemonade.

So that was dinner. Time, after I was finished? Five-seventeen. *Now what, now what,* I was thinking. *I can't go to bed yet.* I went to a double feature at the local theater, two movies I really didn't care that much about, so I made a game of how many times does someone in the movie wear red? Not often, it turns out, not counting lipstick. I had a big Diet Coke (which I believe kills lab rats) in there with me, and every time someone in the movie ate, I drank. My treat. My "popcorn" and "Junior mints." Then I came home and took some NyQuil and went to sleep. And now look. I ought to change the name of this story. Because that NyQuil? It was *good.*

MRS. ETHEL MENAFEE AND MRS. BIRDIE STOLTZ

———

"Seasoned pepper steak over rice," Birdie says. "And Oriental-blend vegetables."

"What's that mean?" Ethel asks.

"What's what mean?"

"*Oriental*-blend vegetables. What was Oriental about them?"

"Oh. Well, I haven't an idea in the world."

"Were there snow peas in there or something? Water chestnuts? Bok choy? Daikon?"

"No. Just peas and carrots. And stop showing off."

"I'm not showing off! But then . . . was there at least soy sauce over them?"

"Soy sauce? Hold on." A moment, and then Birdie comes back to the phone. "No. No soy sauce. No butter. No white sauce. No hollandaise. Nothing but peas and carrots, and the peas are all wrinkled." Her voice is fainter now; she's not speaking into the mouthpiece.

"Birdie, dear, hold the phone up to your mouth."

"I am."

"Well, closer."

"I *am*."

Ethel turns her head away from the phone to sigh. Birdie Stoltz. Stubborn as the day is long. It's a wonder they've been friends for over fifty years. "Do you need me to bring anything today?"

"No."

"*Think* first, Birdie. You might need me to bring something."

"I don't need a thing." She sniffs, punctuating herself.

"All right, then. I'll see you at one." Ethel hangs up the phone and stares out the window. Her kitchen curtains need washing and starching. They hang limply inclined toward each other, loose in their tiebacks. They look like matching beggar girls, each asking the other for a crumb to put in her basket.

Ethel wishes that Birdie would just once request something. Bed socks. A bar of rose-scented soap. A *TV Guide* or a *Reader's Digest*. French fries from McDonald's, a box of Good & Plenty. Anything to show that she still has an interest in something. She needs to show an interest in something, or this time she won't come home, Ethel just knows it. And then what. Then it will be Ethel's turn to wait for the Great Inevitable all by herself.

Ethel considers bringing Birdie something anyway but then decides against it. Too many times she has handed her friend a package, saying, "Surprise!" or "This is for you because I love you" or "Now, don't get all excited, really, this is nothing," only to be met by the flat, nearly accusatory expression on her friend's face. Birdie doesn't like to get gifts when she's in the hospital. As near as Ethel can tell, it's because they remind Birdie of where she is and of other things she prefers not to think about. Gifts make her think people feel sorry for her. And she will not be felt sorry for. Birdie spends most of her time in the hospital staring straight ahead, waiting for the doctor to tell her she can go home. If anyone calls her Birdie, she says emphatically, "My name is Mrs. *Stoltz.*"

It's Birdie's chronic lymphatic leukemia that has her in the hospital again. She's done well for a long time, but now things are starting to act up. She's getting some kind of experimental immune system therapy. If it works, she'll get another reprieve. If it doesn't, well, it doesn't. Birdie tightened her mouth when she told Ethel that last part, then took in a breath and looked pointedly away. She had the air of someone who had just been grossly insulted, and Ethel supposed she had been.

Ethel takes her curtains down and shakes them out. Maybe they're not that bad; when she looks at them now, they don't seem that bad. She hangs them back up and fluffs them out a little. There. Better, if only by virtue of having had someone notice them. "Things have feelings, too!" Ethel used to say, as a little girl; and she still believes it, actually. Why not. Stranger things have been discovered. Plants and *their* feelings. Dogs and their emotions. The health benefits of dark chocolate—that was a *good* one. As opposed to Pluto being stripped of its planetary status, that was deeply disturbing. Though not of course to Pluto, which simply continued to orbit, oblivious of its status, out there until it wasn't. Simple.

Ethel checks her watch. She'll go and run some errands: the bank, the drugstore, a turkey sandwich at Subway, and then she'll go to the hospital. Nothing like having a friend immobilized to make you appreciate your own freedom. She has time to go to the library, too, and she has to quash the immediate impulse to find something for Birdie there, surely her friend couldn't refuse a library book—it was free, it was returnable. But Birdie would refuse it. She would say thank you but she really didn't feel like reading. And anyway, maybe a library book didn't belong in a hospital, where it could get all full of germs. It wouldn't be polite to bring a library book there. Think of the next person who checked it out, catching something terrible.

Ethel wipes off her kitchen counter, straightens the rag rug in front of the sink, centers the fruit bowl on the little round table. "See you later," she tells her kitchen.

Ethel bought her house ten years ago, six months after her husband died. It's on a block lined by tall trees, whose tops meet in the middle of the street like crossed swords at a military wedding. Her place is a little bungalow, Chicago yellow brick, the smallest property on the block, but truly the loveliest, Ethel thinks. She got it for a song, because it had the original bathroom and kitchen, which Ethel preferred. It has a sweet front porch outfitted with a swing, a mature garden out back, small but lush, and art glass high at the tops of the windows that makes for churchlike spills of color on her oak floors in the late afternoon. The closets are small, but what does she need with huge closets? And the closets have glass doorknobs, which she loves. As a girl, she used to pretend the glass doorknobs in her parents' house were diamonds, and they all belonged to her. Her kitchen sink, too, is similar to the one she grew up with, and she likes to wash her dishes there, all her flowered china that she now uses instead of saving. She splurges on

Williams-Sonoma dishwashing soap for her dishes. Birdie does, too. Birdie said once she felt so thrilled and guilty when she got that dish soap, it was like buying marijuana.

"Have you had marijuana?" Ethel asked, astonished, and Birdie said no, not yet. But she *would* have it. She didn't think she would like to smoke it, she had never liked smoking; instead, she would have it in those brownies. She said it would probably help her glaucoma. She'd get hold of some, she said, and she and Ethel would stay in and watch Cary Grant movies and order out for Chinese, wouldn't that be something? They would have to draw straws for who would answer the door in their condition.

"But where do you get it?" Ethel asked, and Birdie said she had no idea and that was that, they had never spoken of it again.

Birdie lives in a high-rise with other older people, and she hates it. She calls it a prison with wall-to-wall carpeting. When her daughter moved to Los Angeles last year, she talked Birdie into moving from her house into the high-rise so she wouldn't have to worry about her, and Birdie is plenty mad at her daughter now. Getting madder every day, too. Her daughter had wanted Birdie to move to L.A. with her, but Birdie had refused. And Ethel had seconded the motion. What would Birdie do in L.A.? Well, what would Ethel do without Birdie, that was the question.

On the bus, Ethel sits on a seat for the handicapped. She doesn't need it, but no one else knows that—wear a hat and some old lady shoes, and you can do whatever you want. She stares out the window at all the different kinds of people walking down the sidewalk: men with briefcases talking on cell phones, kids with backpacks talking on cell phones, mothers pushing strollers that look like lunar landing devices and talking on cell phones. Ethel likes to watch the children best. She was never able to have any, and Ed wouldn't adopt, kept holding out hope that Ethel would get pregnant. Finally, it was too late, they were in their forties, and they made their dog their child. Though not like today! No, no dog bakeries or miniature Harley-Davidson jackets or playdates for their Archie. He just got to sleep on the bed, and on his birthday he got a hot dog.

The hospital lobby is crowded today, a woman dressed in an elegant black pantsuit and quietly weeping, holding on to her husband's hand. A couple of young women laughing about something that's in one of their purses. There is also a group of about ten people all of whom seem to be together, and they look positively giddy—Ethel guesses they're taking turns visiting someone up in Maternity.

Sometimes Ethel thinks everyone should come and hang around in a hospital for a few minutes every day. The things that go on here! The births and the deaths, the miracles and the failures. The anxious questions, the careful answers. The sad conversations about what to do next, the joyful ones addressing the very same question.

Ethel sees the doors of one of the elevators opening, and she walks quickly toward it—sometimes the elevators here can take a long time, and nothing makes her more impatient than a slow elevator. She's one of those who will punch the Up button again and again, though she knows it doesn't help. Well, it helps her.

Inside the elevator, there's an orderly standing beside a gurney on which a patient is sleeping. "Going up?" the orderly asks. He's come from the basement, where the cafeteria is, but Ethel doesn't think he's coming from the cafeteria.

"Yes, thanks," she says and looks quickly over at the patient. He's an old man, his arms full of purplish bruises. Ethel winces and looks away. She wonders if the man is sleeping after all—she hears no sound of him breathing. And that orderly was overly cheerful. She sneaks another look at the patient and sees his chest rise. There. Thank goodness! Well, silly of her to suppose they transport dead bodies on the elevator mixed in with everyone else. Though maybe they should. Really. Because if there's one thing you're aware of in a hospital, it's that people die. They die and probably get sent to the morgue in those terrible body bags with handles that allow you to carry a person like a duffel bag. But maybe they just use sheets, that would be nice. Ethel hopes when she dies she gets wrapped up in a sheet with a decent thread count.

The elevator door opens, and the orderly pushes the gurney out ahead of Ethel, the patient still sound asleep on it, or pretending to be, Ethel supposes he might be pretending in order to spare himself the stares of the other passengers. And wasn't she one of them, someone standing there stealing looks at the poor man: his knobby collarbones, the tiny constellation of moles at his temple, the wedding ring worn thin on his finger.

Ethel walks the short distance down the hall to the station where Birdie is. She smiles at the nurses as she goes past the desk. So young, so pretty, and many of them are really very nice, though they certainly don't spend much time with their patients, not like they used to. And they don't wear white uniforms and caps anymore, either. Why not? What was wrong with those caps? They were badges of honor! And they let people know who was in their hospital rooms. Now everyone wears scrubs, and you can't tell the IV therapist from the psychiatrist from the cleaning staff. Birdie only yesterday asked a woman she thought was a nurse for a pain pill and the woman said in broken English she was just there to "take out it the trashes."

Nurses don't have time for anything anymore. Back rubs? Ha! But they used to do back rubs at least twice a day. Ethel had a friend named Vicky who'd been a nurse years ago, and she told a story about once giving a back rub to a young man as part of his "HS" care, "hour of sleep" that stood for. You changed the draw sheet, helped the patient wash his face and brush his teeth, and finally used the thick, unscented hospital lotion to give him a back rub. After Vicky had finished the man's back rub, she'd asked if there was anything else he needed. "Well," he'd said, "my testicles have been feeling *really dry....*" Ethel shrieked and covered her mouth when she heard that story, then asked from behind her hand, "So what did you *do*?"

"I handed him the bottle of lotion," Vicky said. "I told him, 'Here you go, try this.' And then I walked out of his room."

"For heaven's sake," Ethel said, shaking her head. To have a young man so boldly ask you for . . . Well. Those nurses. They saw everything.

When Ethel comes into Birdie's room, she sees that her friend is asleep. The head of the bed has been raised, and Birdie is bent far over to one side. Her meal tray is still before her, mostly untouched. She has gotten a roommate, Ethel sees, and she smiles and waves to a woman who appears to be somewhere in her thirties. The woman is pale, with dirty blond hair and dark circles under her eyes, but she is cheerful, and attractive, too, in a country-and-western kind of way; she smiles and waves back, then says, "I think she's asleep."

Ethel looks at Birdie. "Yes. She is."

"Not for long, I'm afraid," the woman says. "My family is on the way up, and my kids are *loud*."

"That's okay," Ethel says and goes to sit down beside Birdie. She's going to wake up with a neck ache, positioned that way. Ethel pushes the button to lower her friend's head, and it wakes her up.

Birdie's blue eyes, still beautiful after all these years, open round and startled, but when she sees Ethel, she relaxes. "Oh," she says. "Hi, you."

"Hi, darling."

"What's it like outside?"

"Warm! You'd think it was the middle of summer."

Birdie's face clouds. "What's . . . What day is it?"

"Friday."

Birdie nods. "And the month?"

A flash of cold down Ethel's spine, but she answers normally. "May."

"The twelfth," Birdie says, then rushes to add, "Two thousand and eight. Bush is president. Fifteen, twelve, nine, six, three. You're holding up zero fingers."

"You didn't eat nearly enough," Ethel says, and Birdie says, "Did you meet my roommate? I got a roommate last night."

"Kind of," Ethel says, then calls over to the woman, "I'm Ethel Menafee. Birdie and I have been friends for over fifty years."

"Oh, *wow!*" the woman says.

Ethel shrugs.

"I'm Angie Larson," the woman says. "I'm going home tomorrow."

Well, la-di-da, Ethel thinks but she says only, "Nice to meet you."

"Uh-huh." Angie flips on the TV.

Birdie turns to Ethel and rolls her eyes. She hates television, won't have one in her house. But what can you do. They're starting to put TVs on buses, now.

"You know, there's a McDonald's right next to the hospital," Ethel tells Birdie.

"There's a McDonald's right next to everything."

"What I mean is, I could bring you a Happy Meal. It would stay hot. It would be better than——"

"No," Birdie says. "Thanks."

Ethel settles back in the hard chair and looks over Birdie's IV and the clear green tubing that delivers the oxygen into her nose. As if she knows anything about it. As if she's in charge. Still, it seems one must acknowledge the equipment. Let it know that someone's keeping an eye on it. "So," Ethel says. "Any news?"

"I got a roommate."

From the corner of her eye, Ethel sees the roommate give a little absentminded wave.

Ethel lowers her voice. "You said."

"I *know*. But that's the news. The only news."

There is a great hubbub at the door, and then two little dark-haired girls come running in the room, yelling, *"Mommy, Mommy, Mommy!"*

Instinctively, Ethel pulls back in her chair, and just as instinctively smiles at the children. They appear to be about six and eight years old, and are dressed in look-alike pants and tops—hot pink pants and white, ruffled blouses that expose their midriffs—uselessly, Ethel thinks. She hopes it's uselessly. They have ponytails high on top of their heads, and they wear star-shaped studs in their ears. Their shoes are pink, see-through plastic, with gold glitter embedded in them. Each carries a Barbie doll whose hairdo makes her look as though she's just been ravished, and the older girl carries a pink plastic suitcase with "Barbie!" written across it in silver glittery script.

Ethel feels an old, familiar stirring inside. She would like to see what's in that suitcase. She loved playing dolls as a little girl and in fact gave up doing so only because her family and friends shamed her into it. She pretended she wasn't really playing after she turned twelve, but she was. She played her doll was a flower girl at a lavish wedding. She played her doll won an Academy Award. She played her doll had been told she couldn't play dolls any longer. The doll let her say everything she was feeling, let her *know* everything she was feeling.

Ethel had loved Emma Jean. She loved her just-right length of thirteen inches, her turquoise-colored eyes fringed with thick black lashes, her red lips painted on to look as though she were puckering up or musing, dimples at the sides of her mouth and at her knees. She had a slightly rounded belly and a flat little chest, fat auburn curls that were tolerant of multiple brushings, a faint pink blush on her cheeks. She had dress-up clothes and play clothes: a blue silk dress with a wide ribbon tie; red pedal pushers with a red-and-white-striped shirt. She had a pair of yellow flannel pajamas with light blue piping, and Ethel's mother had embroidered "EJ" on the pocket. She had black shoes and red shoes and white shoes, little plastic Mary Janes; and she had a pair of fuzzy white slippers that looked like little, little dogs. She had a lace-trimmed slip with a rosebud at the bodice and white organdy underpants.

Ethel doesn't know if those Barbies wear underpants, but she wants to know. Maybe she could ask one of the little girls. Maybe she could—

"Ethel!" Birdie says.

"What?"

Birdie smiles. "You didn't hear me?"

"No, what did you say?"

"You're getting worse than I."

Their old battle. They fought about who was getting worse in order to amuse and comfort each other. Starting in their late fifties, they'd begun giving themselves terrible pretend diseases, so that Birdie might answer the phone in those days and Ethel would say, "Today I have diabetes mellitus and essential hypertension. Also gingivitis and a worrisome fatigue." Or Ethel would answer the phone and Birdie would say, "Well, it's uterine cancer, and it's bad, it's very bad." It made them laugh. It made them happy to understand that they didn't have any of those things they were beginning to fear. Yet.

"I'm not worse than you," Ethel says. "You're worse than I by a long shot. Now, what did you say?"

Birdie stares blankly and finally says, "Well, fine, now I've forgotten," and they both start laughing. Oh, what relief, to laugh about such a thing. No, Birdie could never move to L.A.

"That's MIIIIIIINNNNNNE!" the older girl screams, a high-pitched, bloodcurdling scream, and Ethel and Birdie both turn to stare.

"Knock it off!" the girls' father yells. "Didn't I tell you guys you'd have to behave in here? There are real sick people in here!" He smiles at Birdie, raises his hand. "How you doing."

"But it's MIIIIIIINNNNNNNE!" the girl screams again, and, unbelievably, the father ignores her. He grins and sits on his wife's bed. "Ready for a tall cold one?" he asks her.

"I'd say so!"

The man lowers his voice, but Ethel can still hear him say, "Ready for a long, hot thick one, too?" He licks her neck.

"Baby, don't," the woman says, laughing, but it is from a place low in her throat that changes the meaning of "don't" to "yes indeed."

Ethel gets up and closes the curtain that separates the beds. They don't have to *see* it.

When she sits back down, Birdie says, "Why'd you close the curtain? Do you want to LICK MY NECK?"

Ethel's eyes widen and then she begins to silently laugh, her body shaking. Birdie laughs right along with her, not silently. The younger little girl comes over to their side of the curtain and stares solemnly at them. She's holding five dolls.

"Hello," Birdie says. "Can I do something for you?"

"No." The little girl shifts her weight, one foot to the other.

After a while, Ethel says, "Can I?"

Now the girl nods and walks slowly over to Ethel and lays a boy doll in her lap. "Ken's head keeps popping off," she says. And indeed his head has popped off; it falls from Ethel's lap and rolls across the floor and under Birdie's bed. The girl scrambles to get it.

"Ow," Birdie says, and Ethel asks quickly, "Are you all right?"

Birdie waves her hand. "Yes, I'm fine. I don't know why I said that. I guess I thought she *might* hurt me."

Now the girl moves close to Birdie to say, "I wouldn't hurt you. You're sick."

"That's right," Birdie says. "But I can fix your doll. Give him to me."

The girl points to Ethel. "She can."

Birdie says, "Give him to me, or you can't be on my side of the curtain."

The girl looks at Ethel, and Ethel raises her eyebrows, offers up her palms.

The girl places the doll and his head in Birdie's lap as though she is offering a piece of meat to a dog she doesn't trust.

"Wash it off first," Ethel tells Birdie.

"What?"

"Why don't we wash the doll off, it was on the floor."

"Oh," Birdie says. "Right. All right, then, to the shower!"

"Where is the shower?" the girl asks.

Ethel points to the sink in their corner of the room. "Use that sink right over there, honey, it has a control you work with your knee. There's some antibacterial soap right on the wall."

"*Huh?*"

"Tell your dad to help you," Ethel says.

The girl looks at the curtain as though she can see through it. "He's busy," she says, and sighs.

"You can do it yourself," Birdie tells her, and now they hear the girl's sister. "I'll do it!" she says. "Let *me.*"

"No," the younger girl says, doubtfully, but here comes the older one charging over, her mouth open and ready to scream again.

"Don't you dare," Birdie says in a low, authoritative voice that stops the child cold. "You let your little sister do it. You go back over there with your parents. This was not your idea."

"DAAAAD!" the older girl yells, and her father says, "Come on, Jessie. Leave us be for just a minute."

Jessie wrinkles up her nose as though she is smelling something bad.

"Come over here," Ethel says, "and you can sit with me. We'll just watch, how's that?"

"NOOOOOOOOOO!"

"All right, that's it, we're out of here," the father says, and the girls' faces turn quickly toward him, though they do not otherwise move.

"Don't forget your doll," Birdie says, and the little girl says, "I don't want him. He's busted. You can have him." She looks over the other dolls she is holding and lays a brunette with a shorn haircut on Birdie's lap as well. "You can have her, too. Her name is J.Lo."

"Did you cut her hair?" Birdie asks, and the little girl shakes her head no, then points to her older sister.

"She *wanted* me to!" the older girl says.

The younger girl picks her nose and shakes her head. "Nuh-uh, you made me."

"I said, let's *go!*" the father says, and the little girls run over to him. The sounds of their voices carry down the hall and finally disappear.

Ethel gets up to pull the curtain open but sees that Birdie's roommate has closed her eyes, and so she leaves the curtain as it is.

"Yes," Birdie says, when Ethel sits back down. "Keep it closed."

They sit quietly for a moment, and then Birdie whispers, "Did you see how she didn't think I could fix the doll?"

Ethel nods.

"Well, that's it," Birdie says. "That's what happens." She closes her eyes. "That's what scares me." She says nothing more, and shortly her breathing changes to a deep and regular rhythm.

Ethel sits for a while in a room where the two women sleep, and there is something about the sounds they make that reminds her of birds settling down into the nest. Doves. She leans over to whisper into Birdie's ear, "But you did fix it." Birdie has a few fine hairs matted into an S shape at the side of her face. Her skin is the color of pancake batter. Never mind, she heard Ethel. She heard her. After a while, Ethel, too, dozes off.

"Swedish meatballs over multigrain pasta, mashed potatoes, Prince Edward blend vegetables, peaches on a cloud," Birdie says.

"What's the cloud?" Ethel asks.

"Fake whipped cream."

"And the Prince Edward vegetables?" This was the best one yet, better than last week's fiesta blend, which did not even have corn and red pepper but rather broccoli and cauliflower.

"It was a mix of green beans and yellow beans. Oh, and carrots."

"So . . . what is the Prince Edward part?"

"He liked green and yellow beans and carrots mixed together?" Birdie asks. She's laughing. She's in a good mood today.

"He liked to wear green and yellow and orange together?" Ethel asks.

"His yellow hair had green and orange highlights?" Now Birdie's snorting a little in her laughter, an endearing little snort that always makes others laugh more.

"Wait! I know why they're called Prince Edward!" Ethel says. Because they came from a can, she wants to tell Birdie, remember that old telephone joke, where you call someone and ask if they have Prince Edward in a can and if they say yes you say, "Well, you'd better let him out!" and hang up.

So long ago that Ethel did that. She was still playing jump rope in those days, she remembers making chicken calls one Saturday afternoon with her friend Emily Bean-blossom and then going outside to jump rope.

But, "Hold on," Birdie says. "The doctor's here. I'll call you back." Ethel hangs up the phone, worried. The doctor is there to deliver the news. She'd wanted to be there when he did that. Now Birdie will be all alone if it's bad news. And even if it's good news, it would be nice to have your friend there.

Ethel dresses quickly. Never mind waiting for Birdie to call back. She ties a scarf beneath her chin and looks at herself in the small hall mirror. She is crying, just a little, that's the way these things go, good news, tears; bad news, tears. And her hands are shaking! Well, now, this is too much. She needs to calm down. On the way to the bus stop, she chants a jump rope rhyme under her breath, just to keep her from thinking about anything else: "First grade babies, second grade tots, third grade angels, fourth grade snots." What else? "Mabel, Mabel, set the table."

Ethel imagines the doctor clearing his throat, asking Birdie if she has any relatives nearby. Birdie saying, "No. Why?"

"Strawberry shortcake, blueberry pie." And there was "Postman, postman, do your duty"—oh, that was a nasty one, she used to like that one. It ended with "She wears her dresses above her hips."

On the bus, Ethel watches a man sitting opposite her nod off, snort awake, then nod off again. He appears to be homeless: he's wearing layers of filthy clothes and is carrying a variety of plastic, overstuffed bags. His skin is sallow, unwashed. Sometimes homeless people look mean——sometimes they *are* mean, asking for spare change in a way that is just plain threatening, stepping forward to block your way and, if you don't give them money, saying "God bless you" in a way that sounds like "I'm going to *get* you." Other times they look sad, or kind, or even happy. But this man looks like he's trying to understand something that just can't be understood. Even in sleep, his forehead is wrinkled, and there are two deep vertical lines between his brows. Perplexed, that's how he looks. Ethel wonders if he's trying to imagine how he ended up that way. It wouldn't be so hard to get that way, really. Miss a few mortgage payments, start talking to yourself a little too often.

She turns to stare out the window, counts down the three blocks remaining, then quickly exits the bus.

When she gets to Birdie's room, she walks past the empty bed——the roommate has indeed gone home——and kisses Birdie's cheek. She flops down into the chair and fans her face. "Whew. Out of breath."

"I tried to call you back, but I guess you had left," Birdie says.

"Yes. I figured I'd just go ahead and come down. I was coming down anyway."

Birdie nods, staring into her lap. She tears a Band-Aid off the back of her hand, winces.

Ethel waits. An announcement is made over the loudspeaker, code orange, whatever that is. "What's code orange?" she asks.

"Oh, just another soul gone to heaven, I imagine," Birdie says. She sighs. On the bed beside her are the dolls from yesterday. She picks up the Ken doll and, lowering her voice, speaks for him. "Your friend's got some bad news for you, Mrs. Menafee."

Ethel sits with a smile frozen on her face. She looks like an idiot, she knows, but she can't think what else to do.

"It appears the treatment hasn't done her one bit of good," Ken says.

Now Ethel lets some air out of her chest. "So what are you going to do, Birdie? What do you want to do?"

Birdie bites at her lower lip, stares straight ahead. Behind her blue glasses that she says make her eyes look like an owl's, tears tremble, then disappear.

"Birdie?"

"I don't want to talk about it."

But then Ken speaks. "She wishes she were already done with everything. If she's just going to die, why can't she be dead now?" Birdie has been moving the doll up and down while she talks; now she keeps moving him, up and down, up and down, though more slowly. Then she stops.

Ethel picks up the other doll, the one with the shorn hair. "Ken?" she says, in a high voice.

A faint smile, and then Birdie bobs Ken around in the air again. "Yes?"

"I think she should just move in with her friend."

"What a dumb idea, J.Lo. Her friend has enough problems of her own."

"What problems do *I* have?" Ethel asks, and Birdie doesn't answer.

"What problems does Ethel have?" J.Lo asks.

Ken goes up in the air, then down. Up, then down. Then he says, "It would just be too much. Trust me."

Ethel presses J.Lo up to the bed rail to say, "I don't think I *can* trust you, Ken, as you are an imbecile."

"Am not. Don't make me mad. Don't make me pop my head off."

Ethel laughs. Then she lays her hand over her friend's, and they sit for some time in silence. Carts rattle down the hall outside the door. Someone speaks loudly, not entirely kindly, to a hard-of-hearing patient, asking if he needs the bedpan. Announcements are made over the intercom, some serious, some not so. Once, the person making the announcement fumbles over her words, and laughs. Someone comes in to pick up the menu Birdie has filled out: she has ordered the Healthy Baked Fish, the Sicilian grande vegetables, the baked potato, and the apricot halves.

Finally, Ethel clears her throat and says, "Birdie?"

"What."

"What are *Sicilian grande* vegetables?"

Birdie snorts.

Ethel leans forward to say, "I mean it, about your living with me."

Birdie sighs. "I suppose I should go to L.A."

"But why?"

Silence.

"Birdie?"

"Wait. I'm thinking." She laughs, in spite of herself.

Ethel rearranges herself on the chair, centers her purse on her lap. "I have a lovely guest room."

"So does my daughter."

"Well, but . . ." Ethel taps her heel rapidly against the linoleum floor. What to say? *I can imagine how you feel.* No. Too trite. *You're going to die, so why not be with your best friend instead of a daughter who, no matter how much she loves you, has no time for you?* No. Too blunt and, in a way, too mean. What she wants to say is something she is having trouble articulating even to herself.

She studies Birdie, who is not looking at her, who has her head bent down in a way that makes it look like she is praying, though Ethel knows she is not, they neither of them believe in all that. But what relief if they did! If they did, they could be talking about how they'd meet again, how, in heaven, they might be young again, dressed in blue and wearing pearls! But it's not true for them, they've discussed it at length. You're born, you live, you die. We are lonely visitors to a small planet. We are minuscule links in a long, long chain. And yet.

Ethel thinks about her Grandma Mo, short for Moselle, a name Ethel has always loved, her grandmother was named after a river in Germany. But her grandmother was right, such a delicate, feminine name didn't suit her. Grandma Mo used to sit out on the porch in the evening smoking a pipe, a habit that displeased her husband and all her other relatives but Ethel, who loved the smell of the tobacco, loved too the rhythmic puffs of smoke that came from her grandmother's pooched lips. And there was the fact that Grandma Mo let her try the pipe, too, anytime she wanted.

When she was nine years old, Ethel sat at Grandma Mo's kitchen table one day to help peel apples for a pie. She had just started on one when a worm crawled out of it. Ethel shrieked and dropped the apple and the peeler, and when her grandmother looked over at her, her pale blue eyes calm, a bit amused, Ethel said, "There's a *worm* in there!"

"Would you like a different apple to peel?" Grandma Mo asked.

Ethel nodded. Saved again by her grandmother, who was as good as any cowboy.

"Try this one." Grandma Mo handed her an apple from the little pile she held in her lap.

Ethel began peeling it, but it was full of brown spots. "Look," she said, holding up the apple. Her grandmother nodded, and handed her yet another apple. A worm *hole* in that one. "Every one I pick has something wrong with it!" Ethel said, exasperated.

"So should we not have pie?" Grandma Mo asked.

Ethel shook her head no.

"I guess what we'll have to do is cut around those bad parts, huh?"

Ethel said nothing, her lips still in the pout position. But then she sat up straighter in the chair, stopped pouting, and put into the mixing bowl all the apple parts she could salvage.

Well. An overobvious allegory. Sentimental slop, Birdie might say. Still, Ethel wants very much to share that story with Birdie. But when she starts to speak, she hears herself saying a jump rope rhyme:

*"All in together, girls.
It's fine weather, girls.
When is your birthday?
Please jump in!"*

And now Ethel speaks very quickly, as the rhyme used to demand:

*"January—February—March—April—May—
June—July—August—September—October—
November—December!"*

Birdie looks over at Ethel. Her face is hard to read. "I know that rhyme," Birdie says. "You know what comes next?" She recites:

"All out together, girls.
It's fine weather, girls.
When is your birthday?
Please jump out!"

And now Birdie speaks rapidly:

"One—two—three—four—
five—six—seven—eight—"

"I have the finest sheets you've ever slept on," Ethel says, interrupting her.

"Oh, you do, do you?"

"Yes, and I have a mailman I give lemonade to in the summer, and hot chocolate in the winter. He's a very strong young man, a wonderfully good-natured man, and he has told me if I ever need anything to put a clothespin on my mailbox and he will knock on the door, and whatever it is, he'll take care of it."

Birdie considers this. "What about Sundays and his days off?"

"911," Ethel says.

"I suppose."

Ethel sits still. She can't force her. She waits. She thinks of the homeless man she saw on the bus that morning. She thinks of how things could just as easily turn around for him. Really. He cleans up, for God's sake, could it really be so hard, there are people who can help. He cleans up, he gets a job flipping burgers, which everyone makes fun of but which Ethel thinks is perfectly honorable work and she would do it herself. He gets a job flipping burgers and gets promoted a few times. He buys himself some new clothes at Sears, short-sleeved blue polyester shirts, some pants that fit. He meets a woman there, she's the cashier who rings him up, a Hispanic woman with dimples and an endearing little potbelly, for which she makes no apologies. They get married, and he is a better father to her kids than her ex-husband was. It could happen. Or he could deteriorate further, end up a black-eyed, shivering soul sitting over a grate and unable to articulate anymore his request for spare change, for anything. Either way, the birds will sit on the wire and sing.

Birdie has spoken. "What?" Ethel says.

"Deaf as a post."

"But what did you say?"

"I said I have my own sheets I can bring."

"Ah." Ethel's eyes fill, and she sits back in her chair. For one moment, the weight of what she has taken on frightens her. But then she is fine, settled, complete in a way she hadn't known she wasn't.

"I think when you're dying, you can get a prescription for marijuana," Birdie says.

"Everything's still negotiable," Ethel tells her.

Over the top of the bed rail, Ken's head appears and he says, "She can't even say how grateful she is. Why don't you get her clothes out of the closet and you girls can blow this pop stand."

"We have to wait for your discharge order," Ethel says.

"Well, I've got a minute," Birdie says, and Ethel says she knows it.

DOUBLE DIET

———

Last time Marsha was dieting and her husband, Tom, wanted to go out for dinner, she took his arm before they left the house and said, "Now listen. I am fifteen pounds up from where I want to be. I'm going to need you to *help* me, okay?" She had been told at Weight Watchers that people who had supportive partners did a lot better at losing weight. And he said sure, he'd help her, he understood, he didn't like it when he felt overweight, either.

At the restaurant, Marsha ordered a tuna steak and a salad, dry, some lemon wedges on the side. Baked potato, dry. "Anything to start?" the waiter asked, and she said "No, the entrée will be plenty." "To drink?" "Water," she said. "Thank you." The waiter then turned to Tom, who ordered French onion soup as an appetizer. "And for your entrée?" the waiter asked. Tom said, "I think . . . the chicken Kiev and some garlic mashed potatoes." What did he want on his salad, the waiter wanted to know. "Oh," said Tom, "maybe . . . blue cheese, I guess. And hey, how about mixing it with French?" "To drink?" "Scotch to start, and a nice Chardonnay with dinner." Tom started to ask Marsha if she wanted wine, but he saw her arms crossed tightly over her chest and so he did not ask her after all. "Would you like bread and butter?" the waiter asked, and Tom looked meaningfully at Marsha and declined.

She watched Tom eat the stringy, salty cheese from the top of the soup while she nursed her water. She watched him cut into his deep-fried chicken breast and saw the butter come running out while she poked at her salad. She kept her plate with its little tiny bit of tuna left on it so that she might have something to do while he ate his Snickers pie. "Whew!" he said, after a few bites. "Full. I can't finish it. You want it?" He pushed the pie toward her, and she devoured it.

But now, Marsha and Tom are double dieting, and Marsha is very excited about it. It has become a bone of contention between them, though. Tom would prefer that Marsha keep it a secret, but Marsha thinks they should celebrate it. "What's to celebrate about it?" he asks her. "It's not an engagement or anything."

"Actually," Marsha says, "you didn't want to celebrate our engagement, either. You wanted to keep that quiet, too."

"Altogether different," Tom says.

"What is," Marsha wants to ask. "Dieting and getting engaged? The reasons for keeping it, whatever 'it' is, secret?" Oh, but why get started. He was very shy back then, she knows that, he was unsure. For her part, she was pregnant, diffidence was not so much an option, action was her only option. It was the early seventies. And although abortion was legal in some states, although Marsha in fact made an appointment to get an abortion and Tom drove her to the clinic, in the end she could not do it. When they took some blood from her arm before the procedure, she thought, *Don't. That's the baby's.* And then in the waiting room, when she looked around at all the faces of the women who would also be terminating that day, she had a sudden rush of feeling that made her leap up and bolt from the clinic. She stood on the sidewalk, her purse pressed hard against her middle. Tom followed her, took her arm, and said, "Me, too." That was their engagement announcement.

But that was years ago. Now they've been married for so long, the kids grown and gone, and Tom and Marsha are starting to worry about the things fifty-somethings worry about, including cholesterol and blood pressure and carcinogens. Last time Tom went to the doctor he came home with a bad report card and orders to lose at least twenty pounds or else he'd have to start taking medication. He sat glumly at the kitchen table and said, "I'm not going to a goddamn gym, either. I'm not going to bench-press next to some nineteen-year-old who has oiled up his muscles and can't take his eyes off the mirror."

"There might be a lot of men your age at the gym," Marsha said. At which he gave her a look, and Marsha understood that Tom just didn't want to go the gym, period. "We could walk together," she told him. "And you can come with me to Weight Watchers." She had recently reenrolled.

"Oh, no," he said. "I'll take the heart attack. I am not going to Weight Watchers."

"You don't even know what it's like," Marsha said. "You've never been to a meeting. Why don't you just—"

He held up his hand, traffic cop style. "Marsha?"

"Okay," she said. "You use whatever method you want. I'll help you. I've been dieting all my life. I can show you lots of things that will really help. And men lose weight much faster than women; you'll lose a good five to seven pounds a week."

He looked up at her, full of hope.

"Really," she said.

"Okay," he said, sighing, and she clapped her hands together, then pretended it had been to try to catch a fly buzzing around the room. "Missed," she said, pointing to the black speck on the wall.

On Saturday, they go to the mall to buy good walking shoes. "You could be a role model for men," Marsha tells Tom. "By admitting that you're going on a diet, you could give other men permission to—"

"Please, Marsha."

"What."

"Don't get all New Age on me."

"I'm not! This is a vital service you could provide. A great inspiration. A lot of men really need to lose weight, but they don't know how to—"

"Oy." He covers his ears. *"Stop."*

"Fine," Marsha says.

Just this morning, Tom selected his very own weight loss clinic, he won't say where, but it's a place where you meet with a counselor one-on-one, every day, and you get weighed every day, too. He has been given a little notebook where he is meant to record what he eats. To show her support, Marsha has said she'll go on the same diet, and she will rely on Tom to tell her what she can and can't have. She thinks it will keep him from feeling emasculated—he has described the waiting room at the clinic, the plastic roses, the pink walls. But would it be so awful for him to thank his wife for praising him? Couldn't he consider her suggestions instead of covering his ears like a three-year-old?

Marsha picks up the pace, making sure that Tom is continually just a little behind her. They bought their shoes, and now they are going to find a place to have lunch. They pass a few windows where Marsha would like to stop and look at the merchandise, but never mind, it's more important to punish her husband for another five minutes or so. The truth is, he doesn't even know she's punishing him, but Marsha knows, and that's the important thing. Her self-esteem and all. Her ability to confront an issue when it happens. She imagines her therapist sitting in her comfortable armchair in her blue office giving her a thumbs-up. Not that Marsha really likes her therapist, she hates her therapist. She would like to talk about that sometime, but imagine the awkwardness. It would be like a picture in a picture in a picture or something. Anyway, why bring it up; as soon as Marsha gets some more self-esteem, she's going to dump her therapist. God. The annoying way she has of leaning forward, her elbows on her knees, saying, "Can you tell me more about that?"

"I am!" Marsha always wants to say. "I am telling you about it!" But instead she nods and dutifully finds some other detail to include, some other item to add to whatever sorrowful laundry list she has dragged out for the day. Oh, therapy is an awful thing. Who started it anyway? Did some cavewoman go on way too long to another cavewoman who, after she listened, said, "Okay, next time? I'm going to have to charge you for that." A friend of Marsha's recently told her, "You're not supposed to like therapy. It's supposed to be painful. That's how you know it's working."

"Well, I'll tell you what," Marsha began, full of outrage, of argument, but then nothing followed. She was like a car engine that turned over and quit. Sputter sputter stall. Sputter sputter stall. Anyway, therapy *was* helping— Marsha felt happier, stronger, more optimistic. But the magazines she could buy with what she spent on therapy! Once she mentioned that, and her therapist said, "So you feel that you're not entitled to therapy *and* a magazine." Marsha answered by scratching the side of her neck and looking out the window. Then she looked at her watch. "Well, our time is just about up," she said, and the therapist said, "How about if I be the one to decide that?"

Marsha decides to stop punishing Tom and slows down to match her stride to his. "I'm starving," she tells him.

"No," Tom says. "We're on a diet, remember? You can't eat now. It's ten-forty. It's not even eating time."

"Well, then I want a coffee," Marsha says. "I need something."

They go to the stylish kiosk, and Marsha looks at the menu. "A large café caramel, please," she tells the kid, the *barista*, she supposes. Behind her, Tom snorts. She turns around. "What."

"That is not 'a coffee.' That is a liquid sundae." When the kid asks what kind of coffee Tom wants, he says, "I'm fine."

"I can have this," Marsha says. "I just have to count it."

"Uh-huh," Tom says. Then he says, "You're going to be very bad at this."

Marsha feels the blood rise in her face. Who does he think he's talking to, some novice, some rank beginner like him? "Do you know how many diets I've been on?" she asks.

"My point," he says, lightly.

She sucks the whipped cream off her coffee. Chews it. "I'm not even starting today, anyway," she says. "I'll start tomorrow."

At lunch, Tom gets a salad and Marsha gets a cheeseburger with barbecue sauce and bacon, and waffle fries, which she loads up with salt, because she, as opposed to some people, does not have high blood pressure.

On Sunday morning, when Tom comes downstairs, Marsha says, "I can't start today, either. I forgot and ate breakfast."

"What did you have?"

"Grape-Nuts." And a lot of sugar sprinkled on top, she does not add.

Tom scratches his head, yawns. "Well, you can still start today, but I'm going to have to penalize you. That's too much starch."

"Too much starch," Marsha says.

"Right." He pulls out a carton of fat-free yogurt from the refrigerator and closes the door with his hip, which Marsha has never seen him do and finds effeminate.

"Exactly how much starch can I have?" she asks.

"A piece of bread."

"How many times a day?"

"Once."

"Pardon me?"

"Once!" he says. "You get one piece of bread a day!"

"Go to hell," Marsha says. "I'm not doing this diet. It's stupid. I'm doing Weight Watchers, where you eat whatever you want so long as you—"

"I told you it wasn't going to be easy. And *you* said"— and here Tom does his high-voiced imitation of Marsha— *"I* know, but *I* can do it! I want to be on the same diet as *you*, I want to *support* you! And it will be easier to *cook* if we're on the same diet!"

Marsha runs her tongue back and forth across her front teeth, thinking. Then she says, "Yeah, but you didn't tell me that thing about the bread. You know how much I like bread."

"Do what you want," Tom says. He begins eating his yogurt. He makes it look good. It makes Marsha want some, and now she's gone and had Grape-Nuts, a.k.a. Too Much Starch.

"Fine," Marsha answers. "I'll do your diet from whatever cockamamie clinic you go to, which probably isn't even accredited and is staffed by charlatans."

Tom loads up his spoon again, leans over toward Marsha. "A tip: If you cut the bread in half, it seems like more. Piece in the morning, piece at night."

Salads. Salads, salads, salads, that's what they eat. And cantaloupe and pineapple and watermelon and apples cut into little pieces, which they eat with toothpicks in order to make it seem "fun." They eat chicken breasts and chicken breasts and chicken breasts, and one time Marsha puts pineapple and green and red peppers and onions on top and calls it "Festive Hawaiian chicken." She actually says this; she puts the dish down before Tom and says, "Voilà: Festive Hawaiian chicken."

"Aren't you mixing metaphors?" Tom asks, and she tells him never mind, this is just to make them feel excited about eating, for a change.

"Know what would make me excited?" Tom asks. "A three-inch steak, that's what would make me excited."

"Fettuccine Alfredo," Marsha says. "Apple crisp with vanilla ice cream."

"Don't even go there," Tom says. Which Marsha thinks makes him sound both effeminate and Valley Girl.

The next Saturday, when they're out taking a walk, they decide to go to one of their favorite pizza parlors for lunch, but they agree they'll only get a Greek salad. But then Marsha says she thinks she'll get a seafood pocket instead. No potato chips to accompany it, no Coke, nothing like that. Water. Water and a little seafood pocket.

"You can't have that," Tom says.

Marsha lets go of his hand. "Why not? It just has a little mayonnaise on it. We're allowed to have salad dressing."

"Not the same," Tom says.

"Is too," Marsha says.

"Is not."

"Is too."

"Look," Tom says, "I'm not going to argue with you. If you want a sub sandwich, get a sub sandwich."

Marsha stops walking and turns to face him. "I didn't *say* sub sandwich. I said seafood *pocket*! I used to get the spicy *Italian*, extra *cheese*! Now I'm only getting a *FUCK-ING SEAFOOD POCKET!*"

From behind her, Marsha hears the short, tight exhalations of a jogger. Their next-door neighbor, Marty, runs past them. "Hey," he pants, holding up a hand.

"Hey," they say back, together, and watch him run off. Not an ounce of fat on that one. Or on his wife.

Tom turns back to Marsha and speaks quietly. "Either you do this diet or you don't."

Marsha orders the Greek salad. And when she has finished she is no longer hungry and crabby. She is grateful that she stayed on the diet, and she tells her husband that.

"That's right," he says. "A moment on the lips, forever on the hips."

What kind of weird clinic is he going to? Marsha wonders. "You already told me that one," she says.

"Okay, then, how about this: Nothing tastes as good as being thin feels."

Marsha thinks about this. Then she says, "Not true."

"I know," Tom says, and sighs.

Marsha uses the toilet, takes off her pajamas, pushes all the air out of her lungs, and steps on the scale. Five pounds down! She steps off, gingerly, as if the scale might grab her by the arm, pull her back on, and show her her real weight. She dresses and brushes her teeth, thinks maybe she'll skip breakfast, how about *that*! Give 'em the old one-two! She finds herself doing a little dance, and she laughs out loud. From out in the hall, she hears Tom ask what's so funny.

She opens the bathroom door. "Have you lost much weight?"

"Twelve pounds," he says, with something like wonder in his voice.

She stops smiling. Nods. Lifts the hair up off her neck and blows air out of her cheeks.

"You?" he asks.

"Uh-huh," she says and shuts the door again.

Weeks later, at eleven A.M., which is close enough to noon, Marsha is about to sit down to a lunch of eggplant parm; focaccia, which she will dip into olive oil spiced with red pepper; and Caesar salad, extra dressing. She got takeout from her favorite Italian restaurant. You have to cheat sometimes or you crack up. At Weight Watchers, they know this; you can bank points for just such an occasion. Tom's diet is ridiculous; it thinks you're an automaton who can just eat the same thing every day. When the phone rings, she answers in a voice meant to convey hurry; she wants to eat quickly and get rid of the evidence right away. Tom is out of town on business, but still. She didn't even eat at the restaurant in case a mutual friend saw her and let it slip to Tom.

"Hello?" she says, breathlessly.

"Just landed," Tom says. "Are you being good?"

Silence.

"Marsha?"

"Oh, Tom, I was going to cheat. I guess it's good you called. I won't now. I really won't."

"Good girl," he says, like he's talking to a dog. On a diet.

Nine pounds down, and they are out for Marsha's birthday. They have allowed themselves a steak, which they shared so as to have the proper-size portion, and even at that, there's some left over. "I'll bring it home for Ditzy," Marsha says.

Tom raises an eyebrow. "You know what they say at the clinic?"

"What," Marsha asks tiredly.

"The dog doesn't need it, either."

Marsha leaves the steak but tells Tom that she *will* be stopping for an ice cream on the way home, it is her *birthday* and she can have *ice cream* on her *birthday*.

"You need to learn not to reward yourself with food," Tom says.

She stares at him.

"It's true."

She sits back in the booth. "So where's my jewelry, then?"

He grins, reaches in his jacket pocket, and pulls out a black velvet box. Marsha gasps and covers her mouth with her hands.

"See?" he says.

Down the street from Tom and Marsha live two sisters about seven and nine years old, entrepreneurial towheads who perform acrobatics on their front lawn between going in and out of various businesses. They were the Wonderful Weed Pullers until a person who hired them realized they were not so very expert at distinguishing a weed from a plant. They offered homemade greeting cards for every occasion, then porch washing. Now they have gone into the dog-walking business. Just this morning, Marsha found in her mailbox a hand-lettered flyer that began "Does your dog spend the whole day just lownging on the sofa?" But Marsha's favorite part was at the end: "And of course the prices are always lower if you act right away. First person who calls will get to pay only twenty cents for a half hour of dog play. (Our charge for walking around the block will still be a quarter, sorry.)"

Marsha decides to bake brownies for them. She doesn't want any, she truly doesn't, but she wants to bake something, she just wants the smell, and she wants to use her professional-size Mixmaster and her beautiful heart-shaped stainless steel measuring cups and spoons, which she had just gotten at Williams-Sonoma on the very day Tom came home depressed from the doctor's office. He is off golfing; he won't be home for hours. Marsha had planned to pay the bills and clean, and when Tom got home they were going to try a new sushi restaurant. She'll make and deliver the brownies—get them out of the house!—and then she'll pay the bills while she breathes in that heavenly, lingering scent.

She finds the butter, the fancy chocolate, the nuts. She breaks eggs into the big metal bowl, adds salt and vanilla, which she inhales deeply before adding to the bowl. When the batter is done, she has one little taste to make sure there is enough salt, usually you have to add just a bit more salt to the batter than they say. A bit more salt, a bit more vanilla. You can only tell by tasting; you can't rely completely on a recipe, it is really only an approximation. Baking is not a science; it's an art.

Marsha is in the family room when Tom comes home. All the blinds are drawn, and the television is on and Marsha is lying on the sofa watching Bette Davis say, "It's going to be a bumpy night." Well. Truer words were never spoken.

Marsha sits up and uses the remote to turn off the television. Which is part of the problem. A nation of obese people who spend all their time designing labor-saving devices. When what everyone needs is to go out into the fields and walk behind the plow horse!

"Marsha?" Tom calls.

"Everything in this culture conspires against the dieter," Marsha says.

Tom comes into the family room, his golf shirt tucked into his pants for the first time in . . . how long? Who knows. "Why's it so dark in here?" He starts to raise the shades and Marsha says, "Don't. I'm watching movies."

Tom raises the shades anyway. "Marsha? What's wrong?"

"Everything in this culture conspires against the dieter," she repeats, and he sits in his La-Z-Boy recliner (see?) and asks again what's wrong, and now Marsha begins to cry and blubber.

"You have a bad of owies?" Tom asks. "What does that mean?"

"I *ate* a *pan* of *brownies*," Marsha says.

Tom nods slowly. "I see."

"Don't say anything!"

"I didn't. I won't."

Marsha gets off the sofa and moves to the window. Earlier in the day, there had been a beautiful cardinal at the feeder; now no birds are there. "I am fifty-seven years old," she tells Tom.

"Yes. I know."

"Once, many years ago when I was in New York City, I saw a woman on the elevator and she looked really familiar, and I said, 'Are you Helen Gurley Brown?' and she lowered her head kind of shyly and nodded that she was. And then I said something inane, like 'Oh, nice to meet you,' but I was mostly just staring at how thin she was. She was so thin, and really, she was kind of old then. And I had just recently read that she wore makeup to bed, that her husband didn't know this, but that she actually wore makeup to bed because she would never let him see her without it. And I remember thinking, *God, is that dumb. I will never be so dumb.* But you know what, Tom? I am that dumb."

"You wear makeup to bed?" He's very nearly whispering.

"No! But I keep dieting and dieting and dieting and I just . . . I just . . . It doesn't work! I diet; I lose; it comes back on. I diet; I lose; it comes back on. I just can't keep it off, and now *especially* I can't because my body does not *want* me to, estrogen is stored in fat cells, and I need to get estrogen some way because I don't make it anymore because I don't have any more periods, I haven't menstruated for years, I don't even have a single tampon in the whole house!"

"Whoa," Tom says, laughing. "This might be TMI, too much information."

Marsha spins around angrily. "I know what TMI is! And don't say that! Don't *say* it! You don't talk that way, you never used to say things like that! That's a girl thing to say!"

"No, it isn't," Tom says. "Guys at work——"

"Well, you say other things you never used to say, and they are just girl things. I'm sorry, but they are."

"Fine," Tom says.

"And I just also want to say that this is partly your fault."

" 'This' being . . . ?"

"This dieting! I mean, I try very hard to stay attractive to you, and I know I'm just not attractive to you anymore!"

"Yes you are!"

"Oh, don't you dare. Don't you dare. Let's just tell the truth. I know you love me, but you no longer find me attractive like you used to!"

"Well, Marsha. Come on, do you find *me* attractive like you used to?"

"Yes!" This is not so, actually. But she finds, oddly, that at this time of demanding the truth, she herself cannot offer it. She doesn't want to hurt his feelings. And anyway, she doesn't want to talk about him. She wants to talk about her.

She moves to sit on the sofa and leans forward earnestly, just like her stupid therapist. She says, "I look in the mirror now, and even if I lost weight, there's just . . . There's nothing I can do. It's over. My bodyness. My attractiveness in my body. I can diet forever but it will never make me like I was. I'm . . . Well, I've gotten kind of square and melty-looking. I will never be attractive like I was again. In the bodily way of before, which is impossible." Oh, she hates it when she gets this way. When her emotions gobble up her reason, making her wildly inarticulate.

"So why try?" Tom asks, and she wants so very much to go and get the yellow pages and bring it squarely down on his head.

"Because you want me to! You respond to me differently when I lose weight! I can see it in your eyes that you find me more attractive when I'm thinner! My husband! So I feel I have to keep trying and trying—"

"But you *don't* have to keep trying."

"Tom. Do you or do you not find me more attractive when I'm thinner."

He frowns, thinking. Then he says, "Well, I guess you might look a little nicer when you're thinner. I mean your clothes aren't as tight and everything. But, Marsha, don't you know this? I don't care. Do I notice a beautiful woman on the street, even if I try very hard not to look at her? Sure. But do I *care* about her? No. I care about you, sweetheart: then, now, forever. Marsha. I love you. I love you with all my heart, and I always will. Look, I'm overweight, too."

"Not anymore," Marsha says, bitterly.

"No, not anymore. But it will come back, I can't keep this up forever."

"You can't?"

"No! And I don't want to! I'll be reasonable; I don't want to create health problems. But I'm not going to go to that clinic or follow diets or count points or any of that crap."

Oh, Tom, she thinks. *You're back.*

He comes over and embraces her. "Listen, if I don't put the moves on you, it's because . . . Well, sometimes the dog just won't come to the whistle."

She doesn't answer. She knows this.

"But also, I guess I just don't think so much about that anymore. I think about other things. You know?"

Buried against his shoulder, she nods. She feels the bodywide relief of having had a good cry without having had a good cry.

"Suppose we agree to try to be a healthy weight, and that's all," Tom says.

"Okay." She wipes under her nose, pulls away to smile at him. "Okay."

"And suppose we agree to go and get a pizza right now."

"I'm kind of full," she says. "But I guess I could eat a little."

"There you go. And I brought something home for dessert that would make the girls at my clinic hold the sides of their heads and scream." He takes Marsha's hand and leads her to the kitchen, where there is a bakery box on the table from Butterflake, their favorite. He lifts the lid to show her a cake that must have been beautiful before. But it appears the cake must have slid sideways, for it is smashed on one side, and the frosting is smeared so that none of the pretty designs are intact.

"Uh-oh," Tom says.

"What happened?"

"Well, I dropped it."

She laughs. "It's fine. It's better."

"Forget the pizza," Tom says. "Let's eat this."

"We can have pizza for dessert!"

Marsha goes to the cupboard for plates, she knows just the ones she wants to use, the ones she got at an antiques store; they have scalloped edges, and they feature bouquets of violets at the center. Cake forks, of course, they'll use them, too. The very name thrills her: cake forks.

She pulls down the plates and then stands still for a moment, remembering the day she and Tom brought their first child home from the hospital. They were so young, barely twenty-one, they didn't know anything. The baby was in a car seat in the back, and they both kept turning around to say things to her. Passing a memorial site, Tom turned around to say, "We don't believe in war." At a stop sign, he told her, "Art matters. We really believe that. We really like dogs, too, Alice. There will be many, many dogs in your life, so please don't be allergic. There is a dog waiting at home for you. Teddy. Because he looks like a teddy bear, you'll see."

For her part, Marsha leaned over the seat to very gently touch the baby's hand, which was curled into a tiny little fist. She said, "We love you so much. We're so happy you're here. We're so happy we're bringing you home. We're so happy you were a girl, we wanted a girl." She was crying, a little; her voice trembled.

"I guess you could say we're happy," Tom said, and Marsha lightly punched him.

Alice has children of her own now. Marsha wants to say something about Alice, about how many hopes and dreams were pinned to that baby sleeping in the car seat that day. Alice fulfilled many of those hopes and dreams. She brought them joy, and she brought them sorrow, too, but oh, the joy. The joy. Marsha wants to say something about that to Tom, now, it seems to fit the moment. But she decides not to tell him. She doesn't need to. He knows.

THE ONLY ONE OF MILLIONS
JUST LIKE HIM

⸻

It was Monica who began calling the puppy Dogling. At first it was in jest, but then it stuck; even her tough-guy husband, Ralph, used the name with no sense of irony. But the name fit: the dog was small and adorable-looking even into old age, a ringer for the dog who starred in *Benji*, only cuter. Sometimes when Monica bathed, Dogling sitting devotedly beside her, Ralph heard her sing to him in her loud Brooklynese, "You oughta be in pictures, you're wonderful to see . . ."

Dogling really should have been in the movies. He had the kind of dog face that made people act foolish, made them crouch down and speak in a high voice and say everything twice: "Are you a sweetheart? Are you a sweetheart? You are, aren't you! Yes you are!" Then came the inevitable "What's his name?" and both Monica and Ralph always answered "Butchie." No point in everybody knowing everything about nothing that was their business, as Monica's mother used to say. She was an intelligent woman, Shirley, but every now and again she would come out with these head spinners. Once, watching Dogling staring into the fire, transfixed by the flames, she asked, "Do dogs have brains?"

But now Dogling barely eats, he barely drinks, he barely interacts with them at all. When he's not sleeping, he stares off into space as though seeing the canine reaper, ethereal leash in hand. Dogling is thirteen years old and has had a good run for the money, as Ralph says. He couldn't have had a better home, a better time. The way he loved unwrapping his birthday presents? The way he'd slept with them every night? The way he liked riding in the car, running in the woods, eating White Castle burgers? Ralph says the dog doesn't know he is dying, and really, isn't that dying's worst problem?

None of this makes Monica feel any better. She tells Ralph he doesn't understand the relationship she has with the dog, how he really *is* her best friend. All right, so Dogling is thirteen, but a lot of small dogs live much longer than that! Tootsie, that disgusting, runny-eyed miniature white poodle down the block, she's *fif*teen. And why is she alive, anyway? All she does is tremble and bite. Not just strangers and the postman, she bites her owners! And they just laugh! Wave around their bandaged fingers like a trophy! "Oh, boy, you really drew some blood this time! Good girl! Want a cookie?"

On this warm spring afternoon, Monica lies in the chaise longue on the back deck wearing her red pedal pushers and yellow blouse and bangle bracelets and Liz Taylor sunglasses, holding Dogling to her ample bosom, drinking Tom Collinses and weeping with abandon. Her mascara is running, her lipstick has smeared, and her foundation, mixed with her tears, has dripped onto her blouse, making for pale orange spots that have dried stiff. Oh, it is just too much, it is willful hysteria, plain and simple, and she knows it (as do her neighbors), but she can't seem to stop. Finally Ralph tries to take Dogling from Monica's arms, suggesting that, dying though the dog may be, he might want to pee, or have a drink of water, or eat something. *Or for Christ's sake, be alone,* he thinks but does not say. "What," Monica says, "you think I'm not trying to feed him, here? You see this baloney, all cut up? You think I'm not trying to give him water?" She holds up an eyedropper. "What's this, Ralph?"

He squints in her direction. Ralph's vision is shot. Also his hearing. Also his you-know-what, but what the hell. He is not without his charms. A bit overweight, but with kind blue eyes and a full head of hair. "A swizzle stick?" he asks.

"It's an eyedropper, Ralph! An eyedropper! For . . . Well, of course it's for dropping things in eyes." She sniffs and pushes at one side of her hair. "But I remembered something. When I was a little girl, I once found a baby bird that had fallen out of the nest, and I fed it water with an eyedropper. Also I fed it hamburger. With my fingers."

"Did it work?" Ralph says. "Did you get to watch it grow up and fly away?"

Monica shakes her head, and her face screws up into what looks like a human asterisk. "No! It died! Everything *dies!*"

That's right, Ralph wants to say. Everything dies and you are turning what is a completely natural process into a big fat soap opera. Instead, he says, "Well, that's a good idea, the eyedropper. So he's drinking, at least?"

"No! Because he wants to drink out of his *Butchie* bowl!"

Dogling has food and water dishes with his photo imprinted on the insides, one of his gifts last Christmas. More than once, Monica has wondered aloud if it might have been the printing process for those bowls that gave him cancer. And now she starts up again, here she goes, Ralph could say the words right along with her: "Everything in the world is poisoned, Ralph! The land, the sea, the air! *Everything!* And nobody cares one whit!"

"Monica," Ralph says, sighing. "You're just . . . You're making too much of this. You've got to stop."

Monica stares at Ralph, slowly gathering the fabric at the neck of her blouse into her fist. Then, in an oddly matter-of-fact tone, she says, "You don't care. I don't think you ever did." Her words sound suspiciously like lines of dialogue from an old Bette Davis movie.

"Of course I care," Ralph says. "I love him! He's the old Butcheroo!"

"No," Monica says. "As I have said on more than one occasion, Ralph, I'm not sure you really know what love is." She turns away to caress the head of the sleeping dog, then suddenly turns back to her husband. "He farted! Ralph! Do you think he's getting better?"

Ralph comes to kneel beside Monica and stares into the face of the sleeping dog. Well, the dog did fart. But when Ralph looks up at his wife, he doesn't have to answer the question she asked him. Monica begins again to cry.

Ralph stands, watching helplessly, his hands in his pocket. Finally, he says he's going out bowling and to drink a cold one.

"Fine," Monica says.

"I just need to get *out* a bit," Ralph says. "I'll be back in less than a hour. One beer."

"By then . . . who knows?" Monica says.

Well, exactly.

That evening, while Dogling sleeps in his basket at Monica's feet, they watch *American Idol* and eat coconut cream pie that Ralph brought home from the bakery. "You know, you're right, Ralph," Monica says. "You have to do something else. You can't just hold him and . . ." She points at the screen. "Oh, look! Look who's coming, I like her, she's my favorite. She should win. She's kind of weird-looking, but if she wins, they'll fix that. Look what they did for Clay, my God."

Ralph watches as another young hopeful belts out a song—or so they call it, it never really seems like a song to Ralph. What these people call singing Ralph would call . . . what? Riding the scale up and down as though in frantic search of the note, that's what. "The Way You Look Tonight," there's a song!

"Want another piece of pie?" Monica asks, after the show is over, and when Ralph says yes, her face fills with sorrow and he wonders if he's answered incorrectly. "I don't *have* to," he says. "Either way is fine. I could drop a pound or two, God knows."

"No, no, eat the pie," she says. "I'm just fragile right now, Ralph. He's not even gone and I already miss him so much." She lifts Dogling out of his basket and kisses the top of the dog's head. An ear twitches, but he doesn't wake up. "Dogling?" she whispers and then smiles broadly. "*There* you are! Hi, baby! *Hi!*"

"I have to go to the bathroom," she tells Ralph. "Though how I can have anything in me after the tears I've been shedding, I'll never know." She hands the dog to Ralph. "Here. Hold him. Don't let his legs hang down like that! Keep him comfortable! And talk to him!"

"Well, look who's up and at 'em," Ralph says. Dogling's tail wags once, twice. "How about we get the hell out of here?" Another wag. Ralph carries Dogling out into the backyard and gently sets him down. "There you go, pal. Let her rip." The dog stands still before him. Blinks.

"Come on," Ralph says, "pee for Daddy before Mommy comes back."

The dog starts to lift his leg but falls down, and Ralph quickly picks him up and brings him inside. When Monica comes back into the living room, he says, "Sweetheart. It's enough."

She stares at him. "What do you mean?"

Ralph shrugs. "He can't even stand up. He's starting to smell. I think we should . . . you know." He draws his finger across his neck and whistles, then instantly regrets it.

"Oh, my God," Monica says. "Oh, my God." But then she draws in a shuddering breath and says, "Okay. All right. I know. But, Ralph?"

"What?"

"This is our last dog."

"We'll get another one," he says. "In time."

"No," she says. "We absolutely will not. I could never go through this again. I won't! And I want to sleep with him alone in the guest room tonight."

"Go right ahead," Ralph says. Good, then he himself can sleep in peace. Christ. It's a dog! It's a good dog, but it's a dog. Ralph takes his transistor radio out into the backyard and smokes a cigar while he listens to the White Sox cream the Cubs after four extra innings. And no one to celebrate with; Monica would take exception to his happiness.

When he comes back inside, the living room lights are off and Monica has gone to bed. He cracks the guest room door and watches the sheet over Monica rise and fall. Dogling is loudly snoring. For a moment, he regrets his decision. If a dog snores in a forest, should he be put to sleep the next day?

"I'll get our jackets," Monica says the next morning, after she and Ralph have had their coffee and determined that Dogling is indeed no better and probably worse. She goes over to the coat closet while Ralph sits in a living room chair, wrapping Dogling in his blanket for the trip to the vet. At the center of Ralph's chest, a terrible pressure is building. Grief, of course. Only then he feels a rush of nausea, and begins to perspire. He leans back in the chair. The pressure intensifies; he can hardly breathe.

"Monica?" he calls.

"I'm coming!" she says. "Just can't wait to kill him, can you. And cover his ears, that he shouldn't hear that."

"*Monica!*"

"I'm *coming*!" She walks into the room, tightening a brightly patterned scarf around her neck. *I gave her that,* Ralph thinks. She stops abruptly a few feet from him. "Ralph? What's the matter?"

"I just had this big pain in my chest. I think . . . I think I'm having a heart attack!"

She stares at him. "Ralph, you can't! Dogling is dying!"

"Call 911."

"Really? Are you serious, Ralph?"

"*Now!*"

She drops her purse and runs into the kitchen. He hears her giving their address. Then she says, "Well, you know our dog is dying and all of a sudden he had this terrific chest pain. . . . No, my *husband.*"

Sweet Christ in heaven. Does he have to speak to them himself? Ralph starts to stand, then falls back into the chair. Before his eyes, the loveliest violet curtain descends.

Ralph awakens to the sound of chewing. Sitting in a chair at his bedside is Monica, eating a bag of Cheetos and reading a magazine. "Monica?" he says softly.

She stands quickly. "Oh, you're awake, thank God. Listen, Ralph, you're fine. Let's go." She drops the bag into the garbage, picks up her purse, and slides it onto her shoulder. "Come on."

"What are you talking about? I just had a heart attack! I'm not going anywhere!"

"No, you didn't, Ralph. You did not. They did an EKG and checked your blood—cardiac enzymes, don't you remember?"

Ralph smiles. *Cod*iac, Monica says. What a goil. He chuckles.

"Ralph?"

"What?"

"Are you a little . . . Are you stoned? Do you feel stoned?"

Stoned! Now he laughs out loud.

"Shhh!" Monica squeezes his shoulder. "Ralph. Act normal. It was indigestion. That's all it was, indigestion and anxiety. And they knocked you out a little bit, is why you're stoned. But wake up, now. We have to go home. Dogling's all alone."

Ah. He remembers. He thinks, in fact, that he has just been with Dogling. A dream? A vision?

"Get dressed, Ralph, I'm going to find the nurse. They said you could go home when you woke up. So wake up, already."

Ralph nods, then slowly sits up. "Where *are* my clothes?"

Monica comes impatiently back to the bedside, pulls a plastic bag out from the bedside stand, and throws it at him. "Here!"

"How should I have known that?" Ralph asks.

"Oy. Don't start a fight now!"

"Get the nurse!"

"I am!"

Ralph pulls on his trousers but gets stuck trying to figure out how to put a shirt on over his IV. So he sits at the side of the bed, waiting. The bed across from him is empty, pristine-looking. You'd never know that someone had been in it before. Anything could have happened in that bed. He wonders if the beds get washed, if they go down to some gigantic car wash–type thing and then get put back into use. He hopes they get washed. God. Anything could be on them. Maybe somebody died in that bed. Or in the one he is sitting on now. Or gave birth in it. You never knew, from one day to the next what—

"Mr. Aronson?"

The nurse. A short little redhead, God bless her, big smile, real cute. "Hello," Ralph says. He reaches up self-consciously to smooth down his hair.

"What do you say we get rid of that IV?"

"Be okay with me." Ralph watches as the nurse— DIANNE, her name pin says—takes out the IV, then covers the site with a Band-Aid.

"World War Three," Ralph says, referring to the many bruises on his hand.

"Guess you were hard to get a line in," Dianne says, and from behind him Ralph hears Monica say, "He has bad veins."

The nurse instructs Ralph about what to watch for in the future, how he must never ignore such symptoms, he was exactly right to call 911, just sign here and he's a free man. Then he and Monica are out in the sunshine and walking toward the car. Ralph climbs into the passenger side of the car slowly, adjusts his legs with great care, and draws in a long breath. He may not have had a heart attack, but he's been in the hospital, by God! "It seems like so long since we've been out together," he says.

"We've been out," Monica answers. Then, "*Watch* it, you *idiot!*" she yells at a car that has come nowhere near her.

"Only on the deck. I mean, we've mostly been . . ."

"I left him a can of cat food," Monica says.

Ralph nods. The dog loves cat food—they discovered this when friends visited with their Siamese; they put down cat food, and Dogling raced over and vacuumed it up. Ever since then, he's gotten to have a can of cat food on special occasions. He likes the salmon supreme best. Liked.

Monica drives home at speeds well over the limit, and Ralph says nothing. He wants to get there, too. Old Butchie.

When they come into the house, Ralph hears the sound of the TV. "Is someone here?" he whispers to Monica.

"No," she says. "I turned the TV on for Dogling before I left. Animal Planet. First I had on channel five, but what did he need with that crap? It was some comedy that wasn't even funny. And the Food Network, they weren't talking enthusiastic enough."

"Jesus Christ, Monica. I was being rushed to the hospital and you were channel-surfing?"

"He was being left *alone*, Ralph. And he's *dying*!"

"*I* could have been dying!"

"You were not, it was only indigestion!"

"You didn't know that then!"

"You were in the ambulance! What could *I* do? I was coming!" She takes in a breath, calms herself. "Now stop it. The least we can do is give him a tranquil environment his last few . . ." She takes off her jacket and hands it to him. Then she goes into the living room, turns off the television, and calls, "We're *home*, sweetheart! *Hiiiiiiii*, Dogling! Where's my good *boy*?"

It's been a while since the dog greeted them at the door, Ralph thinks, hanging Monica's jacket. She got yellow from the Cheetos on the sleeve, he sees, and he tries to brush the stain off, which only makes it worse.

Yes, it's been a long while since they walked into the house on a normal day and had Dogling run over to them, snorting and turning around in circles, his little tail wagging so fast it was a blur. Ralph tries to remember the last time it happened. A month ago? Two? So often, you never know the last time's going to be the last time. There's so much you don't get to know. Something tugs at Ralph's mind, some memory, some thought. But then he hears Monica cry out, and he walks quickly into the kitchen. Dogling is on his side, lying still in that unequivocal way, and Monica is crouched down beside him, her hands over her face, weeping.

Ralph lowers himself beside Monica and rubs her back. Then he picks the dog up and cradles him against his chest. Already, the legs have grown stiff. "Ah, buddy," he says. "My little man."

And then his heart seems to crack wide open and he sobs, hoarse, choppy sounds he has never heard coming from himself before. The dog died alone. He cries and cries, and snot runs freely down his face and he gets the hiccups. On and on he weeps, for what surely must be only minutes but feels like hours. He hears Monica saying, "Ralph? *Ralph?*" but she might as well be miles away. He cannot see her. He cannot feel her.

Finally she says, *"Ralph!"* and he is able to turn to her and say in his anguished voice, "What? *What*, Monica?"

She nods. "Okay. You know why I'm crying?"

"Yeah. Because he died alone." Another sob, unbidden, unmanly. What the fuck, who cares.

"No. Not because he died alone." She wipes broadly under her nose, then under Ralph's.

"Because he died," he says.

"No. It's because he *ate*, Ralph." She shows Ralph the half-empty cat food can. "He ate, he tried, oh, what a champ, what a *great dog*!"

Through his tears, Ralph smiles, then begins to sob again.

"He was!" Monica says.

"I know he was."

"And . . . see? I'm crying from happiness," Monica says. "I'm so glad that one of the very last things he did was eat that salmon supreme." She folds her hands in her lap and speaks quietly. "Oh, Ralph. Everything's so much more important than we think."

Now Ralph remembers what eluded him before. The sense of peace he'd had when he thought he was dying, how *willing* he was, for whatever came. For whatever had happened, to have happened. He lays Dogling out on his lap. One of the dog's eyes is open, and he gently closes it. "Oh, God," Monica says softly, but there is more relief than sorrow in it. And then—could you believe it?—she begins to laugh a little, and through his tears, Ralph does, too.

"You know, Monica? When I was in the ER and I thought . . . I mean, I didn't know. I heard voices, but I couldn't speak, I felt kind of floaty and I didn't know if I was dying or what. But I felt the opposite of you. I felt like nothing really mattered. In the good way." He takes in a deep breath. He thinks he's done crying, now. "You know?"

"Maybe it's the same thing," Monica says. "Maybe we're saying the same thing." She strokes one of Dogling's ears. "I think we are." She looks over at Ralph, and there is in her face a girlishness, a lucent shyness he has not seen in a long, long time. "Ralph? I'm really glad you didn't die."

Doi. Ah, Monica. Ah, Butchie. Ah, spring day, come to a close, with the night wind rising up.

He kisses her forehead. "I'm glad I didn't die, too."

"I want to bury him under the rhododendron bush," Monica says. "He liked it there. When he was lying under there, he thought he was king of the hill."

"Yeah, he did. Do you want bury the rest of the cat food with him?"

"No. It will get all on him."

"We could wrap it up in foil."

She considers this, then says, "Okay. And . . . Let's get another dog. A puppy." She sighs.

"Okay," Ralph says, the word wide for his mouth, barely able to fit. But yes. Okay.

They sit for some time in the kitchen, in a silence rich with a shared sentiment that gives up nothing of itself to words. Finally Ralph stands and offers his hand to Monica, and she stands up, complaining that, oy, her elbows hurt. "Do they?" Ralph asks, and they head out to the yard together, continuing a quiet conversation up to and including a starlit graveside ceremony, meant to honor and say farewell to a dog who with his life brought them joy, and with his death flapped their future like a rug, straightening it out before them.

TRUTH OR DARE

After dinner, Laura ushers her friends out onto the front porch. It is a Friday evening in early spring, the buds tight on the trees, the grass greening in spots. Joyce settles herself into one of the wicker chairs, still stiff after the insults of winter, and sighs. "It's so light outside," she says. "I'm always so happy when it stays light later."

"Everybody is," Trudy says. She has stretched herself out on the little sofa, hogging all the room, so that Laura has to take the bad chair, the one with one leg ready to break off—when one sits in it, one fears moving. But Laura likes the way Trudy feels so comfortable taking the best seat, likes the way she is so unapologetic generally. It's refreshing, a marked change from many of the women she knows, who routinely begin conversations with an apology.

Even a phone call! *Laura: Hello? Friend: Oh, I'm sorry, were you busy?*

The three of them are relatively new friends, having met a month ago, when they all signed up for Yoga Plus! in a just-opened studio. They were in the back row, next to one another, when the teacher told them to assume a certain pose and shout out, "I love my beautiful face!" (This, Laura assumed, was the "plus" part.) They none of them shouted it. They said it, but they didn't shout it. When they assumed another pose and the teacher told them to shout out, "I love my beautiful rectum!" they all burst out laughing. "Focus!" the teacher said, but they couldn't stop laughing, and finally they left and went across the street and had lunch, where they agreed they *might* have said, "I appreciate my rectum."

The women have a lot in common: they're all in their late fifties, they're all divorced, they all live alone in condos they've bought in this newly gentrified neighborhood, they've all had cancer scares, and Joyce has in fact had a mastectomy. This is the first time they've had dinner at Laura's, and they have found it so agreeable, they've decided to have homemade dinners together once a week, rotating houses. Trudy has volunteered to be next and has already announced her menu: an Indian meal, all vegetarian. And a killer dessert. She complimented Laura on the dessert she made when they were served it; now she brings it up again. "That really was a good tart you made. Lemon curd and fresh strawberry. I really like that combination. And that cookie crust—it was like shortbread."

It is quiet for a moment; the women can hear the sounds of some neighborhood boys playing basketball a few houses down, the ball being dribbled. Then, *"Dude!"* one of them yells. Someone must have scored.

"*Was* it shortbread?" Trudy asks.

"Not exactly," Laura says. "I'll give you the recipe."

"Well, it was really good. Really buttery."

Joyce jumps up so quickly Laura thinks she's been bitten by something. But it's not that. "I want another piece," she says. "I'm going to get another piece."

"Me, too," Trudy says.

Laura follows the women into her kitchen, and they all sit back down at the kitchen table and finish off the tart, thin slice by thin slice. Trudy tells them that she has been thinking about old boyfriends lately, and she has decided to call her favorite one up. Don, his name is, Don Christianson, and he's someone she knew over thirty years ago.

"You haven't seen him since then?" Joyce asks. Her voice is like Georgette's, on the old *Mary Tyler Moore Show*, a high, little girl's voice, innocent and open. She actually looks a little like Georgette, too; blond, vacant-eyed, and dear.

Trudy, licking off her fork, shakes her head. She looks a little like Lucille Ball, red curly hair always tied up on top of her head, big blue eyes, high cheekbones. She was quite a looker not so very long ago. Joyce and Laura weren't bad themselves. They have admitted this to one another, each in her own way, how they used to be pretty. These young girls now? Ha. You want to talk about *hot?* Should have seen *them* thirty years ago. Well, forty.

Laura says, "If you haven't seen that guy for over thirty years, you're going to have to reconcile yourself to the fact that he might be dead. Lots of my old boyfriends are dead." She shakes her head and sighs.

"Who died?" Joyce asks, her hand pressed against her chest as if she might have known them.

"Well, one died of AIDS, one died of cancer, one—"

"You have an old boyfriend who died of AIDS?" Trudy asks.

"Yes."

"Was he gay?"

"Yes. He was."

"Did you *sleep* together?" Joyce asks.

Laura tilts her head, thinking. "Isn't that the definition of old boyfriend?"

Silence, and then the women agree that yes, in the context of what they're talking about, and also considering that they came up in the sixties, when having sex was roughly equivalent to a handshake, "old boyfriend" means "slept with."

Trudy says to Laura, "You slept with a gay guy?"

"He came out after we broke up," Laura says. "I loved him even more after we were just friends. He was so handsome. We always kept in touch, and once when he was making a lot of money and I didn't have anything— I mean, I had *nothing*—he invited me out for dinner at a fancy restaurant. I didn't have anything nice to wear, so he took me shopping and bought me a beautiful green silk dress at this store where nothing was even *out*—they just brought things to your fancy changing room. Which was way nicer than my apartment. But anyway, he bought me a dress there, and he bought me a purse to go with it, too."

"Shoes?" Joyce asks, and her voice is a reverential whisper.

"I actually had shoes," Laura says. "I'd had to go to my aunt's funeral, and my mom had bought me some shoes and some nylons for that. But anyway, he took me to this really great restaurant, and he let me take home all the leftovers, and when we got home my puppy had pooped all over my apartment, I mean all *over* it, he'd gotten sick, and there was Jim in his beautiful gray-green suit looking like the cover of *GQ* and he said, 'I'll help. Where are the paper towels?' And he took off his jacket and folded it neatly over the top of one of my awful chairs, and then he rolled up his sleeves and helped me clean up. On his knees.''

"Wow," Joyce says. "That was a good date."

"That was a good boyfriend," Trudy says. "Even if he wasn't even your boyfriend then."

"I know," Laura says, and she misses Jim so much right then, it is as though all the love she felt for him has been re-delivered to her solar plexus. She remembers the night when he first made exquisite love to her, he was the kind of man who could spend ten minutes describing the beauty of your neck to you, not only with words but with the light touch of his fingers. She remembers the pearl gray light in his bedroom, the moon coming through the window, the clanking sound of the radiator, the brown-and-white-striped sheets on his bed—oh, it's all so *clear*! She remembers how, after they finished, he ran his finger down the side of her face and asked her to tell him something about her that he didn't know. She told him she could make good chicken sounds and not only that, she could imbue the clucks with real emotions. "For example," she said, "Chicken with a Broken Heart." And she made long, drawn-out, sorrow-saturated clucks. He laughed so hard. "Now do Chicken Mad at the Rooster," he said. And she did. Again he laughed. Then he got up and made her linguine with clam sauce because another thing she told him was that she'd never had it and she didn't see what the big deal was.

"He *was* good," she tells the women. "And I miss him so much. It isn't often you find someone so handsome who is also so kind." She sighs and unbuttons her jeans. In the back of her mind, she feels happy to be among people with whom she can do this. In the front of her mind, she's thinking something else, and she asks Trudy, "What if Don is married?"

Trudy shrugs. "So?"

"If you were married, would you want some old girl-friend coming around?" Joyce asks.

Trudy considers this, then says, "Maybe not. But I probably wouldn't care if I didn't know about it."

Joyce's eyes widen. "So this is going to be clan*destine*?"

"Oh, stop," Trudy says. "I'm almost sixty years old. We'll probably meet in a cafeteria and compare lipid levels. I just feel like calling him up again because . . . Well, because I'm almost sixty. Isn't there anyone you ever wonder about, that you'd just like to see again? Just to talk to?"

"Only if it doesn't involve air travel," Joyce says. "I am so through with airplanes. Last time I flew, I was wearing this really sheer top under a suit jacket, it was just to have that little triangle of fabric at the top of the suit. You know. And they made me take my suit jacket off to go through security. I would have refused if I hadn't been running so late. I would have had them pat me down or something. But I was running really late, and so I took it off and then made my excruciatingly slow way through. I swear I could feel the eyes of the guy behind me just boring into my fat. Plus my bra straps were showing because of the cut of the sleeves of that little top, which was *never meant* to be shown in public." She waves her hand, as though pushing the memory away, then says, "Actually, you know what? There's a guy I used to date who lives only an hour's drive away. I just heard from a mutual friend that he moved to Indiana. Roy Schnickleman. Not like it sounds, honest. He looked just like James Dean. He drove a motorcycle, too. God." She smacks her hand down on the table. "Okay, I'm in. Old boyfriend. Lunch. Let's all do it this week and then we'll tell about it at dinner next week." She looks over at Laura. "Want to?"

"I'm telling you, all my old boyfriends are dead."

"*All* of them?" Trudy asks.

"All the good ones," Laura says. Dennis Anderson, who was an artist and a sculptor and a writer, and who asked her to move to Tahiti with him, which she did not do, which was idiotic. But he moved there and married a native, and he had a heart attack at fifty-one and died. Fifty-one! John Terrance died a terrible death from pancreatic cancer. The last time Laura saw him, he was being wheeled about outside on a friend's farm, and he saw the pond where he and his friends used to swim, where Laura in fact had swum with him just after they had begun their relationship. He couldn't talk anymore by then, but Laura saw the look of longing in his eyes. She tried to push him down to the water's edge, but the wheelchair wouldn't go through the mud, so she went down to the pond and filled her hands with water and carried it back up to him and spilled it out all over his legs, which by then had gotten so heartbreakingly thin. And Ted Sullivan, he was in a car wreck, and he was such a good guy, too. So funny. Once they were walking through a park together, through roses, and they were talking about how beautiful they were. Then Laura asked Ted about a movie, and he said, "Laura. The subject *was* roses."

"Well, maybe . . . your ex?" Trudy says. "Would he count as an old boyfriend?"

"He wasn't a good one."

"I have an idea," Joyce says. "Think of someone you wish had been your boyfriend. Call him."

"Right," Laura says. " 'Hello, I used to know you when I was a hot tamale. Now I'm an older woman with liver spots and forty extra pounds, and I wondered if you'd like to have lunch.' "

"How about this?" Trudy says. " 'Hello, I used to know you back in yada yada yada, and I was just thinking about yada yada yada, and you know what, I just wondered if we could get together just to have lunch. It would be fun, wouldn't it? Incidentally, I turned out to be a terrific person who makes one hell of a tart.' " She makes it sound so perky and possible.

"You know," Laura says, "we are becoming good friends, but we don't really think all that much alike."

"Well, then take a chance on something else," Joyce says. "Make your dare be different from ours."

"Why don't I just do truth?" Laura says.

"We tell the truth to one another all the time," Trudy says. "Let's do something different now. Joyce and I will call old boyfriends. You can do something else. You make a lunch date with someone else, okay? Are you in? All you have to do is be scared to ask."

"All right, I'm in," Laura says. "I know someone I'd like to ask. If I can get up the nerve. He's a homeless guy, lives under the bridge on Sumac." The other women start to laugh, and Laura holds up her hand. "I'm serious. I've actually had this fantasy for months, that I'd bring a meal over there and share it with him. I just want to know why he's there."

"Don't give him your address," Joyce says.

Laura looks over the top of her glasses at her.

"So we'll debrief at dinner at my house next week," Trudy says. "Six o'clock sharp." She stands, stretches, then points at her friends. "No backsies," she says.

That night, as Laura washes up for bed, she decides that she will just make up something about her lunch date. The other women will never know the difference. She'll make something up, say it really fast, and then they can move on to the real stories. Already, a false scenario is creating itself inside her head. The homeless man's surprise at her offering lunch. His interesting anecdote about how he landed there, him a former platinum credit card carrier. Some highly placed executive thrust out suddenly because of . . . what? Sexual harassment? A criminal act involving a White Hen? She falls asleep imagining various misdeeds, all kinds of things that can take a life and rip it right up. Then she imagines the man as shoved out of a mental institution that no longer has room for him, for that is the more likely scenario. She imagines saying, "Hi, there. Listen, I know this may seem odd, but I brought you some lunch, and I wonder if I could just sit with you for a while and talk." And him leaning over to say between clenched teeth, "The descent is upon us, Silverado!" then leaping up and flapping his arms and yelling, *"Helllllllllp!"* so loudly she gets arrested. Then she imagines the man saying nothing, just staring at her and breathing oddly. Then she sees him as a poetic genius too sensitive for the world, someone broken by its unyielding ways, who begins to weep when she touches his sleeve. And then she decides that whatever he is doesn't matter; she's not going to approach him or anyone else, either.

In the morning, Laura looks out her office window (she

works at home, for a spectacularly successful gardening service, doing their billing) and sees a construction worker on the roof of the house across the street. He is very handsome—tanned and muscular, absolutely delicious. Could it be that her time for sex, for sensuality, is not over after all? Could it be? Or is this some kind of psychic hangover, the result of too much talk about times gone by, too many memories brought once again into sharp focus but apt to fade by lunchtime?

She watches the construction worker for a while, then moves away from the window, sits at her desk, and opens up her computer. Sips her coffee as she reads her e-mail. Remembers last week, when there was yet another spam filter failure and she had yet another message asking if her penis was big enough. Now she wonders who responds to those e-mails. Who keeps those penis people in business? Are men her age trying to make sure they can still . . . ? And if they are, would it be any fun to try once again to . . . ?

Focus! she tells herself, in the same odd accent her yoga instructor has, and begins her dreary task of calculation— she likes to work on the weekend and take weekdays off. If this new longing has not gone away by five P.M., she'll go out to Panera for an Asian sesame chicken salad for dinner. There she will make a list of old boyfriends who might still be alive and were not horrible. She will Google them, and if she finds them, she will call and propose a lunch, and if they agree to meet her, she will even fly to get there. Might be better to fly there, in fact. No. No, she won't fly. It has to be driving distance, she's not going to use up her miles on what might prove to be a complete disaster. Imagine if the plane crashed after what wasn't even any fun.

Her sons at her funeral, sorrowfully asking, "What was she doing in Kansas *City*?"

Focus! Laura gets to work.

All the way to Panera, Laura has told herself not to get the bread as a side, get the apple. But when she gets there, she goes right ahead and gets the bread. One good thing if she starts to have sex again is that it will be no trouble to get the apple. That's how it goes: good sex equals appetite suppression. Plus your complexion improves, who knows why.

Laura eats her salad and starts making a list of all the boyfriends she's had, from college on. The redheaded guy who came from a really rich family who dumped her after two weeks, the business major who looked like Gregory Peck but was chronically depressed, the Italian guy who loved Apple Jacks cereal and was such a good dancer, the doctor who wanted her to convert to Judaism. And after that doctor, Brian's and her marriage, which lasted for over twenty-five years, then abruptly ended.

The first few months after the divorce, she was ecstatic to be free again. Then, gradually, she became aware of what her freedom really meant; and there was nothing to be ecstatic about—mostly she felt as though she were walking a tightrope all the time. She came to the discouraging realization that many of the demons present in her marriage had moved into her condo right along with her. She realizes now that her ex-husband *is* the old boyfriend she would most like to have lunch with. Would like, in fact, to be married to again. He has a girlfriend named Cassandra, she's heard—five years after the divorce, he finally has a steady girlfriend, but a girlfriend is not a wife, even if she's living with him. Laura has never seen Cassandra; Brian, deeply wounded by the split, wanted nothing to do with Laura after their day in court. They communicated over the phone or e-mail about their grown sons only when necessary, which turned out to be hardly ever.

Laura offered to be the one to move out of the house. She thought that, since the divorce was her idea, the least she could do was let Brian stay in the house they'd built together. But she misses that house. She drives past it now and then, and last time she parked her car a few houses down and went to look at the garden in the backyard that she put in the first year they lived there. There it was, still growing. Everything still alive. It shamed her in a way so elemental her knees actually buckled. She fled the yard with her head held falsely high, a tight smile on her face, and vowed never to go there again. But now she leaves her salad unfinished and walks quickly to her car, keys in hand.

Even on a Saturday the neighborhood is quiet. No one on the street, as usual. It's one of the things that bothered her about this neighborhood, actually, the way you hardly ever saw anyone out. She likes that aspect of condo life better, the way you can't help but see people every day—in the elevator, in the laundry room, at the monthly meetings. If she and Brian got back together, they would move to a bigger condo together. They wouldn't need this house anymore.

So now what, she thinks. Here she is, she sped over here, and now she is just sitting in her car right in front of the house. She looks up to see if anyone is peering out the windows at her. No.

She takes a quick look at herself in the rearview, then marches up to the front door. She will say she is sorry to come over unannounced, but she needs a word with Brian.

She hopes it's Brian who answers the door. And she hopes he will accommodate her request. She thinks he will. She's sure of it, actually. Laura and Brian. The roots remain.

She rings the doorbell and waits. Rings it again and waits some more. Inside, she hears the grandfather clock striking, the clock she and Brian saved so long for, she loves that clock. She rings the bell one more time, waits one more minute. Then she walks down the sidewalk toward her car, full of a kind of misplaced embarrassment. As she moves past the curbside mailbox, she sees that the flag is up, and she looks to see what's inside. It's pathetic, it's wrong, but she just wants to see. There are bills being paid, Brian's familiar script for the return address. The only other thing is a postcard being sent to some kind of catering company; Cassandra is taking advantage of a free consultation. Laura looks around, up and down the block. No one. She puts the postcard in her purse. Then she closes the mailbox and drives away, careful not to exceed the speed limit. Once she got pulled over on her own street. "But I *live* here," she told the cop. He looked at her oddly, then issued her a ticket. She cursed him as he drove away.

On the way home, she resolves to mail the postcard—she'll drop it in the box outside her building. She's horrified that she took it. What in the world is the matter with her. She wonders what she would have done if Brian had been home, or Cassandra, or both of them. She'd flown over there in some kind of trance, expecting that Brian would drop whatever he was doing and say yes to anything she suggested, including getting back together. What is the matter with her. She will mail the postcard, and then maybe she'll try to find Jerry Menzel, who was her teacher for an acting class. She'd had a crush on him, but he never knew, because he had a girlfriend, and so she never approached him. That's how she used to be. What is the matter with her.

On Monday afternoon, Laura calls Cassandra. "Hello," she says. "This is Regan Kennedy from—" She looks quickly at the postcard again. "Home Cook In, and I am calling about the postcard you sent for a consultation."

"You got it already?" Cassandra asks.

Silence, and then Laura says quickly, "Yes, we did, and I'm happy to say we've had a very nice response to this offer, so you'll need to pick a time quickly, now how does this afternoon work?"

"Today?"

"Well, we only have . . . this is a limited offer."

"I can't do it today. But I could do tomorrow morning, say, ten o'clock?"

"That's fine," Laura says. Something occurs to her, and she says, "Now, with whom will I be meeting?" Undoubtedly Brian will be at work, but better make sure. For what she has decided is that she wants to have lunch not with an ex but with that ex's girlfriend.

"Oh, it'll be just me," Cassandra says. "This is a surprise for my fiancé."

Once Laura put salt on a slug. This is what her stomach is doing now. But she manages, "Oh! What fun."

"Yes," Cassandra says. "I'm excited."

Laura hangs up the phone and stares out her window. Fiancée is not wife, she tells herself. She eats nonfat cottage cheese for breakfast. It would be nice if she could lose forty pounds by tomorrow.

She doesn't bother with makeup today. She doesn't want to look into her own eyes in the mirror. Nor does she answer the phone when Trudy calls, because if she does, she'll tell Trudy what she's doing, and Trudy will make her come to her senses, and she doesn't want to come to her senses. She wants to meet Cassandra, who has a low and lovely voice. She could be on the radio, one of those late-night personalities. What she does do is nothing, Laura happens to know. Her younger son told her that Cassandra used to sell cars, but now she's doing nothing. "That's ridiculous," Laura said, and her son said, "I know. She should work." But what Laura found ridiculous was that Cassandra had sold cars. It made Laura mad, because it made her jealous, because she could never do that. She still doesn't know what a spark plug is. She pictures it as a cartoon character with a high voice and a little hat.

On Tuesday morning, Laura parks on the curb a few houses down from Brian's, gets out of her car, then back in it. She drives right up to the house, parks in the driveway, and walks briskly up to the front door. She puts her finger to the bell and takes in a deep breath. Rings it.

Almost right away, the door is opened by an unusually beautiful woman wearing a sleeveless black sweater and tan pants, gold hoop earrings. She is tall and slender, with shoulder-length black hair, green eyes, and a full mouth. She is barefoot, her toes painted a champagne color, and even her feet are pretty. Laura's hand flies up to her mouth, and, helplessly, she begins to laugh. When Cassandra looks askance at her, Laura says, "I'm sorry. Sorry! I was just remembering a joke a friend told me about . . . Well, never mind." She holds out her hand. "I'm Regan. Very nice to meet you."

Cassandra continues to stare closely at her but smiles back. "Cassandra. Thanks so much for coming." She gestures toward the back of the house. "Shall we go into the kitchen?"

"Surely," Laura says. *Surely!* Like some old maid schoolteacher. All she needs is some ugly old satchel-type briefcase, the straps curled up from age. Bad enough the state of her purse. Her older son, who lives in L.A., has a girlfriend who showed her a purse she thought Laura should buy, and Laura told her don't be ridiculous, who would spend that much for a purse? Well, the woman in front of her would. Laura would guess that she paid well over fifty dollars for her pedicure.

Laura sits at the kitchen table and puts her purse on the floor. A lot has changed here—the walls are a different color, the table is round rather than square, a lighter wood. There are curtains at the kitchen window, and it's all Laura can do not to say, "Hey! Brian and I hate curtains— how'd you talk him into that?" Instead, she folds her hands and says, "So. How can I help you?"

Cassandra laughs. "I hope that's what you're here to tell me. All I know is that your company sends people into homes to cook. So . . . What do you cook?"

"What do you want?" Laura asks. It feels a little mean, the way she's said this, and she likes that. She likes being a little mean.

But Cassandra is not in the least offended. She says, "Well, the first thing I should say is that I'm a terrible, terrible cook. Just never had any interest or talent. But I'd like my fiancé to have good, home-cooked dinners every night—his ex was a wonderful cook."

"Was she?" Laura asks.

"Yes, apparently *everything* was homemade—bread, piecrusts, pasta."

"I suppose she had one of those pasta machines," Laura says. She did not. She cut the noodles freestyle and laid them over the backs of the kitchen chairs to dry.

"I guess so."

"Although she might have cut them by hand and let them air-dry," Laura says. "Like when pasta is *really* homemade. I'll bet she did that. I'd imagine she made her own pizza crust, too. And fancy birthday cakes?"

"Oh, I'm sure. I mean, Brian told me she made corn bread from scratch to use in the *dressing* she made at Thanksgiving."

"Gotta love that," Laura says sarcastically and rolls her eyes in what she hopes is a modern, working-woman way.

"Well, actually I kind of admire it," Cassandra says. "But I don't want to do it. So I thought I'd hire you and have my cake and eat it, too. So to speak."

Laura leans forward. "I have to tell you right off that this would be a very expensive proposition. Having everything homemade that way."

"No problem," Cassandra says.

The bitch. "With the shopping, it would be a good five hundred or so a week," Laura says, then wonders if that's enough.

"That's fine."

Laura raises her eyebrows. "Your boyfriend must do very well, if you don't mind my saying."

"He does, but it's not my fiancé—he's my fiancé—who would be paying. I would."

There's a neat trick for an unemployed woman, Laura thinks. But never mind, better let this go; a real person would not be asking these kinds of questions.

"So let's talk about some menu ideas," Laura says, and Cassandra says, "Oh, good, let's." Laura looks sharply at her, but no, there's nothing in her face that makes it seem as though her remark is anything but innocent and true.

"Does your boyfriend like beef?" Brian loves beef.

"Oh, God," Cassandra says. "Yes!"

Well, that's nothing that you know that, Laura thinks. *What about the macaroni necklace he made for his mother in Cub Scouts, I know you never saw that, you never even got to meet his mother.* But she speaks impassively, professionally. "I make a fabulous beef Stroganoff. *We* do, I should say. That dish has done very well for us, everyone loves it."

"Well, Brian has a bit of a cholesterol problem."

"He does?"

"Yes."

"Since *when?*"

Cassandra frowns. "Pardon?"

"Well, I just . . . I just mean that, even if it's a long-standing problem, we can take care of that. We can use low-cholesterol products and still make it taste good." What cholesterol problem? He never had a cholesterol problem when she lived with him. She'll fix that when they get back together. No more omelets, he used to love omelets. She feels a pressure in her bladder and realizes that she's had to pee for a while—speaking of health concerns, she's got to stop drinking so much coffee. "I wonder if I might use your bathroom," she says.

"Sure—right down the hall."

"The door on the left?" Laura asks, pointing. She should win an Academy Award.

Cassandra nods. The phone rings, and she moves to answer it. "Hey, Sarah," she says warmly, and Laura wonders what it would be like to be Cassandra's friend.

Laura goes into the bathroom, also completely changed but for the toilet and the sink. Even the floor tiles have been replaced—what was wrong with the floor tiles she chose? The wall colors? The towels? Although these towels are quite nice—much plusher. If you need that sort of thing.

When she comes out of the bathroom, she hears Cassandra still on the phone, and so she tiptoes down the hall into Brian's office. That at least has stayed the same—the bookshelves she picked out, the desk and easy chair, the lamp. And on his desk, mixed in with pictures of their boys and artful shots of Cassandra (overly artful, in Laura's opinion), one picture of her remains. It is one Brian took not long after they met, and it is of her back as she is leaping over a low fence, her hair streaming out behind her. Laura remembers a night shortly after she'd told Brian she wanted a divorce and they were sitting in his office, he at the desk, she in the easy chair. Brian picked up that picture and stared at it, and Laura said, "I never understood why you liked that picture so much. You can't even see me." He smiled, bit at his lip, and then said, "It's the truest image I have of you, Laura." He set the picture gently down, then said, "What the hell, I think it's a nice picture. The fog. The beach grass. And you were happy that day, you can tell even looking at your back. You still felt free." It was true, everything he said. She hadn't really wanted to get married; she'd felt trapped from the moment they got engaged; she'd even told him early on that she'd never be able to stick it out, and he'd said, "I know. I'm glad I get to have you for as long as I do."

Laura's eyes fill, and now she remembers the last night she was in this house, when she and Brian sat out on the front steps in the dark holding hands, because no matter what they were still friends, they did love each other in this way, and they regretted all the pain. Brian was talking about Einstein, whom he idolized. He said that when the Nazis came to power, they wanted nothing more than to discredit one of Einstein's theories. So they got together a whole bunch of scientists to debunk him, this big group of scientists. "But," Brian said, "if Einstein were really wrong, they would have needed only one." It was something like that, Laura can't recall every word. What she does remember clearly is the way Brian sounded that night, telling her those things. How his tone was plain and simple, utterly lacking in bitterness or rancor. She thought then that he meant all the accusations she made against him in order to justify the divorce were also excessive and therefore false. And now, years later, she sees that her finger should have been pointed at one thing only: herself, a person who drove down her own street recklessly because it was her own.

"Laura?" she hears from out in the hall.

Well. No Academy Award for her after all. She doesn't move, doesn't breathe. Then Cassandra comes into the study and says, "I want you to know that he still loves you, in his way. I think he always will. But he's with me now, and we're happy. We really are. I adore him. We haven't told your sons yet that we're getting married. It will be a very quiet ceremony, and then . . . Well, we have some things planned with them."

Laura begins to cry, an ugly, hiccuping kind of crying, and she coughs against this awful display of emotion. "I'm sorry," she says. "I've never . . ."

"I believe you," Cassandra says. "And I won't tell him. I really won't. I think I understand."

What Laura wants to do is lash out angrily and say, No you don't. You don't know me. You don't know me, you don't deserve him, you have no business being in my house. It is *my* house! But every single one of those things is wrong. Here is a woman who loves Brian the way he always should have been loved, and in a small, undamaged corner of her heart, she is glad.

"So I'll just go now," she tells Cassandra, and Cassandra says, "Thank you," and Laura thinks, *This is the part of the story Trudy and Joyce will like best, if I tell it right. I hope I can describe how elegant she was, saying this. How kind.*

On the way home, Laura drives past the Sumac Street bridge. She pulls over and parks, then walks down the little incline to where the homeless man sits. He sees her coming and looks up when she is standing beside him. "You wouldn't happen to have seventy-five cents, would you?" he asks. He is blond and blue-eyed, perhaps mid-forties, his lashes surprisingly long and dark. He wears brown corduroy pants and a dirty gray sweatshirt and flip-flops, despite the chill still in the air.

"I would happen to." She opens her wallet and hands him a dollar.

"I don't have change."

"That's all right."

"God bless you."

"You, too." She stands there for a minute, then says, "Would you mind if I ask . . . How did you get here?"

"Shelter's too crowded."

"No, I mean . . . Did you ever work?"

He glares at her. "Course I did."

"What did you used to do?"

"That's none of your goddamn business."

Laura nods. "Okay. Well, good luck to you."

"Wait a minute." He looks down, then back up at her. "I'm sorry. Some things I don't like to talk about. Don't like to look back. This is now, that's all. Got to keep walking."

"I understand." She smiles, then says, "You know, I could bring you some lunch sometime. Would you like that?"

He laughs. "Ain't that a kick in the head."

"Really. I like to cook, and I'm always making too much and then throwing all kinds of things away."

"Yeah, you wouldn't believe what some people throw away."

"Oh, yes I would." She thinks of the mountains of food she's wasted: casserole dishes of enchiladas with only two missing; a cake with barely a twelfth of it gone, salads full of carefully julienned vegetables tossed into the garbage on top of coffee grounds and eggshells. She thinks of things she's seen her neighbors put at the edge of the curb: furniture, clothes, lamps, not a thing in the world wrong with any of it. Then she thinks of a time when she and Brian were getting ready to move from their first apartment. It was a move up, no doubt about it, but Laura had a great fondness for the old place; in some ways she was very sorry to leave it. Never mind the cramped kitchen, the crack in the living room wall, the stench of the downstairs neighbor's cat box that drifted up to them; Laura had a sentimental attachment to the place. She lay in the bathtub that night on her stomach, letting the water drain out. Brian was in the bathroom with her, sitting on the closed lid of the toilet. They'd been talking about moving, how they'd have room for so much more, and Laura suddenly began quacking like a duck—she'd moved from chickens to doing very good imitations of ducks. So she began quacking like a duck, and in between quacks, she kept saying, quite plaintively, really, "Let's stay here, bud" (they called each other "bud" in those days). She said it a few times, "Let's stay here, bud, *quack, quack, quack.*" And Brian was laughing, but in his eyes was a soft sadness, because he knew that, no matter how much she loved that place, she was going to have to go.

"I'll see you another time," Laura tells the man, and he grunts and gives her a little wave. A meat-loaf sandwich on homemade white, that's what he'll get, Laura's got his number. A meat-loaf sandwich and some homemade potato chips. Couple of peanut butter cookies from the recipe she found in *Bon Appétit.*

On Friday evening, Laura shows up at Trudy's with good wine, both red and white, and a bouquet of apricot-colored parrot tulips mixed with apricot-colored roses. She loves this particular arrangement and in fact often buys it for herself. On one occasion, she called a florist and had it sent to herself with a card signed, "Guess who?" She does something like this with fancy chocolates, too; she gets them gift-wrapped so that at home she can tear off the paper, then display the box with the top casually off-kilter, satin ribbon coiled beside it: *Gift.* She doesn't really care for Godiva chocolates, but she will buy them for their artful designs and for the cunning little ornaments that come with them. And for their ridiculous price: she subscribes, however reluctantly, to the belief that if something *costs* that much, it *must* be good.

Last Christmas, Laura sprayed a big box of Godiva chocolates with shellac so they would last longer, and then she went and scared away the five-year-old girl who lives down the street and used to come and visit her sometimes. *"Don't eat those!"* she yelled, when Dory reached for a chocolate. The little girl jerked back her hand and said, "I *wasn't*. I was only *looking.*" And then she got all round-eyed and began to hold herself. "Would you like to use the bathroom?" Laura asked gently, and Dory whispered, "No, I want to go home." She hasn't been back to visit since.

Trudy opens the door laughing hard, and behind her, down the hall, Laura can see Joyce, also laughing, bent over with laughter, in fact.

Laura steps in, feeling awkward the way you can when you enter a room with people laughing like that. There is a perfumy scent of Indian spices in the air; Laura feels she's nearly levitating. "Wow, something smells *good,*" she says.

"Chicken tikka masala," Trudy says proudly, and accepts the flowers. "Oh, these are lovely. Thank you." She wipes a tear from laughter off her cheek, then says, "Come on back to the kitchen. Joyce was just starting to tell about her lunch date, but I told her she had to wait until we were all here. What she told so far was *funny,* though."

"Well, now we are all here," Joyce says, "and I want to go first."

"Wait until we're sitting down," Trudy says. She takes off her apron, and the women help her carry dishes of food over to the dining room table. In addition to the chicken, there is saag paneer, lamb biryani, samosas, and naan. There is an ice bucket on the table holding Kingfisher beer.

"Did you *make* all this?" Laura asks, and Trudy says, "Not the beer."

"Ha, ha," Laura says, drily.

"Not the beer or the chicken. Or the rice. Or the samosas or the spinach." She points to the table. "Sit anywhere. Dig in."

"Did you make the naan?" Joyce asks and Trudy looks at the bread as though considering. Then she says, "Oh. No. But I did make the dessert. We're having mango pudding. I found the recipe in the newspaper. It's full of cream. I can't wait."

"Didn't you say this was going to be all vegetarian?" Laura asks, and Trudy says, "Huh. Did I? I can't remember. I can't remember anything anymore, and I'm getting panicked about it, so that makes me remember even less. You know what happened last night? I woke up from a sound sleep thinking, *What does 'fulcrum' mean?*"

Laura feels her palms grow damp. Wait. What *does* it mean, exactly?

"Come on," Joyce says. "Plate up, ladies; I want to tell my story." She looks around the table, making sure her friends have served themselves, and then begins. "Okay. So on Sunday morning, I called Roy Schnickleman, remember? Looked like James Dean only with real black hair, drove a motorcycle, a physique made for tight T-shirts, remember?"

Laura and Trudy nod and grunt, their mouths full.

"Well, he remembered me right away, and he was laughing, and he just sounded so happy to hear from me."

"Is he married?" Trudy asks, and Joyce says, "No, no, but I'll get to that. Just listen. I told him I had to be in Indiana not far from him—I didn't want to say he was the only reason I was coming. No point in going that far. I said I was going to be there that afternoon and how about lunch. He said fine, and then he asked if I was married. I said no, I'm divorced, and he said, Yeah, so am I, and there was this kind of sad, awkward silence, and then he got all hyped up again about how glad he was to hear from me and gave me the address for this restaurant called

Chucky's, and I agreed to meet him there at noon. I told him I'd wear a yellow blouse and a black skirt, and he said fine, he would, too."

"Playful spirit," Laura says, and reaches for another samosa. She could eat the whole pile, she loves these things. She's glad Trudy didn't cook; the homemade samosas she's tasted are never as good as a restaurant's. Somehow they get too Americanized. The Velveeta factor, Brian used to say.

"So I got to the restaurant," Joyce says, and Trudy interrupts her, saying, "Wait a minute. How did you prepare?"

"What do you mean?" Joyce asks.

"I mean, how did you do your makeup?"

"Oh. Well, it was subtle."

"Did you use the expensive stuff?"

"Of course I used the expensive stuff. Chanel."

"Jewelry?" Trudy asks.

"Diamond studs, a gold bangle bracelet."

"Did you wear your Spanx?" Laura asks.

Joyce looks down at her plate. "No."

"*No?*" Trudy says.

"No, because I . . . Because I thought, *What the hell, what if . . . ?*"

"True," Trudy says. "Not the kind of thing you want a guy to tear off you."

"They need to put lace on those things," Laura says, around a mouthful of biryani.

"Even then," Joyce says. "But anyway, I walked into this restaurant—terminally family, but kind of cute—and right away I spotted him, sitting there in his yellow shirt, reading the newspaper. I spotted him right away. I walked up to the table and said, 'My God, Roy *Schnickleman!*' and I leaned over to kiss his cheek, and the man pulled back from me, a little alarmed, and I saw that it wasn't Roy at all."

"That's the part we were laughing about," Trudy says. "Now you're all caught up." She cracks open another beer, and Laura does, too. Then Joyce does.

"Finally I saw the real Roy. He was sitting at a corner table, and he was quite a bit heavier and he was wearing a *toupee,* I could tell from across the room."

"Oh, God," Laura says. Bald is bad enough, but a girl can work with that. Memories of Telly Savalas and all. But a rug. Dead end.

"He leaped up and grabbed my hand and went to kiss my cheek, and we ended up bumping heads. But it was sweet, you know. It was cute.

"Then we start talking, and it wasn't awkward at all, we just blabbed and blabbed and blabbed. I was watching his face, and I saw it kind of go back and forth from how he was to how he is. It was weird. His eyes are still beautiful. Everything else, well . . . I could see that he thought I was still attractive, and at one point I got this image of us making love all those years ago. I remembered the first time we did it, I accidentally *snorted* when we were humping away, and then I was just so embarrassed. Neither of us said a word, we just kept at it, but then he started snorting with every thrust, just to make me feel better, you know."

The women laugh, and Trudy begins rhythmically snorting.

"Yes, like that," Joyce says, "but you know, it was great, it broke the tension, and we had a lovely afternoon."

"It was daytime when you did it?" Trudy asks.

"Well, yes. Yes, it was daytime, we used to do it in the daytime all the time in those days. Remember when our bodies looked good in daytime?"

"Oh yeah," Trudy says.

"It was daytime, and we had Roberta Flack and Donny Hathaway on the stereo, and I think we made love four or five times in a row." She stares into space, sighs deeply. "But anyway, Roy said he had a big crush on this woman, and he was having a hard time working up the courage to ask her out."

"At this age?" Laura asks, and Trudy says, "Oh, come on, Laura. Some things never change."

"I asked if there was anything I could do to help," Joyce says, "and he was just so grateful. He said she was a cashier at Wal-Mart and she was working right now, we could go and see her and I could maybe tell her what a good guy he is. I said sure, what the heck, I needed some things anyway."

"Never shop at Wal-Mart; they're unfair to their workers," Trudy says, and Joyce says, "Oh, stop. It was a social emergency. I had to buy something; it wouldn't be polite to meet her at her store and then not buy something."

"That's not true," Trudy says. "Do you think that's true, Laura?"

Laura finishes chewing her naan, then says, "I guess it depends on how the woman feels about Wal-Mart."

"When you've finished your discussion on microeconomics, let me know," Joyce says.

"Not microeconomics, ethics," Trudy says.

"Isn't it more etiquette than ethics?" Laura asks.

Joyce sighs loudly, and Laura says, "Sorry. Go on."

"*Thank* you," Joyce says.

The phone rings, and Trudy says, "Forget it, forget it, let the machine get it, keep talking," but then they hear that it's Trudy's daughter so she has to take it. Laura and Joyce hear her say, "Is everything all right?" Laura's mother-in-law used to say that; each and every time she called, the first thing she said was, "Is everything gall right?" As though there were a liaison between the "g" of "everything" and the "a" of "all." She was a very nice woman, Rose Goldstein, Laura liked her almost as much as her own mother.

Trudy says, "Okay, well, let me call you back, I've got dinner guests, I love you, good-bye."

"You're never free once you have children," Joyce says after Trudy returns to the table, but there is a note of satisfaction in her voice, and Laura believes her friends are in agreement that there is a sweetness—a great solace, really—in having your children need you.

"So," Trudy says, "you went to Wal-Mart to meet the princess."

"Yes," Joyce says. "And guess how we got to Wal-Mart?" She's pretty excited, and so the answer is obvious.

"Motorcycle!" Laura and Trudy say together, and Joyce squeals, "Yes, a big *hog*! With all this *stuff* on it!"

"Did you sit on one of those high little back seats and wrap your arms around him and let the wind blow in your hair?" Laura asks.

"*Yes*, no helmets, so *Easy Rider*, but listen to what happened: His *toupee* blew off!"

Trudy spews beer out of her mouth, then, laughing, says, "Gee. I always wanted to do that. Sorry. Go ahead."

"So," Joyce says, "he pulled over and retrieved his hair and shoved it in his jacket pocket and said, 'I'll put it on when we get there.' And I thought, *Okay, golden opportunity*, and I said, 'Roy? I hope you don't mind my saying so, but I think you look way better without it.' And he put his hand on top of his head, all shy, and said, 'Really?' and I told him yeah, I honestly think women prefer bald to toupee. He said yeah but the only way she's seen me is with hair. I suggested, gently, that she probably knew it was a toupee, and he blushed and then I felt terrible and I said well, *maybe* she knows. He said he'd decide what to do when we got there, and when we did get there, sure enough, he put the damn thing on. Right out in the parking lot. And I straightened it for him, because the man does not know how to put on a hairpiece, and then we went into Wal-Mart. And I saw her right away."

"Uh-oh," Laura says. "This sounds familiar."

"No," Joyce says, "this time I was right. She was such a stereotype. She had fake blond hair all ratted up, a low-cut V-neck shirt, and blue eye shadow. Killer figure. Killer. Stomach flat as a pancake and a real nice butt."

"Yeah, well, how old?" Trudy asks.

"About fifty, fifty-five."

"Damn," Trudy says, and looks down at her stomach.

"So Roy went over and talked to her, and she looked at me and waved and then she put the Closed sign on her register and came over. And I was thinking, *Wait a minute, how can I talk about what a nice guy Roy is, I don't even know him anymore*. We went over to the little café and got coffee, and Roy and she took out cigarettes—she said she smokes there all the time even though you're not supposed to. She leaned over and looked up at Roy when he lit her cigarette and then she *French-inhaled*."

"Oh, she likes him," Trudy says.

"Right, that's what I thought," Joyce says. "But then Roy said he was going to go pick up a few things, why didn't we ladies just relax, and when he walked away, the woman, Cyndi was her name—as her necklace announced—anyway Cyndi said, 'God Almighty, I wish that man would stop coming around.' And I said all this stuff about how he really is just the sweetest guy. I told her about how we were friends so many years ago when he was a musician and played guitar in a rock band. Cyndi said, 'He played guitar?' and I said oh yes and I said he was really really good, which he wasn't, but what the hell, and I told her about this one time when I was at his apartment and a whole bunch of beautiful girls came over looking for Roy—groupies. True story. That was the night I first slept with him. Of course I didn't tell Madame Blue Eye Shadow that part. Cyndi said she once heard a musician say that he would rather be blind than deaf, and she always thought that was bullshit, but maybe it wasn't. She looked over at Roy, hanging around in the candy aisle, acting like he wasn't watching us, and she said, 'Listen, he's a nice guy, but . . . Can I be honest with you? I just could never go out with a guy that wears a rug.' I said, 'I'll tell you what, why don't I let him know you'd prefer he not wear it, and then would you let him take you out to dinner? Just once?' " She looked at him, and it was the most unfortunate thing because he was bending over rifling through the candy on the lowest shelf and it was *such* an unflattering view. But then she blew out some smoke and kind of smiled and said, 'Aw, hell, I'll tell him to come over for dinner tonight. The only thing is, I got five kids. Three still at home and one of 'em's retarded. Most men, they're completely freaked out by that. Think he can handle it?' And you know, I looked at her in a completely different way then, and I said yeah, I thought he could. For sure, I said, and I really believed it and I hoped it was true. She said, 'How about a hot dog?' I was full from lunch, but I said sure and reached for my wallet and she put her hand over mine—lord, ten-inch nails, I swear—and she said, 'I get them *free.*' 'Oh,' I said, and she said, 'Yeup. I've worked here for a while, now, so . . .'

"On the way home I told Roy to lose the rug, and he said okay. And I told him to let me know what happened, so he called the next day and said, 'No go.' And I said, 'Aw, really? Why?' And I was thinking, *I'll bet it was her kids after all*, and I was feeling so bad for Cyndi. But what he said was, 'She doesn't like that I have four kids.' Can you believe it?"

"Oh, come on," Trudy said, "that was just an excuse."

"I guess," Joyce says. "But I told Roy I'd go out to dinner with him, and he suggested we start a book club and meet once a month to discuss our choices, and I said okay."

"So what are you reading first?" Laura asks.

"*Lonesome Dove.* Larry McMurtry."

"His choice, I assume," Trudy says.

"Nope. Mine. His choice was *Jane Eyre.*"

Trudy frowns. "Get out."

"I'm serious. He said he thought it might help him relate better to women."

"I always meant to read *Lonesome Dove,*" Laura says.

"You can join," Joyce tells her.

"Can I?" Trudy asks, and Joyce says of course, first meeting is May eighth, seven o'clock, Chucky's, they can all ride together and won't it be nice for Roy's ego to be surrounded by attractive women.

"Well. What a nice story," Laura says. "I love the ending. I've really been wanting to join a book club."

"*And* Joyce didn't buy anything at Wal-Mart!" Trudy says. She pours herself a glass of beer. "Can I go next? Because my story is so different from yours."

Laura makes an expansive gesture—*Be my guest.*

"Okay, so as you know, I called Don Christianson. But before I tell you about our lunch, I have to tell you about when I dated him. I was twenty-eight years old and thinking about marrying Jim, but I wasn't quite sure. I signed up to take this adult education class in dream interpretation, and that's when I met Don. He was really handsome, but he didn't have much of a personality—real quiet, not at all witty, which Jim was, and I was very much attracted to witty guys. To mean guys, too, of course, which Jim also was.

"Anyway, in the class, we were supposed to report our dreams every week, and then we would all talk about them. What was really interesting was that, after a while, you saw a pattern; people would dream about the same kinds of things over and over. It got so that you would have been able to tell who had had the dream without anyone identifying themselves. All of us were working out different things: my dreams showed I was obviously ambivalent about getting married, and Don was struggling with whether he should quit his job and pursue his art full-time. He kept dreaming of fish, and then he began to paint them."

"Say, he *was* exciting," Joyce says.

"No, but his paintings were absolutely magical," Trudy says. "He brought them to class. They were watercolors of all these different kinds of fish, and I had never understood until then how very beautiful fish were. I told Don I wanted to buy the lesser amberjack from him—its colors were all these muted pastels: apricot and blue and pink and silver—and he said he'd give it to me if I'd go out with him three times."

"Bold for a shy guy!" Laura says.

"I know. And I really didn't want to go out with him,

but I wanted that painting. So I said okay. For the first date, he took me out to dinner to a really nice French place—I was way underdressed—and then, just as the sun was going down, he brought me to this tiny little park by the river which I had never seen. It was called Lucy Wilder National Park, and it had a lovely wrought-iron entrance with the name on it, and it was about the size of my living room. I mean, tiny, tiny park! With all these pretty flowers growing all over the place! I put a whole bunch of them in my hair, and they kept falling out, I remember Don said, 'And the forecast tonight is for intermittent flowers.' I told Don I'd never even heard of this park and yet I lived only a few blocks away, and I asked him how he'd found it. He said, oh, he just walked around and he found things. He found things, and interesting things happened to him all the time, I really should hang out with him, and I'd see."

"Sounds like a pretty cool guy," Laura says. "What did you not like about him?"

Trudy shrugs. "I just didn't like him. Who knows why? Sometimes you just don't like someone even when you should. You can't force these things."

"It's pheromones," Joyce says. "You have to like their smell. I saw it on the Discovery Channel."

"Anyway," Trudy says. "On the second date, when he took me to an art gallery, I all of a sudden got really annoyed. I thought, *I don't need you to show me art.* I started being really nasty to him. He would say something about a painting, and I'd say nothing back. He asked at one point if I'd like to go sailing with him for our third date, and I said no, I hated boats, but the truth is I love to be on a sailboat; it's one of the most peaceful things in the world to me. I just kept getting nastier and nastier, and finally I decided it wasn't worth it to go out with him again, the hell with the painting, the hell with fish. So I told him, I said, Look, it's pretty clear this is not working for me, so let's just cut bait now, ha, ha. And he got all sad and put his hands in his pockets and nodded and said, Okay, that's okay, he understood, thanks anyway for going out with him the two times I did. There was another couple in the gallery, and they were giving me the stink eye something fierce—of course I deserved it. And I just wanted out of there, so I said I'd get myself home, I was thinking I'd take the bus. He took my hand and said, 'I'm sorry this didn't work out,' and I snatched it back and said, 'Yeah, have a nice life.' "

"Boy, you really *were* terrible to him," Joyce says.

"I know," Trudy says. "I *know*. And then, listen to this, I turned on my heel and started to strut out of there and I fell down. I don't know what happened, I think the floor was really slick or something, but I fell down and broke my ankle! It hurt like hell and I started crying. And Don picked me up and carried me out of there and hailed a cab because it was faster than walking to his car, and he told the driver to go to the nearest ER. He waited for me to get seen, and the whole time, I was bitching about how much it hurt and how I didn't have any insurance and I didn't have any money. Not a word about 'Thank you, Don.' When they called me into the treatment room, he asked if I wanted him to come in with me, and I said, 'No, I do not.' Then when I came out, he was gone. The nurse at the reception desk said he'd left a note for me. I still have that note. He had paid the bill for me, and his note said, *Think of this as something one friend does for another. Repay me as you can, and you can start by taking care of yourself in every way.*"

"Are you kidding?" Joyce asks.

Trudy shakes her head. Tears tremble in her eyes. "And

I never paid him back one cent. I dropped out of the dream class, and I never saw him again. And I was sitting around one day and I thought, *I'm going to find Don Christianson and apologize to him and pay him back the money.* I remember the amount exactly, it was two hundred dollars and eleven cents. So I called a few numbers and found him, and he was such a sweetheart, still; just so warm, and he said of course he'd like to see me, in fact he had something for me."

"The fish painting," Laura says.

"No," Trudy says, "it wasn't that. That's what I thought it was going to be, too, but it wasn't that."

"Is he married?" Joyce asks.

"Yes."

"So was it his *wife* he had for you? Did he want to show you the beautiful and kind person he ended up marrying who is a much better human being than you?"

"Thank you," Trudy says.

"Well, I mean, I'm just looking at this from his point of view. How sweet vengeance would be for him."

"I met him at Paisano's, over on the East Side," Trudy says. "And his wife didn't come, but his kids did. Two beautiful adult children, a boy and a girl, wonderfully good-looking, and obviously they just loved their dad to death. But it was more than that. They were very solicitous of him, and all of the sudden I thought, *Oh, God, he's sick.* He didn't look sick, except that he was quite thin, but then he was thin all those years ago, too. But he ate almost nothing, and finally he revealed that he had stomach cancer, and it wasn't going too well. His kids just sat there when he told me this, being quiet and supportive—I mean, you could feel their love, and a kind of pride they had in him. I was wondering what he'd told them about me. I don't think he said anything bad; they were awfully nice to me. Anyway, he said the treatment hadn't helped and he was terminal now, just kind of trying to enjoy his last days, and he was so glad I'd called. He asked his children to get the car, told me he was sorry but he really had to go home now— I think he was starting to hurt. 'Oh, that's okay,' I said, 'thank you for coming,' and I reached for the check and he tried to take it from me and I said, 'Don't you dare, I still owe you for that hospital bill.' 'Yes,' he said, 'and imagine how much it is now, what with all the interest.' And then he said he hoped I hadn't felt bad about him paying that bill, he'd had a really good job, it had been no problem for him to pay it."

Joyce wipes a tear off her face, then laughs at herself.

"Oh, get ready, there's more," Trudy says. "He said, 'I told you I had something for you.' And of course I was wondering where he had hidden the fish painting. But he reached in his wallet and pulled out a pressed flower. It was one that had fallen from my hair that day in the park. He put it in my hand and said, 'It would mean a lot to me if you'd take care of this.' "

"Oh, God," Laura says, and now there are tears in her eyes, too.

"What did you do with it?" Joyce asks, and Laura hopes Trudy didn't throw it out.

"It's being framed," Trudy says. "I found the most exquisite framing for it, and it will be ready on Monday. I'm going to keep it by my bed to remind me to . . . Well, to remind me to be careful. You know?" She swallows. "So. That was my date."

"Will you see him again?" Joyce asks in a blubbery voice, and Trudy says softly, "I don't see how."

Joyce says, "I had this math teacher in junior high who

really believed in me at a time when everyone else just
called me stupid. And I was so cruel to her. I used to call
her at home and hang up on her. I wrote a story that
ridiculed her and published it in the school newspaper. I
changed her name from O'Brien to O'Reilly, but of course
everyone knew who I meant. She offered to stay after
school to help me with algebra and I stood her up three
times before she stopped offering. Why *are* we so cruel
sometimes?"

"You should call her and apologize," Trudy says.

"She's *dead*."

Trudy picks up her glass and stares into it. "You know
what? I think the reason we're cruel sometimes is that
we're afraid we're going to like something."

"That might be true," Laura says. "I think there is a lot
of fear in cruelty. You were ambivalent about marrying
Jim; you were probably afraid of falling in love with Don,
and so you made sure you didn't."

It is quiet at the table, but for sniffing sounds from
Joyce. And then Trudy clears her throat loudly and says,
"So. Laura. Did you have a date with the homeless man?"

"We're engaged!" Laura says, and then, "No, but I did
go to see him, actually." She tells her friends the story
about the homeless man in as humorous a way as she can,
omitting entirely the part about her ex and Cassandra, and
soon they are all laughing again. Laura excuses herself to
go to the bathroom.

In the little powder room, she sits on the lid of the toilet and looks around. Trudy has a magazine rack holding
mostly home décor magazines but also a copy of Nora
Ephron's *I Feel Bad About My Neck*. Laura would like to
meet Nora Ephron. She has the idea, like so many other
women, she supposes, that they would just hit it off, she

would pick Nora up at her New York condo and they'd run down to the local deli and order blintzes and talk and talk and laugh and laugh. She would like to meet Anne Tyler and Alice Munro. She would like to meet Joni Mitchell, too, even though she admires her so much she's afraid of her, and of course Laura wants to meet and befriend Oprah. She would like to be another friend that Oprah could trust; the woman needs more than just Gayle.

Trudy has a little framed picture on the wall opposite the toilet, a cartoon picture cut out of the newspaper. It is a red spaceship surrounded by the black heavens of outer space, and there is one star that shines more brightly than the rest. It is this star the ship is moving toward. Someone in the spaceship is telling someone else to just trust him; so long as they steer toward that star, they're fine, they won't get lost. What the speaker doesn't see is that, off to the side, en route to that star, there is a huge space monster waiting, mouth wide open, teeth long and sharp.

Laura has a picture in her powder room as well, a miniature oil she and Brian splurged on one day when they were visiting Boston and went into a Newbury Street art gallery. The painting features a violin and sheet music resting on a table, and Laura can never look at it without marveling at how tiny everything is: the pegs on the violin, the dotted eighth notes on the staff. How could anyone have such a sure and steady hand? The painting had cost a lot of money at a time when she and Brian didn't have much. They'd gone to get a cup of coffee before they bought it, they always used to do that, get a cup of coffee at Dunkin' Donuts before they made any major decision. They'd had their coffee and then gone back for the painting, and Brian had said, "Happy Birthday, Merry Christmas, Happy Valentine's Day, and Happy Mother's Day for the next three years," and Laura had said, "I know," and she had been very happy.

She stands and looks at herself in the mirror, wipes away the mascara that has smeared beneath her eyes. Why didn't she tell her friends the whole story, when what she wants is to move their friendship further along, to deepen the trust and intimacy they already enjoy? It is because she has to give up on another fantasy she's been hiding from herself like a bug under a leaf. She has to stop thinking she and Brian will get back together. She has to stop talking about him. She has to stop dreaming about him, though that will be harder. Only last night she dreamed she ran into Brian and Cassandra at the deli case in the grocery store. Cassandra was having a hard time understanding that you could get more than one kind of cheese. Brian told her to look, just look, at the great variety before her. You could pick any kind you wanted. Cassandra looked at all the cheeses, and then she turned to Brian, her head held high, looking very confident and beautiful, and she said, "I don't understand. Repeat." Brian explained again. And again Cassandra said, "I don't understand. Repeat." Laura stepped in between them and very gently said, "Cassandra? Maybe you'd like some cheddar cheese. That's here. Maybe you'd prefer Swiss. That's here, too." "Ah," Cassandra said. "I want Gruyère," and she stepped up to the counter to order. Laura turned to Brian and very quietly said, "What's going on?" "The MRI is very bad," Brian said, and Laura felt a quick rush of joy. If Cassandra died, Brian wouldn't have to feel guilty about getting back with Laura. But Brian has thoroughly finished with her, not unkindly, and now she must finish with him. She must let go. The realization brings her more relief than sorrow, and she is surprised by this. Surprised and grateful.

From the dining room comes another loud burst of laughter, and Laura suddenly remembers the meaning of the word "fulcrum." It is a point of support. It is an agent through which vital powers are exercised.

She opens the bathroom door and starts down the hall. She moves toward the teeth of the monster, and the stars, and the little spaceship with its deep yellow light shining out against all that darkness, all that empty space. When she sits down again at the table, she will propose a toast: to the dinner tonight and the dinners to come, to the forgiving pants they all wear, to the way that all of them have been through quite a bit, really, and here they all are, still walking.

HOW TO MAKE AN
APPLE PIE

Dear Ruthie,

You know I saw your mother over to the Save Way and she asked me would I send you my recipe for apple pie. She gave me your address and said if I'd send it to you right quick, you'd get it by your birthday, I understand your birthday is coming right up and forgive me that I forgot the date. I used to know all you kids' birthdays and didn't we have a time celebrating, you remember those cardboard crowns all loaded up with glitter and the magic wands we made out of sticks and ribbon? And remember how one year you used your wand to try to turn a frog into a prince? You waved your wand over him and you kissed him right on the mouth and then didn't you have a fit when he stayed a frog? I have lots of nice memories from when you and your family lived next door but I sure can't remember dates anymore and there's plenty else has gone down the hopper of forgetfulness! Honey would you believe I am now eighty-six so I'm not exactly running on a full tank these days, and plenty other things have changed, too. You remember you used to come over and play in my closet and try on all my high heels, well, now you would only find Dr. Scholl's and there's even a walker in there but thank God I only needed that temporary. Bunions.

Your mom said neither one of you can ever make a decent pie. That is really just an attitude problem which I will try and explain as long as I'm at it. She said you know it would make Ruthie so happy to get that recipe, it would be her best present. How a recipe would be your <u>best present</u> is beyond me. It makes me worry a bit about your life if you don't mind my saying so. In addition to that, how many times did you sit and watch me make apple pie? Where I told you out every single thing I was doing? I wisht you'd have written down what I said, because I don't have <u>anything</u> written down for <u>any</u> of my recipes. If you'd have written it down instead of staring out the winder the way you always did and can't I just see you now, sitting there with your bare feet up on the chair with you, your arms wrapped around your knees, wearing those baggy shorts and that yellow top with three rows of ruffles your mama would have to practically pry off you to wash, but anyway if you'd have written it down but the one time, I would be spared the effort of trying to write it out and you would be spared the effort of trying to read my writing which never was very good but you know now I have got the arthritis so bad in my fingers I am purt near illegible. Which by now you surely see. But let us get to it.

For the filling it is no mystery. Say I wonder did you

know Nancy Drew turned into a movie? I remember I used to give you those Nancy Drew mysteries for your birthday every year and you would sit right down and start reading with the wrapping paper still hanging on. It never was a surprise when you got those books but it was a pleasure to you anyway. Which is kind of like what pie is like, come to think of it, nothing new but always kind of exciting. And see there, that is what we are supposed to be on is pie. I drift off. I always did, but it's some worse now. I wonder though would you listen to just one more thing. I remember how you and your sister would lie on your stomachs on your beds or on a blanket in the back yard in the summer and read and read and read and I could just about see the heat of your imaginations rising up off you like steam. You can say what you want about movies, but to my mind they leave too little to the imagination, it is always better to read a book. Make up your own pictures, they are always realer because they come from inside out, not the other way around. Most every time you went to a movie you came over afterwards to tell me out the story and I would give you a dime. Sometimes you and your sister both came and told me out the story, each of you busting to get to the end and interrupting each other in a good-natured way, you and your sister got along most times. Though one time when you had a big fight with her I wonder do you remember you came and sat under my kitchen table and said you weren't going home, you would like to move in with us and be an only child. You had that bear with you.

Anyway the filling is a matter of sniff and add a bit of this, sniff and add a bit of that. Number one ingredient is apples, of course, and I have always favored green ones right off the tree if you can get them. Warm from the sun and never seen a refrigerator in their lives. As for the rest of what you add, you must respect the fact that apples are like people, all different, and the same apple can act a different way on a different day. It's true. Lots of foods are like that, maybe all foods are like that. You got to let a thing be itself and work with it. Now say you got tart apples. Then you don't need but a bit of lemon, say a half squeeze of a half of a lemon. But you <u>always</u> need lemon even if it's just a little because a lemon is like a brassiere, it offers support even though you can't hardly see it. Same with salt, you need a little salt always. Even with sweet things, do you see now they make caramels with that sea salt big as boulders right on the top? Acting like they discovered the cure for cancer? Long time ago, we <u>always</u> used to put salt on our caramels, me and all my friends. Not SEA SALT, just the stuff right out the round blue box, and we put it on Kraft caramels and I'll tell you what, it was good. Anyway, add what I said and take a whiff. Then add some cinnamon, a big pinch, and sniff that. Keep adding till you get a good cinnamon smell, but don't let it take over the apples, this is not <u>cinnamon</u> pie it is <u>apple</u> pie. Add just a touch of nutmeg, nutmeg must always work undercover, where you taste it but you don't know what it is. Like mace in sweet rolls or coffee in chocolate cake. Add a pinch of ginger and a wee bit of cloves. Add some brown sugar and some white sugar, just enough to sweeten, but don't deaden the spices. Your nose is your guide, just sniff sniff sniff, don't you remember how I used to shove my nose in the bowl and once you called me the human vacuum. Now if you have a cold, forget making pie or anything else. Go over to someplace like the Olive Garden and load up on the garlic, that you will taste. You remember my husband, Terrence, he used to love the Olive Garden. I think the main reason is that he had a crush on one of the waitresses, which didn't bother me one whit, that girl was about ten minutes old and what was he going to do. I think he just enjoyed looking at her and really so did I, she sure was a pretty little thing. Real shiny hair. I don't know if you know this, Terrence died on me six months ago. I sure do miss him. He had that big rocker on the front porch and sometimes it moves in the wind and it's like he's come to keep me company. I sure do miss him. Now I'll trust you not to tell that I sometimes talk out loud to him when he comes to see me that way, it gives a kind of comfort.

What else. Well, you know you need a lot more butter than you think in an apple pie and what I want you to do when you make one is just go ahead and figure at <u>least</u> half a stick and depending on the personality of the apples it might be more. Put it in the mix in little slices and put some more on the top when you load the apples into the pie shell. About now I'll bet I know what you're thinking. You're thinking, hold the phone, that's a lot of butter, on account of there's also butter in the crust. Wrong. There's no butter in my crust, I think there is something conceited about butter in a crust, for mine it is all Crisco straight out the can and I will stand by that until the day I die. Isn't it funny, I've said that all my life, "until the day I die," and now it isn't that far off! I hope it is, but the truth is that really if you take the long view it isn't. Could be any day, I suppose, what with all that's give out and do you know I have a little touch of cancer to top it all off. Do you think that people ever really do believe they will die, that the world will just go along as always without them? I wonder if we aren't all just a little surprised at the moment of crossover, if we don't look back over our shoulders saying, Now hold on.

But Crisco. Crisco and the crust. Of course we will get to the full crust recipe in a minute though I will tell you now that the most important ingredient in piecrust is something you would never guess in a million years. Not in a million years. I never did tell you out that part, the most important ingredient in piecrust, I just kept it in my head, but now I will write it to you and you can pay me my million dollars either by credit card or cash, ha ha. Oh, but you know what, I should have said first thing to do when you make an apple pie is put on an apron and some good music, big band music is good if you've got it. If not, country and western. Add that right up top. I should have mentioned that right up top. I don't know why you cook better in an apron, but it's true. And if it's at all a nice day out, I suggest you open the kitchen door and cook barefoot. If it's a winter day, why you hope for snow, there's nothing like snow drifting down when your hands are deep in apples and spices, and you should wear a sweater with a pocket with a button and a safety pin and a hankie in it. Just kidding, but you know I swear every apple pie I made in winter I was wearing that sweater, I might could leave it to you in my will. (I hope you're smiling, are you?) Now, I should have said before, too, that you might could <u>eat</u> one of the raw apples with all the spices for taste. Your nose is good, but you might could eat one, too. The taste should be a bright sweet, not a dull one. Put that up higher in the recipe, too. And also I should have told you the reason why you make the filling first, you always make the filling first. That is so the apples have time to meet and greet before they go into the oven, they marinate you might say. And anyway, that filling gives you something good to smell whilst you make the crust. Good smells lift a person's spirits. Sometimes on a day I wasn't baking I'd just boil water on the stove with cinnamon and cloves in it and maybe an orange peel.

What else. Oh! You need flour as a thickener. A good pinch or a little pile in the palm of your hand. We all need something to hold us together, even apples.

Pardon me while I take a rest, my hand is like to fall right off.

Back again and with a glass of sherry to boot. I never did drink much but now I see the point. It's only sherry, and its color is half the pleasure and of course the pretty little glass. I don't drink coffee anymore, that gets my heart wild as a West Texas cowgirl and as one who comes from West Texas I can tell you that is some wild.

I have read this over and I think I should say again that the flavor of your filling must be bright. Terrence used to say when the flavor is right it makes you want to slap your daddy and don't you just know exactly what he means. Remember too to add a little at a time of all your ingredients, you can always add more but you can't take away. Like angry words. After you make a few pies, you'll be an expert, you'll be able to do it in your sleep, which I did once. I made a pie in my sleep. It was when my best friend had her first baby, and she called me at something like three-thirty in the morning and she says, "It's a girl, I'm so hungry I could eat the walls, would you please make me an apple pie and bring it right over?" And I did. Course I woke up to drive to the hospital, but I swear I was asleep when I made that pie. And it tasted fine. A taste is all I got, too, my friend ate the whole dang thing with a tablespoon, and where did she take the first bite from? Right smack in the middle of the pie, and didn't you always want to do that yourself? One day not so long ago I had a hankering for yellow cake with chocolate frosting and I made one and cut me a big piece from the exact middle and ate it and then I cut up the rest of the cake and gave it away to the Dooleys, I wonder do you remember them. Of course cake gets stale faster all cut up, but I didn't want to give them a cake with a hole in the center it would be too embarrassing. I wonder why we are so often embarrassed by things we do that almost any other person would like to do, too, we hadn't ought to be that way.

Are you ready for the crust? Now here comes my top-secret secret: <u>You must not let the crust know you're afraid of it,</u> which you will be the first few times. You must steel yourself inside like your little child is in danger of falling off a high place, he is right on the edge, and you mustn't startle him but rather speak calmly to make him turn around and come to you. You might be nervous on the inside, but outside you keep calm as rain. That summer rain I mean that is so quiet and matter of fact and falls straight down like a curtain.

Now I recommend you use one of those stainless steel bowls if you can, I switched to them a while back and you know there is a lightness to them and you can turn them around with one hand, while you are making the dough, seems like the dough likes to spin a bit, leastwise it makes it easier to mix. But once again I am ahead of myself.

So for the crust, first get your bowl out, and get out a coffee cup and put a bunch of ice cubes in it and add water, that will be your ice water that you add later. Into the bowl put a nice big glob of Crisco, maybe it is a cup, and twice as much flour and a big pinch of sugar and a little pinch of salt. Now use a pastry blender or a fork if you must but a fork is not as good. Nor are the new pastry blenders as good as the old ones, you might could find a good one at an antiques store, the old ones have the wooden handles painted red or green. They are the ones you put your hand on and right away you can feel the history of other hands on them. It lends a comfort and they are just better dough mashers anyhow.

So there you are, and you turn the bowl around with one hand and mash together the ingredients until you have what look like little pea-size blobs. Casually add a bit of ice water, maybe a quarter cup or so, how much water you need will depend on how much humidity is in the air that day. Add enough so that the dough sticks together. NOT TOO STICKY. Make it sticky like it makes you want to play with it. When you have a nice ball of dough, divide it. Then sprinkle flour lightly over the place where you're going to roll the piecrust out. You need a heavy wooden rolling pin and you need one of those ribbed cloth covers for it, you can still find them, and you can roll out on purt near anything, I used to use that old flowered tablecloth, but it's nice to use a pastry cloth which you can also still buy, they have not corrupted them. Put the dough in the middle of the floured pastry cloth and shape it with both hands into a round shape. This lets it know what you expect of it. Flour your rolling pin a bit and then start rolling out the dough. People will tell you you must roll in one direction only. Not necessarily. What's most important is a quick, even pressure, roll that thing out evenly until it is slightly larger than the dish you're going to bake the pie in. Then gently roll the dough around the rolling pin, and unroll it over the dish. You will feel like the Queen of Sheba when you do this, it works out so nice. Pat the dough into the pan and trim off the excess so that you have just a nice little overhang. Now is where you put the apples in and you are almost done. Put the apples in, put a little more butter on the top, and give a good whiff. It should like to make your toes curl. Now roll out the top crust as above and put it over the apples. Crimp the crust, which I'm sure you remember that part at least don't you? I often used to let you do it. You pinch those edges together for a pretty design. And you need to vent the top crust, and for that you can just stick fork tines in here and there or you can make a shape. You one time made the shape of an apple with a leaf on one of my pies, I hardly helped you at all. But you know you can do anything, you can spell out a person's name or make autumn leaves or a dog with a bone or whatever you want, it is your pie, and there's the value of making your own as if the taste weren't enough. Sprinkle the top crust with cinnamon sugar, and you can roll out the extra dough and put butter and cinnamon sugar on it and then roll it up to make what I called roly-polies. I see now that some folks cut out shapes from the extra dough to put on top of the pie but that is in the bakeries where the pie costs around twenty dollars, which if everything else wasn't conspiring to give me a heart attack that about would.

Let me read this over and see did I forget anything. Oh. You should use about six good-size apples, put that part up top. You will have a pretty high pie when it's raw, but the apples will bake down. Use a nine-inch pan. Then the apples don't cook down so far from the crust that it looks like the Grand Canyon in there when you cut into it. Bake at 450 degrees for ten minutes and then at 350 degrees for forty-five. Go and do something else and soon the smell will come and find you and you will feel a great satisfaction.

Some people make a caramel apple pie where they mix butter and brown sugar and chopped nuts and put it on the bottom and then of course you use less sugar in the filling, that is a nice touch and a little surprise. Some will only eat apple pie with ice cream, and I have my doubts about that unless it is the real ice cream you can only find at a few parlors anymore and then I understand. Pie à la mode and a cup of coffee has done a lot for many. It wouldn't hurt to serve the pie on some pretty plate. A piece of homemade pie should never see a paper plate. You might consider polka dots or flowers of any kind, but as for me I always had a soft spot for violets.

Well, Ruthie, that is it and I hope it makes sense, it is as good as I can do. I will say that there has been an unexpected pleasure in passing this along to you, you know I have no family left now Terrence is gone and I hear you have a husband and two girls, one married for heaven's sake. So I hope you will make your own pie and pass the recipe on to your own family through the years. We have lost a lot these days from everything being done for you and fake. I suppose I'm getting old and cranky though most days I still feel in love with the world. I still feel like a young woman on the inside, too, it's the oddest thing. I still feel like Flo with the high-heeled shoes that little Ruthie used to shuffle around in, dreaming of the day she'd be a grown-up. I hope being a grown-up turned out fine for you, honey, you were always a very nice little girl with apple cheeks and a pretty singing voice, and sometimes you sat in my lap like you were my own. You had a kindness about you which I hope remains, it is one thing about us that needn't wither or quit working and thank goodness for that since everything else sure enough does, ha ha.

I'll go out and mail this now. Take my constitutional. It looks like rain. I spect I'll make it back before it hits.

Happy birthday, Ruthie, though I think the gift here

was one you gave me. Here in your old town is someone who keeps you always in her heart and was glad to be reminded of you today.

Your former neighbor lady,

Flo

P.S. You might could put some foil around the edges of the crust if it gets to browning too soon. Move that up where it belongs.

SIN CITY

For years now, Rita has been living a half-a-banana life. Half a banana, half a muffin, half portions at restaurants, half-price movies that she goes to in the daytime, always feeling strange when she comes out of the theater and into sunlight. She doesn't like going to movies in the daytime, but it's safer and cheaper. And you don't have to listen to the half-naked teenagers slouched down in their seats and flinging epithets around; it seems they can't get through a sentence without the F-word. Just the other day, at the mall, Rita saw a pretty young woman come upon an apparent friend and say, "Fuck me, *hi*!"

Rita is sixty-seven and lives in a retirement community in Edina, Minnesota. Her husband, Ben, moved them there when they were only fifty-nine, after he took an early retirement. Then he promptly had a massive heart attack and died. What could she do? She lives there alone; it's a nice place, everything on one level, a fair amount of privacy, a grocery store and a post office on the complex, a golf course and pool, too, though Rita neither golfs nor swims. Ben did that, but Ben's not here.

She has taken to wearing modest, monochromatic dresses bought at Loehmann's, and grinding stale bread up for bread crumbs. She saves tinfoil and plastic storage bags—not just clean pieces, she has begun washing the dirty ones. Although this might be seen as a "green" thing to do, an action for which Al Gore would pat her on the back, it's not for the environment that she does such things. Rather, it is because of the creeping influence of her neighbors, many of whom also save rubber bands and twist ties and every return address label they receive in the mail. They fold grocery bags neatly and store them in the cracks alongside their refrigerators to use for trash bags and for mailing packages and for lining cupboard shelves. They bring home shower caps from motels to cover bowls of leftovers, and wrap thinning bars of soap with net bags from onions and voilà: *scrubbers!* Scrubbers for what, Rita has no idea. Why ask? Ask, and she'll get a half-reasonable answer and then she'll start making *scrubbers!* too. Just like she has started wearing "their" shoes, a light gray ortho-pedic model that makes bowling shoes look like Jimmy Choo. Oh, she knows she can't wear stilettos anymore, but what a comedown! So to speak. She has even begun to em-ulate her next-door neighbor, Elsie, whose perfume is the samples that come on foldout paper strips in magazines.

And don't get Rita started on these people's idea of en-tertainment. Their idea of a good time is playing bocce ball and managing their money so as to be able to leave their children a fortune. Going into the city on the bus to hear the symphony, where most of them will fall asleep. Any theater they see comes with overcooked chicken and undercooked baked potatoes and a salad a rabbit wouldn't eat. Dinner parties start promptly at six.

Peer pressure, that's what all this is. She might as well be back in high school, where she felt obliged to wear multiple crinoline petticoats under her full skirts, and a big wide belt around her midsection. Oh, she hated wearing those uncomfortable things. But you had to! You had to wear those rabbit-fur collars with the pom-poms hanging down. You had to wear nickels in your loafers. You had to wear red lipstick and curled-under bangs and spit curls, and if you went steady, you had to wear your boyfriend's ring on a chain around your neck and his letter jacket over your shoulders. And now Rita feels she's only moments away from getting an elevated toilet seat and storing it in the front hall closet, just so it's there when she needs it— that's what everyone else does.

Well, enough is enough. She is far too young to be living like this, and she is going to bust out. She's going to start spending her children's inheritance. She's going to buy wild salmon and jumbo cashews and Vosges chocolates, and she's going to travel—alone, thank you, not in the company of a bunch of slow-moving people who block her view of whatever it is she's supposed to be seeing and ask each other loudly, "Did you get that? Some guide, you can't hear a word she's saying!" so that Rita herself hasn't a chance of hearing, either. Once, a sweet-faced woman who wore glasses that made it look as though she had compound eyes actually pinched Rita, so exasperated was she by not being able to hear. "Do you *mind*?" Rita asked, and the woman said, "What?"

Rita is going to start buying designer clothes and real

jewelry. She might even move into some hip loft residence in the city and start wearing jewel-colored scarves like babushkas, and she might start drinking espresso. She doesn't like espresso, but if she moves to a loft, she'll probably start liking it.

This decision for radical change came suddenly. Rita woke up this morning and there it was, a psychic billboard: *Your life must go in a totally different direction. Now.* She supposes a mild discontent has been festering inside her subconsciously for a long time, that's the way these things go for her. She's not the kind of person to engage in endless self-analysis, and she is bored by those who do. But on occasion, she surprises herself by doing something completely unexpected that, in retrospect, was not so very shocking after all. As a senior in high school, she had promised Don Trevor one night that she'd marry him the day after graduation, and she meant it with her whole heart and her whole mind and her whole soul. She went to bed that night dreaming of guest lists and simple white wedding gowns, of how their children might look. She was so happy, she cried. Then, months later, she awakened with a sudden clarity that had her breaking up with Don by lunchtime, no regrets on her part, and not even very much guilt. Once she knows, she knows.

She pours another cup of coffee and plans her day. First, she's going to get her hair permed—Dyan Cannon, she's thinking, although she has short hair and looks nothing like Dyan Cannon—and buy a bunch of new clothes; and then she's going to pack a bag and hire a town car to take her out to the airport, where she will get on the next flight to Las Vegas. She'll buy a ticket right there, no matter the cost. She's never forgotten a friend of hers, Patty Obermeier, who drove her friend Linda Schultz to the airport in 1970. Linda was moving to San Francisco, and while they were sitting at the gate waiting for Linda's flight to board, they both started crying—they were going to miss each other so much. Linda said, "Oh, come with me, why don't you. Just go and get a ticket." And Patty did. She called her sister to come and get the car—left the keys under the seat—and she wrote a bad check for a ticket and went to San Francisco with nothing but her purse. She called in to her job on Monday and said she wasn't coming back and told them to mail her last paycheck to an apartment she'd found in the Haight. She got a great job at an investment banking company and did very well, and then married some watercolor artist and then Rita lost touch with her. Rita has always loved that story.

Well, now it's her turn. She isn't going to move to Las Vegas, but she is going there by herself for the weekend. She is going to Sin City, where what happens will stay there. Rita has always thought it disgusting to call a place *Sin City* and to say that what happened there, stayed there. But now that she's going, she thinks it's kind of exciting. It's not *really* Sin City. Lucifer will not be standing there, twirling his mustache. She will not do anything for which she will have to ask forgiveness. She's just going there to put a hand up and stop this noose from tightening. She's going there to remind herself that she's still a young woman. More or less. Well, she's going to remind herself that she's not that old. Some of the women in the retirement center work in nursing homes to prove to themselves that they're not that old, but Rita could never do that. She would feel too bad for the patients, with their little figurines lined up on their windowsills. And she would come home smelling like pee.

In Las Vegas, she's going to try to stay at that pyramid

hotel, she thinks there really is something to the belief that pyramids have great power, but she's planning to gamble at Bellagio. Just quarters in the slot machine, but that's fine. She happens to be a very lucky person. She anticipates winning a fortune. And eating breakfast from those buffets that go on for miles, and if you think she's eating *Egg Beaters* from them, well, forget it. She might go horseback riding in the daytime, if she can find a place that has an old reliable mare. Yes, she might buy a string tie featuring silver and turquoise to wear with a new white blouse and go horseback riding; she bets she can still ride a horse, look at Ronald and Nancy Reagan. And she'll go to a Wayne Newton show and get a front-row seat and wear diamonds and drink Manhattans. One sentence she adores is "Oh, waiter, I'll have a Manhattan." She whispers it to herself now, as she stands at the sink washing her breakfast dishes, and both her big toes jump up.

As she wipes off the toaster, "Danke Schoen" is playing in her head. Bette Midler is in Las Vegas now, too! Rita will go and see her as well. She hopes Bette will sing "The Rose." If she has enough Manhattans, she *might* go and see *A Musical Tribute to Liberace*. A musical tribute. What other kind of tribute could it be?

At a fancy dress shop in the Galleria mall, Rita sits on the little brocade bench of the dressing room trying to read the numbers on her purse-size calculator, which a Lilliputian couldn't read. Well, if she buys what she wants to—the black bathing suit with the pretty pink and black paisley print robe for covering up, the lime green pantsuit with the matching silk shell, the silver sparkly top and sweater and black silk pants to wear to shows, the two wrap dresses that actually look very nice on her, the soft-as-cloud light blue pajama ensemble, the gray jeans and white blouse and black blazer for horseback riding, as well as the denim jeans and jean jacket in case she decides the other outfit is too nice to ride in—she'll spend about a thousand dollars. And she hasn't even gotten shoes or jewelry yet. For a moment, she considers walking out of the store and forgetting the whole thing, but no. No! She has almost two hundred thousand dollars squirreled away here and there. Why should she hold on to so much? So that her children can get talked into buying a finer coffin for her? Or, more likely, so that they can get talked into buying a finer flat-screen TV for themselves? No. She will buy every single item, and then she will hurry and buy some kitten heels. She looks at her watch. Twenty of twelve. She's not sure how many flights there are a day to Vegas. Maybe she'll buy the jewelry at one of the hotels on the strip, that might be fun. She'll buy it with her winnings so that, really, it will be free.

When she puts the calculator back in her purse, she sees a small piece of paper stuck to the bottom. She really must clean out her purse. She'll do that on the plane, she likes to have projects to do on the plane so that the time passes more quickly. She used to embroider until needles and sewing scissors became weapons. She wonders what would happen in a face-off between embroidery scissors and five ounces of toothpaste.

Rita pulls the paper out of her purse and squints at it: it's a ticket stub of some kind. She moves it closer to the light on the dressing room wall and sees that it's from a tour she and Ben took of the birthplace of John Kennedy. So many years ago now, but Rita remembers the day clearly: it was cold and rainy, and after the tour they went to some deli in Brookline that had wonderful matzo ball soup. They'd been a little depressed after the museum; whatever you thought of John Kennedy, his regime *did* at the time seem like Camelot; Bush Senior, who was in office at the time, just didn't compare. And Barbara Bush next to Jackie O? They'd talked about Jackie for a while, and Ben had told Rita she was every bit as beautiful as Jackie. She wasn't, but Ben really believed she was.

She sits back down on the bench, holding the ticket as though it's Ben's hand. She had loved Ben, but they should never have been together. When they met, she told him she loved Elvis and he said he favored Pat Boone: there were their differences in a nutshell. She liked things a little wild, and he liked them Christian. In the way of the times, when men wore the pants in the family and women were subservient to their husbands' preferences, Ben dictated a life that was always too tame for her. And she gave in to it because she thought she had to, but also she wanted to, because she loved him so. A friend once described him as "friendly as yellow mustard," and he was, that was exactly the right way to describe him. And oh, his mild blue eyes. His earnestness. His sentimentality. The way he fathered their children, he had been a wonderful father. Too wonderful, perhaps. For the bulk of Alice's and Randy's childhood, Rita had felt that she was on the sidelines of parenting while Ben ran the plays. Oh, they agreed on things generally, where the kids were concerned, but it was Ben who made the kids pancakes every Sunday and Halloween costumes every year. (The things that man could do with a simple cardboard box! One year the kids were dice; another year Alice was a wrapped present, ribbons spilling from her hair, while Randy was a weatherman on television, wearing a shirt and tie and congenial smile, climate maps pasted behind him.) Ben checked their homework and coached their teams and was the last to say good night. When they moved out, he offered financial advice, and when each of them decided to get married, it was Ben whom they told first. What bothered her most was when they were little and got hurt and ran to him for comfort.

Once, when the kids were ten and eight, Rita told a good friend that she felt her children had drawn a bad number in the mother lottery. She said she had all the flaws of Dorothy's traveling companions in *The Wizard of Oz:* straw for brains, no courage, and not enough heart. And her friend put her hand over Rita's and said, "Sweetheart, that's just not true. Don't be so hard on yourself!"

That night, Rita got in a nasty argument with Ben, and she accused him of stealing the children's love from her— co-opting their affections by never giving her the chance to respond to them first. "Rita," he said, "are you jealous? You sound like you're jealous." And she admitted that she was, and he asked what he might do to help and she said nothing, it was too late, and she spent the rest of the night drinking from that bitter brew. But the next morning, she kissed the kids and sent them off to school and wiped off the breakfast table thinking, *Well, isn't it lucky that they love their father so much? Isn't it good to have a man so open with his emotions, so warm and loving, when so many men keep their feelings so tightly bound they can't even reveal themselves to themselves?* Ben was a good man, through and through, and was that rarest of things: perfectly content with an ordinary life. It comes to her now that he would be horrified at what she is about to do. She feels, for the first time, a rush of guilt, of shame; she has a thought that what she is doing is completely inappropriate, wacky, even—is she getting wacky? People who live alone sometimes do.

Well, she'll ask Ben. She often talks to him in her head, and he often answers her. She closes her eyes and thinks, *Should I go to Las Vegas?* And she hears, *Have a ball, kiddo.* He used to say that all the time, "Have a ball, kiddo." That was him, all right, he's tuned in to her today. She's going to Las Vegas! But she really will have to hurry, now. She puts the ticket into her wallet, tenderly.

After Rita pays for her things, she goes back into the dressing room to change into the gray jeans and the white blouse and the black blazer. She'll wear her silver hoop earrings with this outfit; it's what she'll wear on the plane.

Outside, she walks quickly down the block toward her car and, at a stoplight, turns to regard herself in a store window. The perm looks good; she should have done it long ago. She moves closer to the glass for a better look and sees a charm bracelet in the window. Rita always wanted a charm bracelet but never took the time to put one together. Well, here's one that's already done, and it won't cost much—the place is an antiques store and looks to be a bit down at the mouth. She looks at her watch and rushes in. Five minutes; she won't look at anything else.

A bell tinkles over the door, but there is no one around. "Hello?" she calls out. Nothing. She waits a moment, then says loudly, "Hello? Could I see the bracelet in the window, please?" Again, nothing. Now that it looks as though she might not be able to get the bracelet, she wants it more than ever. She moves to the window and peers over a kind of perforated divider. Oh, it's just loaded with charms, silver ones, Rita can distinguish only a few, they're so crowded together. There's a stagecoach, and a ship, and a cowboy boot—perfect for the day she goes horseback riding—and what looks like an engagement ring, with a real diamond. The stone is tiny, but it shines so brightly.

How wonderful, that someone might put a real diamond in an engagement ring on a charm bracelet! If it is real. She reaches over the divider and nearly has the bracelet in her hand when she hears a door bang open, then the unambiguous sound of a toilet finishing flushing.

"May I *help* you?" a thin, older man asks. He's regarding her suspiciously, her with her armload of shopping bags that might so easily conceal something. Now she'll have to buy the thing.

She offers him her winning smile, not for nothing was she awarded "prettiest smile" in her high school yearbook. "It's . . . I'd like very much to see the bracelet in your window."

The man isn't warming up much.

"The one with all the charms?"

"I know what one you mean," the man says. "I know every single thing that's in that window, believe you me."

Now Rita becomes exasperated. "Listen, I know how this must look. But I have very little time and I really wanted to see that bracelet so I was just going to get it myself. I called out hello, but no one answered."

"I was busy in the back," the man says.

"Well, yes, I . . . *May* I see the bracelet?"

He moves past her, and Rita notices the scent of Old Spice, and this makes her like the man; her father used to wear that cologne. He lifts a latch from the divider and takes slow, careful inventory of everything there. Then, apparently satisfied that she's not stolen anything, he hands the charm bracelet to Rita.

Oh, it's magnificent. So heavy! And Rita thinks that *is* a real diamond on the engagement ring, and there is also a wedding band with three more diamonds. There's an angel on the bracelet, a Mexican sombrero, a tractor, a penny, a Christmas tree decorated with red and green stones. There's a thimble and an owl, and the Liberty Bell. And, oh my, look at this: there is a slot machine, and the arm actually pulls, and the little fruits change. There is a slot machine, and there are dice, and there is a hand of cards: a royal flush. Is this a sign? Is this a *sign?* Oh, yes it is, and Rita will buy this bracelet no matter how much it costs. She looks at the man and tries not to seem too excited. But then she says, "I *love* this! I have to have it! How much is it?"

"It's a hundred dollars," the man says.

Rita nods slowly. Then she says, "I just want to ask you something. If I weren't so enthusiastic, how much would it be?"

The man smiles, revealing two deep dimples. "Four hundred. That's sterling silver. Those charms are exquisitely crafted. It's worth even more. But I see how much you like it, so . . . It's a hundred dollars."

"I'll take it," Rita says, handing him her credit card, and when the man starts to wrap the bracelet up, Rita tells him not to, she'd like to wear it.

When the man hands her the charge slip to sign, he says something.

"Pardon?" Rita asks.

The man looks up, and Rita sees that his eyes are wet. "It was my wife's," he says. "I can't look at it anymore. I wanted someone else to love it for her. So thank you."

Rita touches his hand. "I've been widowed for some time now, but it still seems like yesterday. I think I know how you feel."

The man nods, then says, "I'm Howard Bernstein. Would you like to go out to dinner with me sometime?"

Oh, God. "Thank you," she says gently, "but I don't think so. I'm sorry. I hope that doesn't offend you."

"I'm not offended. I ask any woman who comes in here and is breathing if she'd like to have dinner with me—I don't like to eat alone. I hope *that* doesn't offend *you.*"

"Not at all. Listen, thanks again for the bracelet. Looks like your wife liked to gamble!"

"Did she ever."

"Well, I'm off to Vegas! This very afternoon."

"Put a quarter in a slot machine that's in the middle of a row and has cherries painted on it," the man says. "You'll win big." He stares intently at her. "You think I'm joking, but it's true. I know these things. Kind of psychic."

"I hope you're right!" Rita waves good-bye and rushes down the street, her shopping bags bumping into her knees, her hips. Tonight, she'll be sleeping in a pyramid after she's heard Wayne Newton sing. She wonders how many people in the audience will be seeing him with no sense of irony at all. She hopes most of the audience absolutely adores him. To tell the truth, she does, but she would never admit it. Thank God that what happens there . . .

At the airport, Rita sits at the gate looking at her charm bracelet. It's astonishing, all that's on here. She counts the charms: there are thirty-six of them. Some she might have selected if she'd put the thing together herself: a VW Beetle, she used to have one of those. The four heads on Mount Rushmore, she's been there. The astrological sign for a Cancer, she's a Cancer, too! Other things don't fit her at all: a typewriter, a pagoda, a man leading a donkey, Casa Loma in Toronto, but she likes the mystery of not knowing

what they meant to the woman who bought them. Someone's whole life, hanging on her arm.

A handsome older man sitting across from her has been
checking her out for some time. Now he speaks. "Going to
Las Vegas?"

"I am."

"Been there before?"

"Many years ago."

"Ah." The man smiles, an oily kind of smile, as if he's
in on some joke she's not privy to, and she decides she
doesn't like him. But then she decides to give him a
break—he's just trying to make conversation, trying to
pass the time. "It's built up a *lot* more now," he says.

"Oh, I'm sure. You've been there?"

"Millions of times. Where are you staying?"

What's your Social Security number? she wants to ask
him. Oh, why is she being so nasty? If a woman asked her
this question, she'd answer readily. Then they'd chat about
hotels, and maybe she'd get some tips.

"I don't know the name of it," Rita says. "The place
that looks like a pyramid."

"I know the one you mean. I've heard it's nice."

"Where are you staying?" she asks.

"Not sure yet," he says, and then points to her bracelet.
"That's quite a collection of charms you've got there."

Rita wonders if he's being purposefully evasive about
his hotel, if he thinks she's trying to pick him up. She's
vaguely insulted, the man knows nothing about her. And
then it comes to her how delicious this is, that the man
knows nothing about her. She fingers her bracelet and
says, "Yes, I've had it for many years."

"Is that a pair of dice I see on there?" The man leans
forward, then looks up into her face. "I'm Red Henley, by

the way. Used to have red hair. Lost the color but kept the name."

"I'm Cherise Langley," she says, and offers her hand.

"Pretty name," he says, and moves into the seat next to her. Then, his eyebrows raised, he asks, "Okay if I sit here?"

"Of course." She fingers her bracelet nervously. *Cherise Langley!* That's what she used call her paper doll!

"So, you go on cruises a lot?" Red asks.

She stares blankly at him—she *never* has—and he points to the cruise ship charm. "Oh!" she says. "Yes, I went. Long time ago. I bought that charm on board, in the gift shop."

"Where'd you go?"

"Oh, just . . . you know. Europe."

He nods. "Are you crazy about Paris, like most Americans?"

"I like Paris quite a lot."

He leans back in his chair, and says, *"Ah, Paree. La Pont des Arts, Ile de la Cité, au fond la Cathédrale Notre-Dame."* Then, to his credit, Rita thinks, he blushes.

An announcement comes over the speaker; their flight has been delayed. Only half an hour, they're saying, but who can trust them? She and Red sigh together, then laugh at the same time, too.

"There's a bar two gates down," he says. "Would you like to go and get a drink? Or some coffee or something?"

"I *would* like a drink," she says, and they wheel their bags into the tiny bar. Red orders a scotch, and Rita says, "I'll have a Manhattan," and there you have it, her trip has begun.

"So where do you live?" Red asks, and Rita tells him she has a loft over by the university.

"I'm in St. Paul," he tells her. "Got a real nice condo on Grand Avenue."

"Oh, that's a great area," Rita says. "A lot of nice stores and restaurants."

"Good walking street," Red says. "I go up Crocus Hill to the cathedral every day. I love that place. I'm not religious—just appreciate it for art's sake. When I was a kid, I used to wish I could be locked up in it overnight."

"Why?" Rita asks.

He shrugs. "I don't know. The candles, the mystery. I never felt like I got enough of the place, plus I wanted to see it all alone. I've always been kind of a loner, I never got married or anything. How about you, you married?"

"Divorced," she says.

"Kids?"

"Just one."

"Grandkids?"

"One on the way, actually. Three more months." Oh, wouldn't that be lovely, she can't wait to have grandchildren. Once it occurred to her that the reason she'd like it is that it would be a relief not to have to compete with Ben, but then she felt terrible thinking that, felt terrible that he would never see his grandchildren, nor they him. He always said that he wanted to read his grandchildren *Uncle Wiggley*.

Red studies her face. "You don't look like a grandma."

"Oh, sure I do; grandmas don't look like grandmas anymore."

"More's the pity," Red says, and picks up his coat to make room for another woman who sits beside him. She's about their age, quite pretty, and apparently finds Red attractive. She smiles at him, pulls a cigarette from her bag, and says, "Light my fire?"

"You can't smoke in here," Red says, and turns his attention back to Rita. He rolls his eyes, and Rita smiles into her drink. Which is almost gone.

"Would you like anything else?" Red asks, and she says no, she thinks she'll go back; maybe they're boarding.

"Hope springs eternal," Red says. He pays the bill, then walks back to the gate area with her. Now the departure time has disappeared from the board altogether, and just as they are about to sit down, here comes the dreaded announcement: "Well, folks . . ."

Three hours later, Rita's section gets called, and she makes her way to her seat. She's had some dinner with Red, she's told him she loves to ski (she detests it) and that as a little girl she had wanted to move to Montana and be a cowgirl. This is true, actually, and when it slipped out she had the odd feeling of doing wrong by telling the truth.

Red's section came after hers, so when Rita boarded, they said good-bye and shook hands. Red said maybe they could share a cab into the city and Rita said maybe so.

The flight is light; it looks like Rita is going to have no one next to her. She can sit by the aisle or the window. This seems such a luxury to her, given the way airline travel has changed from people getting dressed up to people wearing what amount to pajamas and being crammed on board like the cattle who ride in those awful slatted trucks you see on the highway. Rita must dissociate when she sees those trucks, those bawling, white-faced cows, their big eyes full of terror, or sorrow, or both. That's what flying is like now, cattle cars. Even first class has an air of weariness these days—no more gay mimosas on the morning flights, complete with flowers. No more pretty, smiling flight attendants wearing tasteful makeup and simple jewelry, their hair in neat upsweeps.

Window first, she decides; later, she'll switch to the aisle. She doesn't like to sit on the aisle when they bring those carts through; once, her elbow got banged and the flight attendant acted like it was Rita's fault, didn't even apologize. She puts her purse under the seat, leans back against the headrest, and closes her eyes.

"Cherise," she hears. Then, more insistently, "Cherise!" She opens her eyes, remembering that she is Cherise, and looks for Red. He's a few rows up, waving at her. She waves back, smiling, then closes her eyes again. She doesn't want him to move and sit beside her; lying is peculiarly exhausting. She wants to go to sleep, so she can stay up late tonight. She wants to find the slot machine with the cherries, and when she wins big, she wants to set aside at least a couple hundred dollars, which she will use to buy more things from Howard Bernstein's store.

She is awakened by turbulence severe enough that many passengers cry out. Rita grips the arms of her seat and holds on. She's not afraid, she is never afraid of turbulence. She feels confident that she will not die in a plane crash, she doesn't know why, but she is absolutely sure of this. The woman across the aisle from her is white-knuckled; the man with her looks angry and in fact begins to quietly swear. Rita looks for Red. There is the back of his head; he's holding perfectly still. Funny how you can tell from behind when a person is afraid. She gets a strange notion. She tears a strip of paper from *Hemispheres* magazine and makes a spitball out of it. Then she throws it at Red, and it bounces off him. He puts his hand to his head and turns around. She holds up her hand and flutters her fingers. He smiles. She gives him the thumbs-up and he returns the gesture. *Don't be afraid*, she has said, and he has understood her. She likes that. The plane bucks again, the captain makes the usual announcement about searching for calmer air, and soon Rita is nodding off again.

"Cherise?"

She awakens to see Red sitting beside her, smiling. She straightens up and tries to secretly wipe her mouth off: much to her horror, she sometimes drools when she drifts off on airplanes. "Some ride, huh?" Red says. "I was a little nervous, I don't mind telling you. Until you fired that spitball at me."

"Sorry," she says.

"No, it helped! Little humor in the midst of terror, that's a good thing."

"It seems so," Rita says. When Sally Wall got breast cancer and told her best friend, Annie, about the diagnosis, Annie said, "Well, don't buy any green bananas," and Sally loved it; she said it was such a relief from all the doom and gloom.

"You don't mind if I sit here for a while, do you?" Red asks.

She does, actually, but not enough to say so.

"I can go back to my seat, if you want to sleep some more."

"That's okay." She pushes back the sides of her hair, remembers that it's permed. She has a perm and she's on the way to Las Vegas. She's Cherise Langley.

"You know," Red says, "I have to confess something to you."

"Oh?"

He's married. He's gay. He's just out of jail.

"Yeah. It's kind of embarrassing."

Jail. White-collar crime. Bookkeeping.

He looks away to say, "You know those ads for Las Vegas where the girl keeps giving herself a different name?"

Oh, my God, he's on to her. "Yes, I've seen them," she says evenly. One of her hands begins to knead the other, and she separates them, makes them lie innocently on her lap. She'll never admit it. She won't admit anything. It's none of his business.

But now he looks into her face to say, "My name isn't Red Barton."

"Henley," she says.

"Pardon?"

"You said your name was Red *Henley*."

"Oh. Right, I was trying to decide between Barton and Henley. But neither is my name."

Rita smiles. "You know what? I lied to you, too. I guess . . . Well, I guess we were kind of up to the same thing. *Sin City*."

"My real name is Herman Miller."

"I'm Rita Thompson."

"You look like a Rita," he says.

"You don't look like a Herman."

"Thank you. I've hated that name all my life."

"I could call you Red. I'm kind of used to it."

He sighs. "Nah, I'm Herman."

"I'm glad to meet you, Herman," she says. "Did you lie about anything else?"

"Everything," he says, and she says, "Me, too!"

"This would make a great 'how we first met' story," Herman says.

"Well," Rita says.

The flight attendants are coming through with their

cart, and Herman puts his tray table down. "May I buy you another drink, Rita?"

"Sure, but I'll pay this time."

"Modern woman!"

"It's only fair."

"Let me buy. It's my pleasure. And then I'd like to tell you only the truth."

"I'd be happy to hear it."

"In fact," he says, "I have a radical idea. Let's be the friends who *only* tell each other the truth, no matter what." Rita says she likes the idea—she does!—and he goes on to tell her that he lives in a duplex on Dupont in South Minneapolis, that he has never been to Las Vegas or Paris, and that he was happily married for twenty-eight years, then widowed. He says, too, that when they had that turbulence—the worst he's ever experienced—he got so frightened, he began to sweat profusely.

"Bullets?" Rita asks, and he says no, just your basic salt water, and she laughs.

"I really thought we might go down," he says, "and I was thinking of writing a note to my children. But I didn't know what to say, because I had too much to say. And then, after everything calmed down, I kept thinking about it, you know? What if I had only one sentence that I could say to my children? One sentence that tried to let them know everything I wanted to tell them. Something more than 'I love you.' "

"Interesting thing to contemplate," Rita says.

"What would you say to your child?"

"Well, I have two, actually," Rita says. "And no grand-children on the way."

"Oh, you'll love grandchildren," Herman says. The cart

has made its way to them, and he orders a scotch. Rita gets
a beer. After he's paid, Herman tells her, "I love a woman
who likes beer," and Rita says, "So do I."

"So what *would* your sentence be?" Herman asks.

"Ummmm . . . You go first."

"All I could come up with was 'You are the best part.'
Dopey, huh?"

"I think it's nice."

"Now you," he says. "And remember, we're the friends
who tell the truth."

Rita takes a long swallow of beer. As soon as Herman
suggested such a sentence, one had popped up in her brain
as though coming out from behind a curtain where it had
been waiting for a long time. She's not sure she wants to
share it. Still, she does. She says, "My sentence would be:
'Please come to me for comfort.' "

"Huh," he says.

She shrugs.

"That's . . . I mean, don't they?"

Rita looks at her watch. Plenty of time to tell him.

Late Sunday morning, Rita awakens in her pitch-black
Egyptian hotel room and opens the drapes. It is a child's
drawing of a day, the sky nearly navy, the clouds so puffy
and well-defined, it seems they are there for the plucking.
She is going to meet Herman at the buffet for breakfast,
then they're going to get in a little more gambling before
they have to leave for the airport. They gambled last night,
as they did on Friday night. Rita sticks with the slot machines, but Herman is game for anything, though he does
not appear to be reckless—he seems to know when to cut
his losses. Rita has lost fifty dollars thus far, no big deal in
this city, but it is to her, as she expected to win immedi-

ately. She puts it to not having found the right slot machine, the one with cherries, in the middle of the row. She'll find it today; she just knows it. And she'll win. The victory will be all the sweeter, for having had to wait for it.

After she showers, she puts on her lime green pantsuit and silk shell, and sprays herself liberally with perfume, Herman having told her how good she always smells. She applies her makeup with care and surprising accuracy, given the fact that there's no magnifying mirror in the bathroom. Rita has taken note of the median age of the ·gamblers here; they really ought to put magnifying mirrors in the bathrooms. She packs her bags, regretting only a little the fact that she didn't go to any of the shows after all; they were harder to get into than she'd thought; you really needed to call ahead. "Next time," Herman told her, when they were at dinner last night. "Next time we'll see Johnny Mathis and Jerry Seinfeld and Elton John and Bette Midler and Barry Manilow *and* Liberace."

"I don't want to see Barry Manilow," Rita said, and Herman said, "I don't want to see Liberace," and so she said okay, if they came out here again, she'd see Barry Manilow, even though he seemed to her the kind of performer who would pad himself, if Herman knew what she meant.

"No," he said. "What do you mean?"

"*You* know," Rita said. "Remember John Denver?"

Still Herman stared at her blankly.

Rita leaned over and spoke quietly. "He put Kleenex in his crotch."

Herman looked down at his own crotch and then up at her. "Is there something wrong with that?" Then he said he knew what she'd been talking about all along and she punched him and he said not so hard, his padding might fall out. And then they ordered sinful desserts after what had been a sinful dinner: steak and lobster, potatoes au gratin, broccoli with hollandaise. Helping himself to the hollandaise, Herman had asked her if she knew CPR and she said she had just been going to ask him that very thing.

In the lobby of the hotel, Rita sees Herman standing by a statue of a sphinx, waiting for her. He hasn't spotted her, so she is free to take full appraisal of him. He is handsome, but in an unself-conscious way that she likes very much. He is manly, but sensitive. He is financially stable, but not rich. Last night, he had asked if he might kiss her good night. She said she wasn't sure; she would hate to ruin what seemed like it was going to be a beautiful friendship.

Herman said, "My seven-year-old granddaughter says it's okay to kiss someone if they're rich." And when Rita asked if he were rich, he looked into her eyes and said, "Right now I am," so what could she do, she kissed him. But first she said, "I have to warn you, I'm way out of practice." He leaned over and very gently put his lips to hers and she grabbed the back of his head and pressed him hard into her and kissed him but good. And he stepped back and said, "Wow. If this is you out of practice, I'd love to see you when you're not."

Rita licked her forefinger, put it on her rump, and made a sizzling sound, and they both laughed. Then Rita made her face get as serious as three Manhattans would allow, and she said, "I'm not kidding." And Herman said, "I'll bet you're not." He looked at his watch and winced. "Breakfast at noon?" he said, and she said, "*Thank* you."

He started to walk down the hall, then turned around to say, "Oh. One last thing I need to tell you the truth about. That French I spoke at the airport? I memorized that off some postcard. I don't even know what it means. I don't speak French."

"Well," she said, laughing, "I know. I do speak it."

He put his hands in his pockets, embarrassed. Then he said, "Will you go to Paris with me sometime?"

She nodded. Nodded again. Then once more.

And now, the next day, free from the influence of alcohol, she looks at him and says yes all over again. Then she calls his name, and there is such gladness in his eyes as he walks toward her. *Oh, Herman,* she thinks, and then, just for the briefest moment, *Oh, Ben.* It is a sweet moment, though, only a step away from hearing Ben say, *"Have a ball, kiddo."*

"Here it is!" Rita says. She is standing in front of the slot machine she was destined to find. They are at Bellagio, the machine is in the middle of the row, there are cherries painted on it, and Rita has five quarters and about ten minutes left.

Herman pulls up a stool and sits down beside Rita. She takes in a deep breath, and deposits the first quarter. Nothing. The second. Nothing. After she puts the last quarter in, she hits. Coins come rushing out, and Rita puts her big cup beneath the mouth of the machine and yells to Herman to go get another cup and she begins jumping up and down and then the coins abruptly stop. Rita looks into the cup, then up at Herman.

"Well, how much?" he asks.

She counts the quarters and tells him: seven dollars and seventy-five cents. "Seven dollars!" she says. "What can I do with that?"

"Why don't you call your children with it, and tell them your sentence?"

"Oh, for——" Rita says. But then she thinks of Howard Bernstein telling her, "You'll win big," and wonders if he meant something besides money. "Can you still do that?" she asks Herman. "Are there still pay phones?"

"Of course," Herman says, and they go off in search of one, the coins rattling in the cup.

It isn't until they get to the airport that they find a pay phone. It is in a dark corner, in a part of the building that it seems time has forgotten. It ought to be in black and white; that's the feeling. Rita will call Alice's number; she happens to know that Randy will be there, too; once a month the siblings and their spouses get together for Sunday dinner. She has sent Herman away to wait for her at the gate——this is private.

She deposits over half of the quarters for the first three minutes, and when Alice answers, she tells her daughter where she is, and then says, "Honey? I don't have much time, but I wonder if you'd put Randy on with you. I want to say something to both of you." Her heart is hammering inside her.

"Is something wrong?" Alice asks, alarmed.

"No, no," Rita says. "I just want to say something I've been meaning to tell you for a while."

When Randy comes on the line, Rita says, "Okay, I just . . . I would like to say something to both of you, this one thing. Just one sentence. I would like to say, Come to me for comfort."

Silence. "Please," she adds.

"What do you mean, Ma?" Randy asks. She can practically hear him scratching his head.

"I mean . . . Well, I just want to offer you that. I always wanted to offer you that and it seems I never did. Or I did, but you didn't know I did."

"Mom," Alice says. "We knew that."

"It's just that your dad was always the one to . . . He did everything, and I think it must have seemed to you that I didn't care or something. But I always did."

"We knew that!" Alice says. "Mom!"

"I know what she means," Randy says. "He did always do everything before Ma had the chance. And remember that time we were both calling for her, I think it was a Saturday morning, and Dad came in and told us, 'Shhhh! *We don't wake Mommy up!*' Remember?"

"No," Alice says.

"Well, I do, and I remember it made a big impression on me."

"Obviously," Alice says. She's miffed that she can't remember something Randy does, Rita knows. Alice is proud of her usually infallible recall.

A recorded voice asks for more money and Rita puts in more quarters. Alice says, "Are you on a *pay phone?*" and Rita says yes and they all for some reason start laughing and Rita thinks of how good it is to be in a family where certain things are shared, where there are common genes that make you all laugh about being on a pay phone.

Randy says, "Mom, I think we thought of Dad as being both of you, you know? But we *never* doubted that you were there for us. Then or now."

Alice starts to sing: *"You were always on our minds . . ."*

"Uh-oh, gotta go," Randy says, but then he says, "Seriously, Mom, you were."

"You know what?" Alice says. "I can think of a million times you offered me comfort as a child. I'm going to make a list for you for your next birthday, would you like that?"

Rita presses her fingers to her mouth and nods; then,

realizing what she is doing, blurts out, "Yes! Yes, I would love that, Alice."

"You in on this, Randy?" Alice asks.

"I . . . I'll do something equivalent," he says. And then, "Hey, how are you anyway, Mom? How was Las Vegas?"

Again a voice asks for more money, and Rita puts in the little she has left. "It was wonderful," she says. "And next I'm going to Paris!"

"Good for you!" Alice says, and Randy says, "It's about time you started living it up! Hey, eat some snails there. *Eww.*"

"What a coincidence, that's what we're having for dinner," Alice says, and then the connection is lost. Rita looks at her watch. She needs to go to the gate. She'll call her kids back later. For now, she wants to hold what they've told her inside herself; she wants to unwrap it more.

At the gate, she sits down in the seat Herman has saved for her. "How'd it go?" he asks, and she nods, tearful.

"Told you," he says.

She turns to face him fully. "If I go to Paris with you, will you eat snails with me?"

"Well, of course I'll eat snails with you!" A beat and then, "Are they good?"

"*I* don't know!" She laughs. Leans back in her seat. Crosses her legs and e-x-h-a-l-e-s.

As a surprise, Herman has upgraded them to first class. Rita sits in the wide seat and slips off her shoes. "Ahhh," she says.

"I only put us up here because there are fewer people to witness my cowardice if we encounter any turbulence," he says. "If we start bucking around the sky again and I start weeping, remind me I'm a man, will you?"

But it is Rita who becomes misty-eyed on the ride home. It is not because of any turbulence; rather, it is because of a series of thoughts she has as she stares out the window at the land far below. From this vantage point, it always seem to her that the earth is being offered up by a benevolent force that understands nothing belongs to anyone unless it belongs to everyone. She presses her forehead against the glass. There is the sky, there are the clouds, there is the red setting sun, there are the fields plowed with such touching precision. She glances over at Herman, who, in sleep, looks boyish, and she resists the urge to pick up his hand and kiss it.

She thinks about being with him in Paris and sees them at an outdoor café just down the street from Notre-Dame, eating croissants after a night of very sweet—and also, my goodness, *surprising!*—intimacy. She is wearing a well-cut dress, beneath which is a bejeweled garter belt (here she begins to giggle and must put her hand to her mouth and stop, lest she awaken Herman), but yes, a garter belt and black silk stockings, *French* black silk stockings, a miracle of near-weightlessness in the hand, an elegant statement on a woman's leg, and, as they are in enlightened Paris, an even more elegant statement for being on an older woman's leg. She thinks about what Herman's duplex might look like, if they might have goulash there one winter night and sit on the sofa watching old movies and holding hands. It is so possible, it seems as if it has already happened.

She thinks of her children, comforting her on the phone, when she had called to ask to comfort them, and then she thinks of a diorama she saw at a natural history museum not long ago: a cavewoman holding a baby and the hand of a toddler, the father with a club over his shoulder heading off for his job of finding food. Rita stared at that scene, remembering the perfect weight of a baby, the feel of a toddler's hand in her own, and wished time could hold still, so that she might have relished a little longer the sweetness of loving small children mixed with that fierce, unequivocal protectiveness. But time does not hold still, and Rita thinks now that it's a blessing, she thinks that what it means is that your life is free to make or unmake every day. And then she thinks of a time she cut open a red pepper and stood studying the hundreds of seeds there, thinking that before her was the potential for creating many more red peppers—for free!—but what she was going to do was throw all the seeds away. It made her feel bad, it made her feel she was neglecting some essential message; but then she decided she was just premenstrual. That's how long ago this incident happened, but she remembers the moment vividly. The red flesh of the pepper, the tiny white seeds, *here you are*. She looks again at Herman, bathed in the pink light of dusk, a nice light for people their age, and smiles. Then she thinks of the people in her retirement center and sees them for the generous and good-hearted people that they are: love makes you love. She will tell her next-door neighbor Elsie that she met a man, and Elsie will be so happy for her she'll probably bake one of her sour-cherry coffee cakes to celebrate.

Rita closes her eyes and gently rests her head against Herman's shoulder. She thinks of Oscar Wilde's purported last words: *Either that wallpaper goes, or I do*. For her part, she hopes she might say, "Would you mind lifting the shade a bit? I want to see more."

ACKNOWLEDGMENTS

Many thanks to Kate Medina, my editor, and Suzanne Gluck, my agent. They are stars in the industry, and it's no wonder. Thanks for your guidance and support.

I am lucky indeed to be published by Random House, where everyone seems to do their job with joy and extreme competence. Barbara Bachman, Susan Brown, Barbara Fillon, Gene Mydlowski, Beth Pearson, Abigail Plesser, Robin Rolewicz, and Jane von Mehren: thank you.

The following read some or all of these stories and offered kind and perceptive criticism: Amy Bloom, Veronica Chapa, Nancy Drew, Leah Hager, Alex Johnson, Judy Markey, Mary Mitchell, Pam Todd, Jessica Treadway, Michele Weldon, and Betsy Woodman.

A special thanks to Phyllis Florin, not only for being a terrific reader and writer, but for being a friend who can be counted on to always tell me the truth, even when it's hard.

ELIZABETH BERG is the author of many novels, including the *New York Times* bestsellers *Dream When You're Feeling Blue, We Are All Welcome Here, The Year of Pleasures, The Art of Mending, Say When, True to Form, Never Change,* and *Open House,* which was an Oprah's Book Club selection in 2000. *Durable Goods* and *Joy School* were selected as ALA Best Books of the Year, and *Talk Before Sleep* was short-listed for the ABBY Award in 1996. The winner of the 1997 New England Book-sellers Award for her work, she is the author of the nonfiction book *Escaping into the Open: The Art of Writing True.* She is also a playwright, having adapted her novel *The Pull of the Moon* for the stage. She lives in Chicago, where she is at work on her next novel.